ONE UNEXPECTED ADVENTURE

SOFIA SAWYER

CITY OWL
PRESS

ONE UNEXPECTED ADVENTURE
Her Journey, Book 2

CITY OWL PRESS
www.cityowlpress.com

Cover Design by MiblArt. All stock photos licensed appropriately.

Edited by Mary Cain.

For information on subsidiary rights, please contact the publisher at info@cityowlpress.com.

Print Edition ISBN: 978-1-64898-201-9

Digital Edition ISBN: 978-1-64898-200-2

Printed in the United States of America

To those facing a fork in the road:
I hope you find the courage to embrace the adventure.

ALSO BY SOFIA SAWYER

One Stormy Night

No Place to Hide

Always, Ella

Saving the Winchester Inn

CHAPTER ONE

AVA

STANDING outside Iceland's exclusive Blue Lagoon spa after some much-needed pampering and a four-hour soak, Ava had an inkling of hope that all of her trip hiccups were well behind her. The two-hour delay in her flight, her suitcase being damaged beyond repair, and her airport shuttle to the lagoon getting a flat tire were child's play compared to the twists and turns of the ten years she'd spent helping transform a scrappy tech startup into a multimillion-dollar market leader. ZettaBytes had become recognized as a premier database software company in the world.

She'd been part of that journey every step of the way. Now, Ava had become its newly appointed chief marketing officer, effective January 1.

In only a month, she'd finally step into the role she'd tirelessly worked for. She'd done it. Her meticulously planned career trajectory had paid off, manifesting beautifully right after her thirtieth birthday, just as she'd expected. Every sacrifice she'd made now meant something.

Ignoring the restless feeling weighing in her stomach, Ava

checked the time again and wondered if her travel woes weren't as far behind her as she'd thought.

She shook it off. Although traveling for the sole purpose of relaxing and recentering herself wasn't her usual style, she could figure it out.

People do it all the time. It can't be that hard.

She refused to let a few minor imperfect moments take away from the purpose of being here in the first place. She *needed* this. She *deserved* this.

If she'd believed in such things like fate and destiny, she'd think they had a hand in helping her find Jónsson Tours. With Iceland becoming a popular travel destination, it was a miracle they'd had availability last minute, especially with their rave reviews. The robust excursion options made planning the trip that much easier—and that's what she needed right now: simple. Everything was done for her in this private three-day adventure, including transportation and exclusive tours. She had her own personal guide to show her the beauty of Iceland without her having to worry about a thing.

Forty-two minutes late. The endorphins from the healing geothermal waters were starting to fade fast. No amount of positive thinking would be enough to outweigh her rising annoyance.

Ava peered out of the waiting area's expansive windows, watching the sun dip lower toward the horizon. She tapped her foot against the hard concrete floor as people flowed from the waiting area to buses, vans, and cars. After another rush of people exited, she realized she was one of the few people left.

There was a reason Ava liked to take control and plan things down to the second. Had she'd just done it her way rather than letting her younger sister, Jess, shame her into "winging it," she wouldn't be standing alone in a foreign country.

Likely stranded, by the looks of it.

Maybe this was one massive mistake.

No call. No text. No email to let her know they were behind schedule. Maybe she misunderstood and was supposed to meet them in the designated tour bus section of the parking lot. For all she knew, they could have been waiting for her too. That had to be it.

As she rolled the oversized and overpriced suitcase she'd been forced to purchase at the airport to the parking lot from the safe confines of the waiting area, a gust of wind took Ava by surprise, catching her luggage and dragging her with it. She dug her heels in, trying to get it under control, but she lost her footing when her flats slipped on black ice.

A car screeched, its headlights nearly blinding her as it stopped mere inches from her. She let out a breath, her heart pounding from the near miss.

The driver's side window rolled down. "You okay?" a baritone voice asked.

This bastard almost mowed me down, and he doesn't even have the decency to step out of the damn car?

She straightened, stomping around the side of the car with her luggage in tow to give the guy a piece of her mind. Her footsteps faltered when she read the signage on the side of the SUV: Jónsson Tours.

Great. Just great.

But the guy sitting in the driver's seat looked nothing like the man splashed all over their website. For starters, he wasn't rocking thick, white hair, nor did he have a mischievous twinkle in his eyes as if he was bound for the next greatest adventure.

This man was likely in his mid-thirties, probably half the age of the tour guide she thought she'd hired. Then again, it was hard to tell with those aviator sunglasses blocking most of his face.

His permanent scowl definitely didn't match the warm smile of the site's mascot.

"You're not Jón Jónsson."

"Nope." He popped the P.

She blinked, waiting for him to elaborate, but he didn't. "I scheduled a tour with Jón. I'm Ava Espinosa."

The man grunted, and she could have sworn he muttered,

"Figures," under his breath. "He's recovering from knee surgery, so you've got me."

He slipped from the driver's seat, practically knocking her over with the door, and tugged her luggage from her hands, carrying it to the trunk and unceremoniously tossing it inside.

"And you are?" *The nerve of this guy.*

"Brooks. His son."

Ava couldn't quite place his accent. There were hints of Icelandic, but a few words also had a bit of a twang to them, like he'd grown up somewhere in the southern United States.

He slipped off his sunglasses, revealing midnight blue eyes that looked nearly indigo under the fleeting sunlight. He crossed his arms, a frown still firm on his face, reminding her of Indiana Jones.

Tanned skin, dark scruff, full lips, and an intense stare.

The same attitude problem too.

Maybe he could have passed for Indy had he been donning a leather jacket, hat, and whip. Instead, he wore a thick winter jacket, a beanie that covered his dark hair, and heavy snow boots.

He towered over her—nearly two heads taller—his broad frame imposing. Her mouth went dry. Ava would almost admit he was sexy in that rough-and-tumble kind of way. The type of man who would give a woman the adventure of her life, searing the memory in her mind before she never saw him again, keeping that rendezvous positive before real life could ruin it. Something to cling to during cold, lonely nights.

The sight of him nearly knocked her breathless. She sucked in air as an act of defiance.

His dark eyebrows knitted together. "Is something wrong with you?"

Of course, his rudeness had to go and mess up that fantasy. Why did attractive men always ruin it by opening their big, stupid mouths?

I might kill him.

His gaze trailed her body, making her flush under the scrutiny. She shifted on her feet, both uncomfortable and slightly aroused by his perusal. Something about the way he looked at her made her feel naked under his stare.

"Where are your boots?"

"Uh, what?" she asked, her mind still lingering in the gutter.

"Boots. What are those stupid things?" He nodded at her ballet flats.

"Shoes."

"Those won't stand a chance out here. You'll freeze. Or crack your head open."

"I was hot after the lagoon." She would have died if she'd put on her boots. Those things would have kept her warm even if she was standing in the Southern Ocean in the dead of winter.

He raised an eyebrow. "You getting in or what?"

She tapped her watch. "You're late."

Brooks rolled his eyes and dropped his arms, pushing past her to swing open the back door before hopping into the driver's seat. "We're on Iceland time, sweetheart. I can't control nature," he said as she slipped into the back. "Got delayed fueling the plane."

"Maybe so, but for the price I paid for this tour, I would've expected you to plan better. Shouldn't you schedule contingency time for the unexpected? And wouldn't you have known to fill your plane well before you needed to get me?" Ava huffed out a breath. "Also, don't call me sweetheart. It's condescending and unprofessional."

"Whatever, lady." He threw the SUV into drive.

"Don't call me that either."

"Listen," he said as he pulled out of the parking lot and onto the main road. "If you're unsatisfied with your service so far, I'm happy to refund your money. Just let me know where to drop you off."

For a second, Ava was tempted to follow through on that. In all of five minutes, her experience with Brooks had been a miserable one. It was amazing how a practical stranger had sparked such a visceral response in her.

A murderous response.

"I'm just saying to give yourself time to go with the flow. Vacation is meant

to explore." Jess's words floated through Ava's mind. *"You don't need to control or manipulate every little detail of your life. Maybe by being open, you'll find exactly what you need."*

Ava had thought she was happy. Upon further reflection, she began to wonder.

For starters, this was the first non-work trip she'd taken in nearly five years.

She promised herself to embrace this vacation. She needed it to rekindle the excitement of becoming a CMO and all the challenges she'd tackle as soon as she got back to Boston. She'd leave a legacy. A mark. This trip would help her recenter herself to take that head-on.

So maybe Brooks wasn't what she had in mind when she booked this tour company, but it was only a few days. They'd travel along northern Iceland for the next three days, and then he'd drop her in Reykjavík where she'd continue the rest of her trip solo. Far, far away from this infuriating caveman.

She could survive a few days. She'd dealt with people like this before and always came out on top.

"That won't be necessary," Ava finally said.

From the side mirror, she could have sworn she saw him wince.

CHAPTER TWO

BROOKS

HE DIDN'T SIGN up for this. Sure, he offered to help his dad while he recovered from his surgery, but Brooks hadn't expected there to be so many obnoxious tourists. He could handle the drunks who were looking to have a good time and the people just wasting money on tours to get the "perfect gram" for their Instagram profiles.

He could even almost deal with the people who seemed utterly clueless about respecting Iceland's incredible landscape, trapezing over its natural spots like they were stomping along the grimy streets of New York City.

But he couldn't deal with a woman like Ava Espinosa. How far was the stick up her ass?

You're late.

As if a few minutes mattered. There were more important things he should be dealing with than carting around another pretentious, well-off tourist who would be too glued to her phone to stop and appreciate what was in front of her.

Too many people took Iceland for granted.

As nice as it was to travel around the island leisurely like this sometimes, he needed to figure out what was killing the fish in his town, and therefore disrupting their economy.

Those who relied on the fishing trade had suffered these last few months.

So, basically, more than half the town. And it was only getting worse.

Brooks knew something was wrong. He'd heard about other northern Icelandic coastal towns experiencing the same thing this past year, but no one could identify what was killing their trade.

In his gut, he knew there was something going on, and he'd do anything to get to the bottom of it. No stone left unturned and all that.

After parking the SUV in his designated spot at the airport, he hauled her luggage down the runway, tossing it into the small storage area of his Cessna 172. She trailed behind him, making critical remarks he chose to ignore.

He patted the light commuter plane as a surge of pride rushed through him. "Here we are," he said, turning to Ava. She tilted her head. "What now?"

"This...doesn't look like the plane on the website." She pointed to the Duct tape on the wing. "Is that even safe?"

"The plane on the site is my dad's. This is mine."

She wrinkled her nose. "And you couldn't have borrowed his?"

Oh. Those are fighting words. Of course, someone as stuck up as her would be too shallow to see a diamond in the rough.

"I'll have you know that Darlene and I have done just fine. This is quality craftsmanship. It could be the end of the world, and she'd be the last thing standing."

"Darlene?" Her lips clamped tight like she was trying to hold in a laugh.

He narrowed his eyes. "Get in the damn plane, princess."

"It's Ava," she said with a scowl.

Walking to the passenger side, Brooks lifted Ava into the seat, clenching his teeth when her sweater slipped up and his fingertips met her bare skin. For a flash of a second, he ached to run his fingers along her soft skin again.

Her bossiness annoyed the crap out of him, but he'd have to be dead not to appreciate what a gorgeous woman she was. Petite, but curvy in all the right places. Thick, layered dark hair that flowed past her shoulders. Naturally tanned skin—even in the winter—that only highlighted her dark eyes, making them seem both mysterious and calculating.

He'd made the mistake of looking into them a second too long, causing him to wonder what went on in that head of hers. She clearly had an agenda, but what was making her so uptight?

This was vacation, for fuck's sake. He'd never met someone so tense on vacation in his life.

After settling in and putting on his headset, he noticed Ava struggling with the seatbelt. Leaning over, he roughly pulled the belt to dislodge it from whatever it was stuck on and secured it across her soft, warm body, clicking it in place. The Blue Lagoon's signature scent—the same fragrance he smelled every time he picked up someone from the tourist hot spot—lingered when he shifted back to his side. He'd inhaled that scent a million times, yet somehow it was intoxicating on her.

He sighed and shook his head. Maybe she smelled good, but she still was a pain in the ass.

"Put on your headset so we can hear each other," he instructed as he prepared for takeoff, noting the worried expression crossing her features.

"Okay, I guess."

"Have a little faith. I've been flying since I was a teen." He flicked a few switches and checked the gauges, the pre-flight check coming to him like second nature.

She huffed out a shaky breath. "Fine. Fine."

Starting the engines, he positioned the plane on the runway, getting the all clear from the air tower at Keflavík Airport. Within seconds, they were barreling down the runway.

Ava's hands gripped her knees. Her eyes squeezed shut.

"We're in the air. You survived takeoff."

She bit her bottom lip and slowly opened her eyes. "I've never been in a plane like this. Is it supposed to feel this rickety? I thought the bottom was going to fall off and we'd be plummeting to our deaths," she yelled over the loud engines.

His lips twitched. "Even my dad's plane would have felt like that."

Checking the altitude levels, he adjusted the plane until it was steady. The retreating sun flashed in his eyes. Even with his aviators, the sun was always on the horizon this time of year, just in his vision, blinding him whether on land, sea, or air.

Ava rustled near him. She pulled out a mini-binder from her oversized purse and flipped through the pages. "Okay. So our homebase will be Örugg Höfn," she struggled to say, "and we'll spend the next couple of days exploring the northern side of the island? What does Ör...Öruuu—"

"Örugg Höfn," he said slowly for her. "It translates to Safe Harbor in English." Brooks eyed the planner. "Did you print an itinerary?"

She narrowed her eyes. "So what if I did? I like to prep."

"Again, sweetheart—"

"What did I tell you about that?"

"Miss Espinosa," he said through gritted teeth. "The weather will dictate our schedule. I'll do our best to hit all our spots, but things are fickle here." He nodded to her planner. "That's not set in stone."

She slammed her planner closed. "Okay. Whatever. But Örugg Höfn is a sure thing."

"Yeah."

"Tell me about it."

"There's not a whole lot to tell." He shrugged. "Small town. Known for whale watching and fishing. A couple geothermal pools. Had a bit of a tourist spike after that blockbuster movie came out a couple years ago."

"With James McAvoy and Emma Stone?"

"Yup."

The tiny town might have been thrilled to have their fifteen minutes of fame thanks to the movie, but it only boosted tourism. Not the worst thing in the world, but their infrastructure couldn't handle the unexpected increase. Not to mention, these tourists weren't the typical tourists. They were rude, disrespectful, entitled, and looking for a quick picture of where famous actors had been, oblivious to the town's most beautiful features just around the bend.

He scanned her impractical outfit and planner from the corner of his eye, making the quick assumption she wouldn't be too different from those people.

At least before, people had come to see the majestic mountains, the gentle whales, and the playful puffins. They wanted to see all Iceland had to offer, not to say they'd been somewhere a movie had been filmed.

Brooks glanced over at Ava again when she remained quiet. For her, that was unusual it seemed. She was like a statue as she looked out at the vast world below them.

"Good?" he asked.

She leaned closer to the window on her side, her warm breath fogging the glass. "I've just never seen anything like this. All that open land. Untouched. It's stunning."

The breathlessness of her voice tugged at him. She *actually* appreciated the things so many people took for granted.

Maybe she wasn't so bad after all.

"Huh," she said.

"What?"

Ava shrugged. "I don't know. There's some sort of construction or something going on down there." She tapped on the window. "I guess it looks out of place. A little speck in all the emptiness."

His eyes searched the direction she was pointing to. The descending sun made it hard to see. Shadows were playing tricks on him, but just as he was about to give up looking, he saw it.

Big machines. Smoke.

Drilling?

That's not right.

Jerking the handles of the plane to the right until they were nearly sideways, he circled back around.

Ava shrieked. "What the hell are you doing, Brooks?"

Tuning her out, his sights were set on whatever was going on down there.

"Brooks. Do you copy?" his father's thick Icelandic accent crackled through the radio.

"Copy."

"A squall's coming in. Winds are picking up. You need to land. Over."

He regretfully eyed the machines plunging into the ground. He needed to investigate it. It could be the key to what was going on with the northern part of the island, but he knew better than to test Mother Nature, especially around these parts.

"We're about thirty kilometers out. Over."

"See you soon, son."

He could feel Ava glaring at him. "What?"

She waved her hands around. "Was it necessary to nearly flip us upside-down?"

"Can you relax? You're fine." He cocked his head ahead. "See those lights? We're almost there."

"Thank God."

Within minutes, he descended into Örugg Höfn, closing in on a small airstrip outside of the main town. After a bumpy landing, one that Ava complained about the whole time while nearly breaking Brooks's arm in half with her death grip, they'd made it.

He ignored her questions as he tossed her bags into the truck parked near the hangar, his mind racing as he wondered what he'd seen as they flew in, eager for the squall to pass so he could get back into his plane and investigate.

As the thought crossed his mind, the wind picked up, shaking his truck back and forth and whipping Ava's hair into her face. She swatted at the wild strands, grabbing her hair by the base of her head to stop it from blowing everywhere.

"Can you not manhandle my luggage? There's fragile stuff in there."

He knocked on the hard outer case. "It'll survive. Let's go." He slipped into the driver's side and slammed the door behind him, not even bothering to open the door for her.

His dad would be pissed over how he was treating her. He'd been "talked to" a couple times since he'd offered to help, feeling like a teen again. Although his father was a great guy—a kind man—Brooks could admit he hadn't been the easiest kid to deal with.

His mom had met his dad while studying abroad in Reykjavík. They had a romantic tryst that left her pregnant. Born and raised in Atlanta, she had no desire to live in frigid Iceland full-time. Born and raised in Iceland, his father had no desire to live in a busy, humid city.

They'd found themselves at a stalemate, but they remained friends.

It was Brooks who had to deal with their reckless behavior and their disagreement on how to navigate it. He'd grown up mostly in the States, visiting his father during holidays and summer breaks. But it was only the last couple of years, after his mother had died, that he'd made Iceland his permanent home.

Although he and his dad had gotten into a certain rhythm they'd never quite mastered during his formative years, his dad still took it upon himself to scold him when necessary.

Like when he was being a dick to the tourists.

Couldn't his dad appreciate his mission? As a search and rescue pilot, his goal was to help those in need. That also included understanding what the hell was affecting the marine life of these surrounding towns.

He zoned out on the trip from the hangar into town, driving on autopilot to the small B&B in the town's center next to his father's business.

The same business Brooks's apartment sat right above.

"Here we are." He hopped out of the truck, grabbing her things, and ushered her to the front door. "Ava Espinosa checking in," he said to Helga, the warm, motherly owner of the inn.

"Why are you rushing me?" Ava asked as he grabbed the card key and herded her up the stairs to her room.

"I'm sure you had a long day."

"I did."

"Then don't let me keep you from resting." He all but dumped the luggage in the middle of the room and hightailed it to the door, nearly knocking her over in the process.

The determined set of her jaw eased, her bullish instincts now transforming into a look of uncertainty. Something about it made his chest ache. "Um. Okay." She shook her head. "What time will I see you tomorrow?"

"I'll be here around eight or so."

"Eight? Or *so?*"

Brooks took off his beanie and shoved a hand through his thick, dark hair. "You're one of *those*. Sticklers for times and details."

She crossed her arms and popped a hip, the vulnerability he'd seen a second ago disappearing. "So what if I am? Sorry if I want to plan accordingly."

He shook his head, not in the mood to argue with her. The sooner he got back to his apartment to survey the area where he'd seen the activity, the better. "Fine. Eight." He pointed to her feet. "Boots tomorrow."

"Okay."

"Okay."

He couldn't stop staring at her. Not only because she was alluringly beautiful, but also because she looked out of place and a little lost.

Maybe he should feel bad. He'd been harsh, but she hadn't been on her best behavior either. They'd started out on the wrong foot. He should throw her a bone.

"Talk to Helga. She'll tell you where to get something to eat." He slipped on his beanie, stuffed his hands into his pockets, and raised a shoulder. "Though the fish and chips or the chowder at the pub are pretty good. Don't let the looks of the place fool you. It's a total dive, but the locals love it."

"Thanks, Brooks." A smile lifted her lips, brightening those suspicious eyes and melting away the tension. His breath caught for a moment. He silently sucked in some air.

"Sure." Maybe it was a truce, but he didn't have time to feel it out. He had to get back home and figure out his game plan. "See you tomorrow."

"See you at *eight*."

He resisted the urge to roll his eyes, spinning on his heels and waving her goodbye as he hustled down the stairs of the inn.

It figured that when he had his first lead on what was going on, he had to cart her around. Maybe he could improvise though. She might be a control freak when it came to her itinerary, but he'd told her it's all about the weather. If he planned it right, he could knock out two birds with one stone. Give her the trip she'd been looking for while uncovering the reason his town was suffering. He was confident he could make it work.

All he had to do was make sure Miss Anal-Retentive could relax enough to let him, and that meant following her perfectly detailed expectations...at least to start.

He'd show up on time. Maybe even early. Gain her trust. Then, wing it from there.

Easy enough.

CHAPTER THREE

AVA

"Just to make sure we're on the same page, you need my team to come up with a global integrated marketing campaign to launch before the end of the year...for a product that doesn't exist, and our R&D team doesn't have a proof of concept? Not even a general road map?"

What the hell am I even marketing here?

Ava kept her voice steady and firm, not wanting to tip off her CEO that she thought what he was asking for was a miracle.

After attempting and failing to take a power nap to shake the jet lag, she finally started to drift asleep when her cell phone rang with a call from Benson Whitlock, founder and CEO of ZettaBytes. Although they'd worked together countless times over the years, this was the first time she and Benson were more or less equals. There was no longer a layer between them. If his marketing request succeeded or failed, it all fell on Ava now.

Benson had spent the last ten minutes explaining how he'd gotten credible intel that one of their core competitors, DataX, was launching a new product in early Q1. This product would propel them in the race for market share, blowing ZettaBytes out of the water. If what he was saying was right, this would be a huge hit to the company.

"Yes and no. The chief product officer has already instructed the engineering teams to prioritize the new product launch," Benson said. "They had the product in their pipeline, but they've accelerated the timeline now. You need to connect with him to get up to speed on the key features and benefits as they become clearer."

"I see."

She may not be an engineer, but she at least had enough understanding to know the timeline was aggressive for only having a loose idea of the product. Even if they somehow figured out the direction for the product and got something up and running, they still wouldn't have enough time to launch proper user testing and get feedback from beta users to ensure it worked.

Benson always took big swings, and they usually paid off. But this was a huge risk, even for his standards. If they went to market with a buggy product, it could destroy the company's reputation.

The very reputation she'd built and worked tirelessly to protect.

"What was that? You cut out." Benson's voice crackled across the line.

Ava watched as her cell service bars faded from one back to three. "Sorry. I'm in Iceland. I think the storm is messing with my signal."

"That's right. My assistant mentioned you were out of town." He cleared his throat. "I'll need you to present your game plan next Tuesday. I know you're away, but time is money. We can't chance a delay in our announcement. We've gotta beat DataX. For all my contact knows, their announcement could come earlier in January. We need to get it out before the end of the month. There's a lot riding on this."

"I understand." Her head started pounding, making it feel like someone was drumming on her brain. Her forehead twitched in response.

She returned to Boston late on Sunday. That only gave her one solid day to get her strategy together, which wasn't realistic. She'd have to work while in Iceland if she was going to launch a strong campaign as her first project as CMO. She wasn't about to let Benson regret his decision to promote her, but she'd need to voice her concerns up front and level-set with him.

"Listen, Benson—" Her phone beeped. She pulled it away from her ear and checked the screen.

Call Dropped.

"Shit."

Holding up her phone, she paced around her room, looking for stronger reception. The service bars didn't budge. Clicking on the settings, she plugged in the password for the complimentary Wi-Fi, finding it to be equally unreliable.

A laugh filled with disbelief escaped from her lips. Ava had thought she'd been a good person throughout her life. She tried to be kind to others. Got good grades and stayed out of trouble. Kept her head down, worked hard. Volunteered or donated when she could. She even helped her parents pay off their mortgage when her company went public and she made a killing on her stock shares. It was the least she could do after all the selfless sacrifices they'd made to ensure she and her sister had the opportunities they never had.

And yet the universe didn't want her to have one single day of relaxation. Not even on the vacation she specifically took for that very reason. Nope. Karma had other plans. They gave her a rocky trip, a tour guide who seemed determined to argue with her about everything, and a boss who didn't fully believe in the benefit of paid time off.

She wasn't even technically in the CMO position yet, but here she was dealing with a massive project already...while she was on vacation. A project she didn't quite have faith in.

"Chief marketing officer," she sighed to herself.

Always the one willing to take on the tough and obscure roles, and usually the last one to leave the office. Always ready to jump on a flight for a product launch or event. Always the one they could count on, no questions asked.

It was a pivotal moment in her career. One she should be proud of.

Yet she couldn't stop ruminating the same damn question since the day she'd gotten the news: *Was it worth it?*

When she'd signed the employment paperwork, she thought she'd feel more...something. *Anything.* Instead, it felt like just another day. Another milestone to check off, barely registering it as she focused on the next thing on her to-do list.

"It's the price you pay to get to the top," one of her mentors had told her years ago. "Sometimes it's lonely up there, but you'll have all the accomplishments you've gathered along the way to keep you company."

She remembered the warning bell sounding in her head, alerting her that the advice didn't sound quite right, but she'd ignored it. Her mentor had a successful track record. She'd known what she was talking about. Now, Ava wondered if maybe she'd missed a glaring red flag.

She tossed her phone onto the bed and paced the small area of her room, shaking her arms around to release some of the tension.

Pressure. What she was feeling was pressure. And not just any kind of pressure, but the kind of pressure that made it abundantly clear that the future of the company depended on how well she could sell a nonexistent product.

Something about it felt...wrong. Yes, companies sometimes marketed products and services that didn't technically exist, but she'd never been in that position before. Those companies always pulled through, usually. It was up to the engineering and product teams to hit deadlines. If they couldn't, then the company's failure wasn't on her.

But you're the one selling a potential lie. People might not get what they're paying for.

She stopped pacing as discomfort washed over her. She needed to talk to Benson and figure out another option.

After layering on an obscene amount of clothing and her boots, she snatched her phone off the bed and descended the creaky stairs of the quaint inn, hoping by some miracle the reception would be better outside.

Wind and snow blasted her as she pulled open the front door, taking her by surprise. She tightened her scarf and raised her hood to protect her from the cold as she made her way to the sidewalk, feet crunching atop the rapidly accumulating snow.

She kept her eye on her phone, stopping every so often when a service bar flickered in and out. Spinning in circles, she lifted her phone in the air, willing it to get any sort of signal.

"C'mon. C'mon," she muttered when the signal flickered out again. Sighing, Ava continued walking, still fixated on the screen.

So fixated, by the time she looked up, she had wandered far from the inn and couldn't remember the path she took. She searched for her footprints in the snow, hoping to backtrack, but the wind had already wiped them away. Her heart pounded in her chest.

She was lost.

It's a small town. How lost can you be? She took a deep, calming breath and tried not to let the sense of panic overwhelm her again.

The sun had disappeared, and many of the local businesses had closed up for the evening, leaving the quiet road in darkness aside from the streetlamps. Deciding to ask for directions at the first shop she saw open, Ava continued down the road. Hopefully, either her service would return or she'd find an open business before she froze to death.

She stared at her phone as she raced down the road, oblivious to her surroundings—the exact reason why she didn't see the person before she plowed into them. Running face-first into his hard, unmoving frame, Ava started to fall backward. A hand grabbed her arm and yanked her to her feet, drawing her flush against his steady body.

"I'm so sorry—" The words died on her lips when she lifted her chin and saw who she'd bumped into. Of course, it would be the *one* person she didn't want seeing her in her frantic state. It would only fuel his poor opinions of tourists.

She took a step back, ignoring the comfort she felt for the brief second he held her against him.

"Ah. So you're one of those," he commented, nodding at her phone in her hand.

She straightened, trying to hide how frazzled she was. "One of what?"

"One of those people who spend a lot of money to stare at their phone someplace else," Brooks said, as if he'd been inside her head, witness to her conflicting thoughts about what this trip was supposed to be and how it was turning into anything but.

Ava bristled at the comment and narrowed her eyes. "I was taking a work call. I know it's a foreign concept to you, but some people actually want to be good at their job."

He frowned.

"Speaking of which, here's a tip for you. As a tour guide, maybe try making your clients feel welcome. That should be Tourism 101. Maybe you missed that memo."

"Thanks for the tip. I'll be sure to take it into consideration," he said, sarcasm lacing his voice. "Tourism isn't exactly in my wheelhouse."

Her hand went to her chest as she feigned surprise. "You don't say," she said, matching his sarcasm.

"I've been...distracted." His gaze locked onto hers.

Her pulse raced, wondering if it was her that was distracting him. Could he be attracted to her, despite their obvious oil-and-water dynamic?

Why does it matter?

She stood there speechless as she processed her unwelcome hopeful thought, praying he'd send another jab her way that would piss her off to no end. Something to remind her that although she found him sexy, he was a grade A jerk. Something to add logic back into the equation so maybe her body would stop reacting so intensely to his touch. His stare. His baritone voice. And his sense of capability and confidence only someone who had earned it could possess.

Instead, he tightened his hand on the leash he'd been holding, bringing her attention to the dog sitting patiently by his side.

"Didn't take you for a dog person," she said, ramping up to stir the pot a bit more. To create a little distance.

"What's that supposed to mean?" Brooks eyed her as if he looked hard enough, he could see past the veil of her comment to the insult she'd really wanted to lash at him.

"They say dogs can sense when someone's a decent person or not. Just surprised she's stuck around."

Okay. You took it a little too far. His face turned stone cold and distant. Guilt ate at her. She wasn't sure why she was being so rude to a virtual stranger or why she was itching for a fight. Wanting to blame it on their rough start, Ava knew it went deeper than that. There was a restlessness churning inside her, overwhelming her, making her want to lash out on someone who likely didn't deserve it. Judging by the look on his face, she needed to apologize and fast.

"C'mon, Stella," he said to the dog, tugging on her leash to walk past her.

Ava spun on her heel, calling to his retreating back. "Brooks, I—" She started to apologize, but there was no point. She may not know the man, but it was painstakingly clear he wanted nothing to do with her.

She couldn't blame him.

He continued walking away, leaving Ava alone on the quiet road. The snow fell in thick blankets around her, layering the streets and sidewalk with at least another inch since she'd left the inn. She took a step forward, her boot sinking into the snow under her weight.

"Brooks, wait!"

He turned to face her. "What?" he growled.

"I'm...I'm a little lost."

"As far as I'm concerned, I'm not on the clock, so it's not my problem."

Heat flamed under her scarf. "You can't be serious."

"You seem like a resourceful woman," he said drily. "Why not use that phone you're so attached to and find your way back to the inn?"

"My phone has no service. I've already tried."

Ava wondered if he was debating on whether to leave her there. After her low blow, she would have deserved it. Brooks stared at her, his eyes dark in the dim light of night. His tense, angular jaw worked as he stood in silence. For a moment, she was distracted by the movement and how that simple ticking muscle near his jawline caused a rush of arousal through her.

Pull it together. Don't even entertain that ridiculous thought.

"See this road coming up?" He jerked his thumb to a cross street behind him, pulling her from her wandering thoughts.

"Yes." Her voice sounded hoarse to her ears.

"Take a right and then your first left. Follow that all the way down until you see the inn. You won't miss it."

Relief washed over her. "Thank you, Brooks."

He gave her a tight nod and said nothing as he and Stella disappeared down the road, leaving Ava alone with her thoughts. As much as they frustrated each other, she couldn't ignore the nagging feeling that there was something to him, deep below the surface. That there was more complexity than the brutish, arrogant, standoffish exterior he shared with the world.

Something about it made her want to poke at it. See what lay beneath it. She wasn't sure what compelled her to push his buttons. Maybe sheer curiosity. Maybe retaliation for all the times he'd done the same to her.

Whatever it was, the unspoken truce she'd thought they'd made earlier at the inn now seemed like wishful thinking. This sparring round was her fault—she'd admit that much—yet he didn't make things easy either.

He got under her skin, igniting an uncontrollable response from her. Impassioned. Irrational.

Not like her, at all. At least, not these last few years. Controlled, centered, and logical had been her approach. It was how she'd been able to fast-track her career as quickly as she had. She kept her eye on the prize, stayed the course, and didn't let her emotions get the best of her.

Brooks stirred up all those emotions and reactions she'd manage to dilute and restrain over time. He made her want to fight. To speak unfiltered. To have a raw opinion about things without worrying how it came across to someone else.

But if there was one thing she absolutely didn't need in her life, it was a man like Brooks getting the best of her. That was exactly why she should keep him at arm's length, even if they were stuck with each other for the next few days.

All she needed was to not rock the boat. To let his jabs and looks and judgments bounce off her. Maybe if he stuck to the facts while giving her the tour instead of getting personal, she could follow through on that.

Maybe if she could ignore the curiosity that made her want to know who the real Brooks was, she'd get through this just fine.

CHAPTER FOUR

AVA

THANKS TO BROOKS, Ava had found her way back to the inn before she froze to death. After another hour of failed attempts trying to reach Benson, she finally gave into the hunger pangs that had been growling excessively at her.

She never thought clearly when she was hangry. A little food would help her come up with a new game plan in case she couldn't reach anyone from work while in Iceland.

After throwing on her jacket, scarf, and boots again, Ava walked gingerly down the creaky stairs of the quaint inn, getting directions from Helga to the local pub Brooks had mentioned earlier.

It took all of her strength to battle the relentless wind and pull the front door closed behind her. The storm had picked up in the last few hours. Judging by how thick and fast the snowflakes were falling, she had no doubt that the town would be buried by morning.

Brooks had said the weather in Iceland was fickle, but how could they not have seen this coming a mile away? She'd checked the weather religiously while planning her trip, and even looked it up again while she was at the Blue Lagoon. None of the forecasts showed snow, other than a ten percent chance. Yet here she was walking down the road as a wall of white made it almost impossible to see.

Zipping her jacket to her chin, Ava pushed through the biting wind and snow toward The Chantey. Thankfully, the pub was only a few storefronts down.

A tinkling bell chimed overhead as she entered, and the smell of a delicious home-cooked meal instantly engulfed her. Her mouth salivated at all the possibilities. The warmth radiating from the fireplace heated her cheeks, luring her in further.

Upon initial inspection, Brooks had been right. The pub wasn't flashy like many places she frequented in Boston, but there was a certain atmosphere to it that made her comfortable. Maybe it was the way all the patrons seemed to disregard their table in favor of mingling, as if they were at a family gathering. Or maybe it was the way the blonde woman at the bar smiled at her like they were best friends. Whatever it was, it made the trek through the storm worth it.

"Halló. Velkominn," the woman greeted as she wiped the bar top with a wet rag. A few patrons turned to look at Ava, who suddenly felt out of place. "Komdu inn. Komdu inn." She gestured for Ava to come in.

Weaving through the groups of people standing around with a beer in hand and returning polite smiles here and there, Ava made it to the bar, took a seat, and pulled off her gloves and scarf.

The woman placed a menu in front of her and smiled before pouring a beer for someone at the other end of the bar.

"Shit," Ava muttered.

The whole menu was in Icelandic. If this was a locals' place, she worried that she couldn't order in English. What if she chose the wrong thing by accident?

The bartender returned and said something Ava couldn't understand.

"Um...Talar þú ensku?" Ava asked, biting her bottom lip and shrugging.

The woman and a man sitting next to Ava at the bar laughed.

"I am assuming you meant to ask if I spoke English? It is hard to tell by how badly you butchered that. But, yes. In school, we are taught to speak Dutch and English." She smiled warmly as she flipped the menu to the other side. "Here you go. I'm Freyja, by the way."

"Sorry. I tried my best, but learning Icelandic isn't as easy as I thought." Being bilingual in Spanish and English made it easier for her to navigate other Romance languages, but Icelandic was a whole other beast. "Thank you," she said gratefully as she scanned the English side of the menu. "I'm Ava."

"Where are you visiting from?"

Freyja gave off such a welcoming vibe that Ava instantly relaxed, forgetting all about her language faux pas. "The States. Boston."

"Ah. Boston. Nice city. I visited a few years ago," she said as she poured another beer for a woman waiting at the bar.

"Yeah. It was a great place to grow up." Ava looked at the menu again, feeling slightly overwhelmed by the options. Although the menu wasn't extensive, there were plenty of things she'd never heard of before. "What do you recommend I get?"

Freyja rested her elbows on the bar and leaned closer to look at the menu. "How about Hákarl?" She raised an eyebrow and bit her bottom lip.

Ava scanned for that and cringed. "Rotten shark?" She tried not to gag. "I may be all for trying new things, but I don't think I'm quite ready for that."

Freyja let out a full belly laugh. Her blue eyes sparkled in the dim light. "I was just messing with you," she said, wiping away a tear that escaped her eye. "Although it's considered a delicacy here, we don't serve it all too often. It's mostly for the tourists who want to say they've done it. Or..." She nodded to a rowdy group of men arm wrestling a few tables away. "For some of our more competitive regulars. When the winters get long, they like to find ways to entertain themselves. Sometimes they drink a little too much and see who can stuff as much of the shark into their mouths without puking."

Ava's stomach turned. "Oh God."

"For you, though, I recommend the fish soup in a bread bowl." Freyja straightened and took the menu from Ava. "It's a family recipe and very popular, especially on nights like this."

"*That* I can handle."

"Very good. Coming right up." Freyja pushed through the swinging doors and disappeared into the kitchen.

While waiting for her meal, Ava pulled out her phone and instinctively clicked on her email app. Hope blossomed as the app loaded slowly. Ava's eyes widened as the number of unread messages creeped up each second that passed. When it finally was done, she was left with 487 emails she needed to review.

The tightness in her chest hit her again. She rubbed at it. She'd been gone less than a day and had left on a Saturday. How did she have this many messages already? If her colleagues were blowing up her inbox on a weekend knowing she's on vacation, what was next week going to look like?

With more service than she'd had all night, she pulled up Benson's contact information. It rang once before the call failed. She watched helplessly as her service bars flickered before it read No Service. She dropped her phone on the bar and massaged her temples.

This wasn't the vacation she'd envisioned. Maybe she should cut her losses and head back to Boston early. She could meet with Benson in person and try to talk sense into him.

"Service can be a bit spotty here, but it should get better once the storm passes," the older man next to her said. "Nothing much you can do about that now. All you can do is be patient and wait for Mother Nature to be finished."

"So I've heard."

Ava thought back to what Brooks had said about being on Iceland time. She'd thought it was just his excuse to write off his poor planning, but now she could see it was a way of life here. She didn't even know what it was like to sit and wait. When Boston was hit with harsh blizzards that buried everyone in several feet of snow, the city never stopped. As a tech hub, high-speed internet was an absolute must. Come hell or high water, every person stayed connected, never missing a beat.

The disconnection was a little uncomfortable. She couldn't control the weather here or how it prevented her from getting work done. Despite it being out of her hands, she couldn't shake the feeling that she was a slacker.

It was stupid to beat herself up over it. She couldn't snap her fingers and suddenly make the internet work, but here she was. Sitting in a snowstorm in a quaint Icelandic town on her first vacation in forever...and feeling guilty because she couldn't work.

Ava had prided herself on her work ethic. However, she couldn't help the nagging feeling that maybe she'd taken her career a little *too* seriously. And maybe her work ethic had created some unhealthy habits. She should be taking in the sights and sounds of Iceland. She should be in the moment. She should embrace the unexpected for once instead of strategizing how to overcome the possible challenges of the unknown. Maybe even apologize to Brooks so they could survive the next few days together in some semblance of peace.

A random trip wasn't going to completely change her life or who she was at the core, but she could at least salvage what she could of the trip before she went back to the breakneck pace of Boston. That *had* to be enough.

"If you don't mind me commenting, you seem a little tense," the man said, pulling her from her thoughts. Normally, the unsolicited comment would peeve her, but his earnest look just made her feel cared about. He gave off a fatherly vibe that made her want to tell him her deepest worries.

The man waved down Freyja and rattled off something in Icelandic. She nodded and came back, placing a steaming mug of red liquid in front of Ava. Scents of spice, cloves, and citrus wafted around her, causing the tightness in her chest to ease.

"What is this? It smells amazing."

"It's a type of mulled wine. Another family recipe." Freyja winked and disappeared again.

"Figured something warm could help." The man offered his hand. "My name is Jón. Pleasure to meet your acquaintance."

"Ava," she said as she shook it. "Thanks for the suggestion." She lifted the mug and took a small sip. The spice and heat warmed her insides, doing their magic to relax the rest of her tensed body. "Oh my God. This is pure magic." She thanked Freyja, who stopped by with the fish soup.

Jón's playful smile made him look twenty years younger. "It always does the trick. A good drink, a good meal, and some good company. That's all you need in life." He shifted in his chair to face Ava. "I'm happy to lend an ear if you need to talk."

Ava waved him off as she tried to process the conflicting feelings coursing through her. On one hand, it was unnerving to open up to a stranger. On the other hand, his open and sincere demeanor made her think there wouldn't be any harm indulging him a bit.

When was the last time she'd put it all out there, raw and unfiltered? She'd spent so much of her adult life keeping up appearances. Hiding flaws, insecurities, and weaknesses. It'd become second nature at this point, but trying to show the world that she had it all figured out had become exhausting.

"Oh, I couldn't torture you like that."

"Nonsense." He patted her arm. "We take care of our community here, even those who are just passing through."

Part of her was relieved that he didn't give up so easily. She couldn't deny how nice it was to fully focus on a conversation without her phone or computer distracting her. "Fine," she said with a smile and turned to face him. "But just remember that I warned you."

Ava spent the next hour enjoying the soup, wine, and Jón's company as she talked about her job and what led her to take the trip to Iceland. A few others stopped by to talk to her, and Freyja hung out when she could.

"Everything was going fine until I met my tour guide," Ava started to say as she took a large gulp of her second mulled wine, the drink washing away the perfect persona she normally shared with the world. Here in this bar, thousands of miles away with not a familiar face in sight, she was simply Ava.

Whoever that was. Regardless, it was the best she'd felt in a long time.

"I just wanted things to go smoothly, you know?" she continued. "I didn't want to think about it. I just wanted to enjoy my time here before I went back to the craziness of running a whole marketing function and the pressure that comes with it. But...then...ugh." She hiccupped. "Then he nearly *runs me over* and manhandles my luggage. Makes these stupid comments. Nearly flips the plane upside-down. If I was smart, I'd just cancel the tour altogether, but now it's about principle. He clearly doesn't want to be my tour guide, but I'm not going to let him ruin my trip."

Ava took another huge gulp of her wine and frowned. She could have sworn Jón and Freyja shared a conspiratorial look with each other. Freyja giggled and shook her head before disappearing into the kitchen again.

Jón nodded, recognition twinkling in his eyes. "I see you've met Brooks." He took a sip of his lager.

Panic and embarrassment rushed through her. She covered her face with her hands. "I'm so sorry. I completely forgot how small this town is. I'm sure you know him, and here I went on and on about how much of an arrogant ass he is." She dropped her hands. "That was rude of me, especially after you were kind enough to listen to me rant for the last hour."

"Dad?"

Ava whipped her head in the direction of that all-too-familiar voice, her gaze locking on Brooks. God, she couldn't get away from this guy. All she wanted was a minute where she didn't have to be on edge. Brooks tended to make her feel hot all over.

One second he was making her pulse race, and the next he was making her blood boil. She didn't have it in her to handle the whiplash from those two intense reactions.

Then it sank in.

"Dad?" Ava loudly whispered to Jón.

"That would be me." His playful smile returned, and it was then that Ava realized why she felt like she knew him. The man's image was splashed all over the tour site she'd booked. The only reason she hadn't placed him was because his face was now covered with a thick, white beard.

"Jón Jónsson," she breathed out. "You let me complain about your *son*." She buried her face again. "I am so so so so so sorry."

"It's no bother. Brooks is a pain in the ass, that's no secret. He shoulders the burden of taking care of everyone—those he knows and strangers—and it can make him a little...cranky." Jón winked. "But his heart's in the right place. He's a good kid."

Ava assessed the larger-than-life presence walking toward them and concluded he was definitely not a "kid." Not with those broad shoulders, that tall frame, that determined set to his jaw, and the intense dark stare that seemed to be searching for all the secrets she hid in her soul.

A scowl flashed across his face. A pang of guilt hit her in the gut. She really should apologize for what she'd said earlier.

"Hey, cowboy," Freyja greeted him as he approached the bar. "Coming for a bite?"

"Not today. I came to collect Dad." Brooks shot Ava a suspicious look. "You two seem awfully chummy. What were you talking about?"

"Nothing," Ava said at the same time Jón said, "You."

Brooks lifted an eyebrow, his stare not leaving Ava's. "What about me?"

"Only good things, of course," Jón said in an exaggerated tone, causing Freyja to sputter out a laugh she failed to hold in. Ava finished the last of her wine, trying to do anything to avoid his scrutiny. Her face flushed from the rush of alcohol and Brooks's proximity.

Her body hummed with awareness.

Brooks's eyes narrowed.

Ava swallowed.

"Miss Espinosa has been very forthcoming with her opinion of me, so I highly doubt that," he said before pulling his gaze away and looking at his dad.

The guilt only intensified. "Brooks, I'm sorry—"

"I came to get you," he said to his father, ignoring her. "The snow's really coming down now, so you won't be able to drive until they plow. I want to make sure you don't hurt your knee when you're walking back."

Feeling like an outsider again, Ava dug into her purse and retrieved enough kronas from her wallet to cover the meal and leave a generous tip. Whatever hope she'd had to fix things with Brooks wasn't going to happen tonight. There was no point in her staying where she was unwelcome.

She stood to put on her jacket, wobbling off to the side. Brooks caught her by the arm and steadied her.

He closed his eyes and let out a frustrated breath. "Looks like I'm going to have to take you home too."

"It's fine. I'll be okay."

"Judging by your slight slur, I doubt it. Plus, another foot of snow has dropped. It's not safe. I don't need you getting lost in the storm and finding you frozen to death blocks in the opposite direction. That's a lot of insurance paperwork I don't feel like dealing with."

"Oh. How chivalrous." Ava rolled her eyes. "Well, we wouldn't want you to drown in paperwork, now would we? Funny how that didn't seem to matter much to you earlier. I thought you weren't *on the clock*," she said, making air quotes.

"Are you always this difficult, or am I just the lucky bastard?"

"You just bring it out in me."

Good job at apologizing, Ava. She was hopeless.

Brooks's gaze traveled down her body the same as it did before, making her feel like he could see every inch of her bare skin. It stopped at her feet. "I see you took my advice and put on boots."

"I *chose* to put these boots on. It had nothing to do with you."

His lips twitched more as he tried to suppress a smile. For a moment, Ava thought how handsome that little hint of genuine playfulness made him. He almost seemed human.

She wanted to see it again.

"I'll come back to grab you after I get her settled," Brooks said to his dad as he guided Ava through the crowded bar and out to the street.

The frigid wind blasted her with snow, stunning her for a moment. Brooks held onto her arm, helping her shuffle along the snow-covered ground that was now as deep as mid-shin.

"Can you stop grabbing me like I'm an inmate?" Ava complained, trying to pull away.

"It's impossible to see a few inches ahead of us, and that's without the mulled wine."

"I might not be a heavy drinker, but I can handle a few glasses of wine. You don't have to treat me like a college student after a night celebrating her twenty-first birthday. I only had two drinks," she said as she started teetering to the right.

Brooks steadied her again. "Okay. That's wine. Not *Freyja's* wine."

"I doubt warm wine and spices make that much of a difference." She spit out a bunch of snow that'd blown into her mouth and walked ahead, out of his reach.

"No, but the brandy and Amaretto mixed with it will. And Freyja doesn't have a light pour."

Well, that would explain why she felt way drunker than expected. She'd blamed it on jet lag. Rather than comment and let Brooks know he was right, she kept marching ahead.

"Ava, slow down."

As soon as he said the words, her foot slipped. She flew into the air and landed hard on her back, legs splayed above her head.

Brooks rushed to her side. "Jesus. Are you okay?" His hands roamed her body, checking for any broken bones.

She swatted at his hands. "Stop coddling me." She hated herself for liking how he touched her, even if it was merely for safety reasons.

He grabbed her arm to help her up, but she swatted him away before she let the effects of Freyja's wine make her do something stupid. Like pulling him down on top of her and exploring how his mouth tasted.

"I've got this."

Standing, Brooks crossed his arms as he watched Ava try to stand. Just as she thought she'd gotten it, her feet slipped again, causing her to come crashing down face-first into the snow. She tried to ignore Brooks's laugh echoing through the quiet night.

"Okay, so maybe I had a little too much to drink," she conceded as she rolled onto her back, watching the snow glitter in the light of the lamp post nearby.

"Probably, but it's more likely that you keep slipping on ice hidden under the snow. That's why I wanted to make sure you got home safe."

"Noted." Ava grudgingly took his outstretched hand. He lifted her to her feet as if she weighed nothing and helped her a few more yards down the sidewalk before she slipped again.

"You're an accident waiting to happen. This isn't working."

"What are you talking—" Ava squeaked as Brooks lifted her into his arms bridal style. Resting in his arms, the warmth from his neck and face contrasted with the cold air. She shifted slightly, growing more intoxicated by his fresh, earthy scent than the mulled wine.

"Stop fidgeting, or you'll knock us both down." He gripped her tighter. Even under his thick winter jacket, his body radiated heat.

She'd never been a damsel in distress. In fact, she was the complete opposite. Always the one to offer a hand, to protect those who needed it, to fight for her place in the world. It was rare, if ever, that she'd let someone help her. Ava's strength and independence were her assets. The reasons she'd achieved so much.

If she were honest, though, the way people put her on a pedestal in the workplace made her feel alienated. Like at any moment, she'd tip right off the side and fall helplessly to the ground, proving she wasn't as amazing as they made her out to be.

That she was just an imposter who faked it really well.

Their high expectations only added to the pressure she'd felt all these years, as if she didn't already have her own impossibly hard expectations to live up to.

She couldn't mess up. Ever. All eyes were on her at all times.

Under normal circumstances, she'd demand to be put down and create some space between herself and Brooks.

She'd show him she didn't need him. Make it clear she was perfectly capable on her own.

And yet...

She couldn't deny how nice it was to be taken care of for once, being scooped into his arms so effortlessly. For a moment, she embraced the feeling of just *being* and accepting help without shame, even if it was as simple as carrying her so she didn't fall on ice.

For that second in time, she didn't feel the pressure weighing on her as it had been since she was a teen. When she'd been old enough to understand the struggles her family faced—financially and otherwise—and all her parents had done and sacrificed to ensure Ava and Jess would get the things in life they'd only dreamed about when they came to the States.

It had been exhausting pretending she didn't need someone to lean on. For a selfish moment, she'd enjoy it...even if it was Brooks who was giving her the brief reprieve.

She let out a long sigh, breathing in the cold fresh air. Breathing in the man determined to drive her insane for the next few days.

A man who didn't even want to deal with her but was carrying her to the inn as if he was about to consummate their wedding night.

She flushed.

It's the wine. Definitely the wine.

Brooks made it up the steps of the inn's porch and pushed through the wooden and glass door with his booted foot. Rough and determined. He definitely couldn't be described as having grace or charisma. Not by a long shot.

Helga came rushing around the front desk. "Is everything all right?" she asked as she followed them through the lobby, rattling off questions in Icelandic.

"Freyja's wine," Brooks answered as he stomped up the steps.

Helga's laugh traveled up the staircase.

"There are pain relievers in her nightstand drawer!" she shouted up after them.

"I could probably walk now," Ava said with reluctance. "No ice in the inn, I'd hope."

"We're here anyway."

He eased her to her feet, and she felt awkward and hot all over. His warm breath fanned the loose hair around her neck, making her aware of how close he was.

She dug into her purse, fumbling with the card key a few times.

"You've seen me to my door. I think I can take it from here." The card key slipped and fell to the floor a second time.

"Apparently not." He snatched it up with the agility of an athlete, scanned the card, pushed open the door, and herded her inside.

He followed.

"Okay...I'm inside. I think you've gone beyond the call of duty. I'll give you five stars, okay?" she said as she ambled around the room, looking for something to busy herself with but feeling disoriented.

"I'm assuming a five-star review won't overshadow whatever you said to my dad."

She turned her back to him and cringed, pretending to search for her phone cord to charge her very charged phone. "It was nothing. Really. Just a little venting. He'll probably write it off as drunk talk. He was fine about it."

Brooks sighed. "Dad's good-natured about everything." He spun her to face him, stopping her from her erratic fidgeting. "How many fingers?" He lifted his hand.

"Ummm." Ava shut one eye and focused. "Twoish?"

"Oh, for fuck's sake," he muttered. "You better not die in your sleep. You're not the type to puke when you've gotten sloshed, are you?"

"First off, I'm not *that* drunk."

Brooks crossed his arms and shot her a disapproving look. "Regardless, I don't need you choking on your vomit in your sleep. Promise me you'll at least sleep on your side. I don't need—"

"Insurance paperwork to fill out. Yeah. Yeah. I got it." She huffed. "You know," she went to argue, but paused when he dropped his arms and stepped closer, his thumb and index fingers gripping the tiny zipper of her jacket, pulling it slowly down. Her heart leapt to her throat.

"You know, what?" His voice was low. Gravelly. His dark blue gaze followed the trace of the zipper as it traveled the length of her.

She shook her head and straightened, trying to avoid the zing coursing through her or how absolutely sexy she found his intense stare.

Would he have the same look on his face if she was lying naked on a bed in front of him? Would his eyes explore every peak and valley of hers, making her feel like the most desirable woman alive?

Her eyes darted to the bed in the center of the room and back to him. *Ridiculous. You're ridiculous. He's insufferable and rude and the worst and just stop.*

She lifted her gaze to focus on his face. "You know, it's your mouth that's the problem." Instinctively, her stare dropped to his lips. His full, beautiful, very inviting lips. "That...that..."

Those lips twitched into a smile. "That what, Ava?" The way he said her name was almost like a cross between a growl and a purr. So seductive. So intimate.

Her brain stopped working.

"Ava?"

She shook her head again. "It's men like you who ruin it with their stupid mouths."

An amused expression filled his face. She hadn't expected that.

He'd been cagey, disagreeable, and standoffish the moment she met him. His smile eased the hard, tense lines of his jaw.

There was that grin again. It was unfair how attractive he was.

"And how would you prefer I use my mouth?"

The heat traveled between her legs, and she clenched. *Oh, no no no.*

"Don't be gross," she chided as he laughed.

He actually *laughed.* Somehow, they'd crossed into laughing territory.

It was short and quiet, but she loved the sound of it and how it made his eyes sparkle in the dim light.

Ava pulled away from him as he finished unzipping her jacket. She tossed it to a chair near the desk. "Let's keep things professional. You being in my room late at night has to be crossing some lines."

"I'd beg to differ," Brooks said, cocking his head. "Plus, it's barely eight."

Ava checked her watch. He was right. "Oh." Between the time difference and the fact that it got dark by four in the evening, Ava's natural clock was all out of whack.

"My job is to keep you safe these next three days, no matter what. And that's what I'm doing. Not only did I make sure you didn't get lost in the snowstorm, now I'm making sure you're not going to suffocate or overheat during the night in that ridiculous puffy jacket."

She sat on the bed, her resolve waning as exhaustion filled her, making her eyelids heavy. Flopping onto her back, she worked to ignore the fact that Brooks was untying and pulling off her boots, placing them neatly to the side. "I don't think you need to do all this though."

"It's all a part of this five-star service you booked." He bowed before retreating to the bathroom and bringing back a glass of water. He held it out to her with a pack of travel pain relievers he found in the nightstand. "I'm at your beck and call, even to make sure you don't suffer from a hangover." He nodded at the glass. "Bottoms up."

Ava rolled her eyes like a spoiled brat and lifted to her elbow to take the glass. She tossed back the pills and chugged the water. "Now you're just doing this to piss me off."

The truth was she liked how she could speak her mind with Brooks. No pretenses. Maybe they were lobbing insults at each other, but his wit was growing on her. Half the time, people were intimidated by her. Or saw her as competition. Or made the assumption they should keep the boss-employee boundaries firmly in place.

Not that she'd done anything to show them that she was open to being more personal. She'd thought her open-door policy had been enough, but after having normal conversation with the townspeople tonight, she'd realized how little she'd done to connect with people on a *real* level. The thought made her chest ache.

Brooks chuckled again but didn't disagree. This side of him was only confusing her more. It was easier to not want to give into the strange pull he had on her when he was being a dismissive jerk. This version of Brooks only made her more curious about who he was underneath it all.

In any case, the least she could do was apologize now that he wasn't shooting daggers at her. Maybe this time he'd hear her out.

"Listen. About before. I really am sorry. I shouldn't have said the things I had. I don't know you, and I had no right."

He shook his head. "Let's just forget it. You gonna be okay?" he asked, the serious concern a stark contrast from his semi-flirty banter moments ago.

She waved a hand limply as the rush of exhaustion threatened to consume her. "Sure."

"See you at eight?"

Inwardly, she groaned but wouldn't admit that she'd be a hungover mess after all the shit she'd given him about punctuality. "Yup. See you at eight."

CHAPTER FIVE

BROOKS

"WELL, YOU'RE A DELIGHT," Brooks said as a zombie-like Ava swung open the door to her room and grumbled a rough greeting. Her gaze dropped to the steaming cup of coffee in his hand.

"Perfect." She swiped it from him and took a large gulp.

"Hey!"

Ava sputtered and pushed the coffee back to him. "Good God, that's disgusting. Why would you bring me that?"

"I didn't. It was mine." He scowled as he noticed how much lighter the cup felt.

"That's strong enough to wake the dead. I wouldn't be surprised if the acidity burned a hole in my esophagus." She slipped a pair of sunglasses into her oversized purse and stepped into the hallway, closing the door behind her. Although he didn't envy how she was feeling—he and many others in town had accidentally had one too many of Freyja's family's drinks over the years and knew the level of suffering that came the next day—he was grateful for the advantage it offered.

She was still a spitfire, but her hangover seemed to have toned down that perfect, control freak veneer she'd been hiding behind since the moment he'd met her. Against his better judgment, he was curious to know who Ava Espinosa was when she wasn't busting his balls.

Maybe this was his chance to learn a little more.

When he'd walked into The Chantey the night before, he'd hung back in the doorway, watching how she charmed the rest of the town with her stories. Something about seeing how she and his father hit it off warmed his heart—a heart that had felt cold and closed off for longer than he'd like to admit.

He couldn't keep his eyes off her. He was captivated by the impassioned rise and fall of her voice as she shared her tale, even if it was venting her grievances about him. He'd known if he'd walked in right then, he'd have broken the spell. Jealousy had twisted his insides, surprising him.

He couldn't blame her for her frustration. He'd been less than welcoming from the second he'd met her, intentionally provoking her a time or two.

Okay, so maybe more than a couple times.

He'd figured she was going to be another tourist who would turn into a massive pain in the ass, especially with the stubborn defiance radiating from her.

But he had started to realize that the stubbornness that *should* have pissed him off was drawing him in.

Made him want to know more, and he didn't know why.

If anything, sparring with her shined a spotlight on how predictable life had been. Safe. Calm. And for a good reason, he needed that.

But Ava...she felt *not* safe. That had been a good enough reason to keep his distance, or so he'd tried to tell himself.

The fact that she clearly didn't need or want him pulled at him, tempting him to dig deeper. He'd spent most of his life protecting and shielding people. Finding ways to keep them happy and safe. For once, it was nice to know he didn't have to walk on eggshells or be in a constant state of alert, in search of the first sign of danger.

This woman could hold her own, and that did things to him he wasn't quite ready to address. The harder he tried to convince himself not to cross the line, the more he wanted to test those boundaries. It was the last thing he needed. He couldn't get distracted. Finding out what was affecting the town's fishing trade demanded his focus.

He'd thought he could survive three days without getting sucked into her orbit. Now, he wasn't so sure.

"Can we make some ground rules for today?" she asked as she followed him down the stairs.

Ah. There's the ballbuster. Even a hangover couldn't hold her down.

"Of course. Because nothing says a fun day of vacation like rules."

"Ha ha. How about just *one* rule then? Can we negotiate that at least?"

He nodded. "I can work with that."

"Under no circumstances will you jerk and flip the plane again. Honestly, my stomach and head can't handle that. This rule is doing us both a favor. Trust me." She groaned.

"Lucky for you, we won't be riding in Darlene today."

"You get your dad's plane or something?"

He frowned and whipped around, finding a slight smile playing on her lips. "Very funny. No, we won't be flying today because..." He paused as he pulled open the inn's door, unveiling the winter wonderland outside.

Ava took a slow step past him onto the porch, peering down the quiet main road. Her face softened, giving him a glimpse of what she looked like when she didn't have her guard up.

Stunning. She was stunning.

"Wow. This is gorgeous," she said, her voice breathless.

Brooks stood next to her and admired the view from her perspective. For her, the sight of the quaint town covered in snow would be breathtaking. Like a snow globe come to life, complete with billowing smoke rising from the chimneys as far as the eye could see. Above that, the clouds had moved on, leaving an inky sky full of twinkling stars.

Even at eight in the morning, Iceland was still dark at this time of the year. With only roughly five hours of sunlight each day in December, it would be another couple of hours before the sun rose. When it did, the snow would sparkle in its light. Brooks was sure that would also take Ava's breath away.

However, his reaction to the snow was quite different. When he'd woken up this morning to discover the unplanned squall had dumped a foot and a half of snow and that the town plows hadn't been out yet to clean up, he'd been frustrated.

Örugg Höfn was no stranger to snow. They had their cleanup system down, but Brooks knew from experience that the town's main roads were the primary focus first. Then the side roads and the more rural roads.

Finally, they'd work on some of the outskirt sections, like the hangar.

It would be hours before they made it that way, and by the time they'd cleared it out, the sun would already be setting.

It meant losing a day to investigate the suspicious activity they'd seen while flying back to town yesterday. Ever since he'd spotted it, his insides felt twisted with adrenaline and tension. After months of coming up empty-handed, he finally believed they'd gotten a promising lead.

Now, he was anxious he would lose it as soon as he found it. Time was ticking.

"Where to?" Ava asked, breaking his thoughts.

"Figured I'd show you around Örugg Höfn since we're grounded here today. Then we can explore the other towns tomorrow when Darlene's been dug out."

He strolled down the steps and made a left onto Hafnarstétt, enjoying the gentle sounds of water rhythmically lapping against the boats in Örugg Höfn Port just across the way. "Judging by your current state, we should stop for breakfast to soak up whatever booze is left over in your stomach," he added.

He knew just the spot. Emilia's coffee shop was only a few

minutes' walk down the road and would be the perfect opportunity to talk to some of the townspeople who were being affected. They were always there for their morning meal before they sailed off for the day. Even during the off-season, they'd show up like clockwork.

People in Örugg Höfn liked their rituals and traditions. Brooks had discovered that quickly as he'd gotten older and spent the summers here. He found comfort in it. It was something he could count on. Up until recently at least.

"Surprised you aren't throwing me over your shoulder so I don't break my neck." Ava followed him, nimbly avoiding patches of ice. A teasing smile brightened her face.

"The sidewalks down this road are shoveled. Figured you could handle it." He tried his best to ignore the unfamiliar feelings stirring inside him as he remembered how it felt holding her in his arms last night. Soft and warm. Her perfume wrapped around them. The same perfume that lingered on his jacket, which he may or may not have sniffed this morning.

"Wow. Who would have gone through the effort to shovel this much already? They must have been out here early."

He, in fact, was the person who'd been out there shoveling the snow at four in the morning, after the snowfall had slowed to light flurries. But he wouldn't tell her that. He didn't need her looking at him all funny if he admitted it, and he didn't want the barrage of questioning that would likely come after.

Ava was a stranger just passing through. He *needed* to remember that, especially during those moments that made him want to lean in rather than push away.

She didn't need to know Brooks always shoveled the snow, with pleasure. Although there were plenty of younger people in town, a lot of residents were older. Or, as in his father's case with his knee surgery, struggling with mobility.

Brooks had been a punk-ass kid most of the time he'd visited his father over the years. Each visit, he'd caused enough trouble and headaches in hopes his father would send him back to Georgia.

Brooks hated leaving his mom alone, especially when she'd sent him to spend time with his dad during the duration of his summer breaks.

That left nearly three months of his mom unprotected.

As hard as he tried to be an outsider, the people of Örugg Höfn weren't having it. They all but killed him with kindness, breaking his ways until he just accepted it for what it was: a town full of people who cared for one another.

When he moved here permanently two years ago, he only then saw how deep that love went. The least he could do, after all they'd done for him, was make sure they had a clear sidewalk to safely make it to wherever they needed to go. Every person here was a hard worker in one way or another. He was glad to take something off their plate.

The aromas of freshly brewed coffee, buttery eggs, and fatty bacon cooking on the griddle greeted him and Ava when they pushed through the door of the small breakfast spot. The familiar smell always reminded him of home.

Brooks grabbed them a table by the large front windows so that Ava could enjoy the views of the harbor. She settled her small purse on the chair next to her and unzipped her jacket before taking a seat and flipping over to the English menu.

"No mammoth purse today?" Brooks looked at his menu, though he already knew he was getting his usual. "Guess that means you don't have your ridiculous planner with you. Maybe I can actually show you around without you barking orders about efficiencies and timelines."

"Why would I need to carry around my planner when I already know it by heart?" She smiled sweetly at him and fluttered her eyelashes.

Great.

Leaning back in his chair, he surveyed the room, spotting Viktor, Lars, and Kristofer at their usual booth. Each of them drank black coffee as they read their newspapers in silence. Just like always.

After making sure Ava didn't accidentally order something weird when Emilia came by for their orders, he stood. "I'll be back in a minute. Just need to say hi to some people I know. You gonna be okay?"

Ava pulled out her phone and let out a breath as her shoulders sank. "It's fine. I have hundreds of emails to review anyway, so I'm sure I can entertain myself for a few minutes."

She was already immersed in her phone before he could respond. Feeling less guilty leaving her, he crossed the small cafe and slid into the booth with the rest of the men.

Viktor lowered his paper enough to peer at Brooks. "Any news?"

The other men folded their papers and placed them on the wooden table, focusing on Brooks. He leaned forward. "I think I've got a lead. When I was flying back to town, I saw some suspicious activity about forty kilometers south from here. Almost looked like drilling."

Kristofer, the owner of a whale-watching tour charter and the youngest of the group, cocked his head. "Drilling? Out there? There's nothing out there."

"If it's the area I'm thinking of, drilling is prohibited," said Lars, a local seafood restaurateur.

Viktor, always intensely serious, held Brooks's stare. "How does drilling inland affect the fish?"

Viktor was the biggest fishing tradesman in town and the surrounding areas, having taken over his father's business nearly thirty years ago. The town's food scene relied heavily on seafood, and with the hit Viktor had taken these last couple of months, many places of business, including Lars's restaurant, were suffering. Some worried they'd go out of business if things didn't turn around soon.

"It's not this particular one that I think is causing the issue," Brooks said. "But if what Lars is saying is right, this might mean whoever's behind it doesn't play by the rules. Maybe they're tapping into areas that affect the rivers that flow into the ocean."

"That's a bit of a stretch." Kristofer straightened in his seat and took a sip of his coffee.

"Maybe. Would make sense though." Lars rubbed his chin. "It

could explain why Viktor's catches have been sick or dying lately. Or why the animals seem to be retreating from the area."

"Shit," Kristofer muttered. "The whale pods do seem to be migrating away. Maybe they can sense something is in the water."

"The specialist who tested the water didn't capture anything concerning," Lars said.

Brooks shrugged. "Perhaps it was trace amounts. Something his tests couldn't identify, but something the animals are able to sense."

"Hey, Brooks," Emilia stopped by their table, pulling the men from their intense conversation. "I think your American is having an aneurysm. Take care of it before she scares away the customers."

Brooks turned.

Ava's eyes were closed, and she was roughly rubbing her temples and taking in deep, shuddering breaths.

One problem at a time.

"I better get back to Ava," he said as he stood.

"You'll tell the others?" Viktor asked.

"Yeah. I'm making my rounds today."

Viktor nodded. "Good. Keep us informed."

Brooks had taken Ava to some of the highlights of Örugg Höfn, strategically selecting tours, museums, and architectural marvels that conveniently allowed him to slip away and consult with other townsfolk who either worked at the sites or nearby.

It also acted as a great buffer. Her perfume was like a siren song, calling for him to spend more time alone with her. To soak her in.

He needed to stay the course. Damn it. No getting tangled up with someone just passing through.

After a soak at the geothermal pool, which seemed to revive Ava from her hangover and allowed Brooks an hour to check in with the last of the group, they'd walked down the main road to grab some dinner.

"So...that was a weird day," Ava said after a few moments of silence.

The sun had set a half hour ago, and the temperature had dropped significantly. Her breath came out in tiny white puffs as she spoke. He looked down, noting the way the cold air had made her cheeks turn pink.

It reminded him of how she'd blushed last night when her gaze had dropped to his mouth and lingered there. How she'd leaned slightly forward as if she were a second away from rising to her tiptoes to kiss him.

In that brief moment suspended in time, he'd wanted to kiss her too. Was praying for it. But before he could act on it, he had reminded himself that the flush could've simply been from the rush of alcohol coursing through her veins, not because she felt this attraction too. And the tilt closer to him could have just been a drunk wobble.

Plus, if he was going to kiss a woman, he wanted to make sure she was in her right mind to remember it. Not that he had any business wanting to kiss her. They'd be a disaster together, even if it was only sex.

He had a feeling nothing would be simple with her. Even more of a reason to get the idea of it out of his head.

"Not sure what you mean."

"Do you think I didn't notice all your hushed conversations today? I wasn't sure if you were showing me a tour of the town or if we were on some errand. There were a few questionable stops that you claimed were locals-only, but I'm not sure I believe that."

Okay. So maybe he hadn't been as discreet as he'd wanted to be, but he was thinking on his feet. The town was relying on him.

"It was a very authentic experience."

Ava stopped walking. There was a determined look on her face, which only meant a headache for him. "Brooks, tell me what's going on. I wasn't eavesdropping, but I heard some of it here and there. Is something killing the marine life? Did it have something to do with what we saw when we flew here?"

Brooks chewed on his inner lip, battling the desire to be honest, but reminding himself she had no business knowing. This was his problem. Not hers. "Don't worry about it."

"It sounds serious."

"Ava, just leave it alone. You're not one of us. This isn't a problem you need to be concerned about. If anything, it's people like you who probably have caused the issue to begin with."

His words came out angrier than he'd intended, and he instantly regretted it, but he didn't take them back. The truth was she was leaving in a matter of days. The town didn't need an outsider muddying up all their hard work. It would waste more of the precious time they didn't have.

This was for the best.

"*You* people? What the hell does that mean?" She put her hands on her hips and took a power stance, trying her best to make her tiny frame seem dominating.

"Tourists."

She threw up her hands and shook her head. "That's right. How could I forget how much you hate tourists? I love how you group me in with them. Maybe I was a little rude to you at first, but I don't deserve this level of hostile judgment. I thought maybe we were getting past this." Her chest heaved under her thick jacket, and the pink of her cheeks turned a shade darker. She looked away. "I just wanted to see if I could help," she added, her voice barely audible.

He took a step toward her. "Why? So you can share some lame post on social media patting yourself on the back for all the good you did on your vacation? This problem is bigger than pitching in to volunteer for a couple hours and calling it a day. More importantly, this problem doesn't involve you. We don't need you or your help, Ava."

Her mouth fell open, and her eyes went wide. He'd expected her to be pissed. To argue back. Instead, the expression that flashed across her face looked more like hurt.

That quick flash gutted him.

"Fine," she said, her voice quiet but strong. "Clearly, you have bigger issues to focus on than showing me around, and I have a presentation to deal with anyway. How about you take me directly to Reykjavík tomorrow instead of continuing this tour?" She pushed past him and stomped ahead before spinning back around. "And don't worry. I won't expect a refund. Your very kind father needs any business he can get, especially with someone like you destroying his reputation."

Fuck. He'd pushed it too far.

"I'll find my way back to the inn. Call me when Darlene is dug out and we can go. Otherwise, leave me the hell alone."

Brooks stood there as she stalked off, wanting to be glad that he got her off his hands so he could focus on his mission, but a stronger emotion washed over him.

Regret.

CHAPTER SIX

AVA

SHE SHOULDN'T HAVE BEEN HURT by Brooks's dismissal, and yet the feeling of being discarded ate at her more than she'd expected. Even when she'd accidentally ran into him hours later on her walk to find cell service, the weight of disappointment sank into her stomach like a lead ball.

She couldn't even stick around to hear whatever he had started to say to her. It sounded like an apology—or whatever could be considered a Brooks-type of apology—but she wasn't having it. Her chest tightened up, the sensation overwhelming her to the point where she needed to get back to her room. To be alone.

To not see his face and remember what it was like to be pushed aside, like so many people had done in her life growing up. Brooks's words bubbled up some of the things she'd felt and feared most of her adult life: she didn't offer anything of value. She wasn't worth anyone's time. It was why she'd worked so hard to advocate for herself. To be strong and independent. Too many people had held her back or looked past her potential.

The bite in his words only brought up years of insecurity when she had felt like an outsider. When she was reminded constantly that she was never enough. Of having to fight harder for everything she'd earned in her life. And when she'd finally achieved those things, of feeling like she had to defend why she deserved to have them and work even harder to keep them.

She thought she'd gotten past that. She'd spent her whole life proving herself, but in that simple interaction, she saw that no matter how much success she had, she would never be done trying to show people her worth.

After their run-in, Brooks had left her alone like she'd asked, but he still managed to find a way to invade her thoughts. First came a knock at the door later that night. Helga stood on the other side with a tray full of food from one of the local eateries. Too angry and hurt to venture out for a meal earlier and not wanting to run into him again, there was no way Helga could have known she'd skipped dinner.

Unless Brooks had something to do with it.

Judging by Helga's darting gaze and evasive responses to her questioning, Ava was almost certain the meal was his idea.

Which only confused her more. The second she'd met the infuriating man, he'd kept her at arm's length. He'd been gruff, reserved, and clear about how much he didn't like people like her invading his town.

When he didn't think she noticed, she saw glimpses of what was underneath that prickly exterior. She'd heard parts of the conversations he'd had around town that day, offering some of the kindest and most comforting words to those who struggled to keep the tears from falling.

He helped with odd jobs as she perused the museums, moving boxes to a back room and grabbing something from a high shelf for the older man running the place on his own.

While Ava lounged in an outdoor thermal pool, Brooks had told her he was running an errand and he'd be back. Little did he know, she'd had a vantage point to see him assist an elderly woman cross the road so she wouldn't slip on ice. The woman had patted Brooks's cheek with affection, and the beaming smile he'd returned had transformed his face in a way that warmed Ava more than the geothermal pool had.

It piqued her curiosity even more when she'd learned he'd been the one to dig out the sidewalk. Yet when they'd talked about it earlier that morning, he'd said nothing.

As the day went on, Ava had started to think she'd misjudged him and that maybe if she let her guard down and was kind to him, he'd show her the side to himself that he'd only reserved for those he trusted.

Based on what she'd heard all day, the problem affecting the town was important to him and those he cared about. She'd thought maybe if she'd offered help, he'd let her in.

Why wasn't I good enough to be let in?

Had she gotten him all wrong? Maybe he was one of the good guys...just not with her. That realization stung, and she didn't know why.

As she stomped back to the inn and started stuffing some of her clothes into her suitcase to prepare to leave tomorrow, she'd berated herself for being so stupid to think he was anything more than any of the other assholes she'd constantly had to prove herself to.

From his somewhat playful banter and making sure she was safe to his harsh comments meant to push her away, the man was giving her whiplash, and she didn't know what to make of it. More importantly, she didn't know why it even mattered. He was a stranger. She had nothing to prove to him.

In less than twenty-four hours, she'd never see him again.

When she settled in bed later that night, she wondered why that thought ate at her.

Ava rubbed her eyes, trying to ease the dryness from staring at the computer screen for hours the next morning. Brooks had sent her a text earlier to let her know the plane was still inaccessible but would be ready to go later that afternoon. With time to kill, she started working on the strategy her CEO had tasked her with.

She pulled her gaze from the laptop and leaned back in her chair, capturing her reflection in the mirror hanging above the desk. She looked just as miserable as she felt. After two hours of reading through competitor research, the product road map documents, and the sales strategy, her brain had turned to useless mush. Words like *revenue, renewal rates,* and *subscription models* swirled around her head. As soon as she'd cleared one email out of her inbox, two new ones appeared in their wake. All urgent from her CEO. All ambitious from her chief product officer. All demanding from the head of sales.

All of them relying on her to see their vision come to life and entice customers and prospects to buy their product over their competitors'.

Ava had known taking the CMO job was going to be hard work, but she'd had grand dreams to make an impact and leave a legacy. Her goal was to focus on ethical marketing practices. To feel good about what they put out in the world. To believe in every single word she placed in her marketing campaigns.

Somehow, she'd barely gotten into the role and that vision already felt like a pipe dream. Nothing about it felt right. Yet it was her job. Sometimes that meant making tough choices and working on projects that didn't spark as much joy as she'd want.

She hoped this was a fluke. Maybe the timing of her new role and the pressure of being competitive had lined up wrong. Once they got this out in the world, she'd have more freedom to put her vision into motion.

Her stomach clenched, as if telling her that her gut instincts didn't believe that one bit.

Convinced that part of her dissatisfaction was due to exhaustion from tossing and turning all night, thanks to dreams of dying fish and Örugg Höfn storefronts being boarded up, Ava rose from her seat and grabbed her jacket. A caffeine jolt would get her in the right headspace to tackle this. Luckily, she'd seen a coffee shop only two stores down when she'd first arrived in town.

Quick, close, and easy. She'd grab a coffee to go and get back to her work.

"Good morning, Ava. How are you today?" Jón asked as she passed by his business on her way to the coffee shop. He wiped down the front door's glass with cleaner and flipped the sign to "Open."

"Hi, Jón. I'm doing well. Yourself?"

"Can't complain." His wide smile turned into a concerned frown. "Uh oh. You have that look on your face. Brooks isn't giving you more trouble, is he?"

"Not exactly. Just didn't get much sleep last night." She bit her lip. "Do you mind if I ask you something?"

"Not at all."

"Is Örugg Höfn in some sort of trouble?"

She wasn't sure why she asked. Brooks had told her to stay out of it. He'd told her it wasn't her problem to deal with. After the hurt from his rejection had subsided, she'd thought maybe he was right and it was for the best to let it go.

But she couldn't stop the question from tumbling out of her mouth. She wanted to believe it was some sort of rubbernecking syndrome, like when you can't help but slow down and stare at an accident on the highway.

Her stomach twisted again, making it clear it wasn't basic curiosity.

The blood in her veins seemed to be carrying electric currents as something within her sparked to life.

Jón offered a small smile and placed a hand on her shoulder. "Why don't you come in and we'll talk?"

Although Jón had been kind the moment she'd met him, she half-wondered if he'd shut her out on such a personal topic. Instead, he filled a mug of hot coffee for her and sat with her in the lobby's small seating area, welcoming her to talk.

For the next few minutes, Jón sat quietly as Ava explained what she'd seen and overheard yesterday, ending on the warning Brooks had left her with before she'd walked away.

"Oh God. I did it again. I wasn't saying anything bad about Brooks. I just wanted to explain what happened." She shook her head, feeling like an idiot for unloading on him, especially when it didn't exactly paint his son in the best light. Jón's gentle and patient presence made it so easy for her to be open and honest. If the tour guide business didn't work out, he'd make a killing as a therapist.

When she'd finished, he nodded and patted her knee. "It's fine, Ava. My son can sometimes cause friction, whether he means to or not. As I said to you the other night, Brooks has a tendency to take on all the problems of the world, but he does it alone. He'd been a little too serious for his own good even as a kid. Then, everything with his mother a few years ago happened and—"

Jón shook his head. "I'm getting ahead of myself. All I'm saying is that Brooks has always believed it was his calling or his duty to carry the heavy weight of these burdens and never has been willing to share the load with anyone, no matter how much we try to help. He wants to take care of everyone around him, but that's too much for one person. I've told him time and time again, he's stubborn as hell though. All that burden leads to pressure, which leads to his unfiltered responses. He doesn't mean much by it. He just wants you to not worry about it."

Every word Jón said about Brooks hit Ava right in the heart. She'd known that pressure and burden all too well. Flashbacks of childhood memories flooded her brain. Those times when her family struggled to make ends meet. How her mother cried when they ran out of money due to an emergency, which meant she couldn't pay for Jess to join the soccer team she'd so desperately wanted to be a part of. How her father's hair seemed to have turned gray overnight because he couldn't take a single day off work.

As a kid, she'd felt helpless watching her family work tirelessly, only to barely get ahead. Sometimes even their hard work and sacrifice couldn't stop the unexpected backslide that made her parents believe they'd never pull themselves out of that financial hole.

When she'd gotten older, she'd vowed to never leave her family struggling again. Her parents hadn't known she'd secretly overheard their conversations as a kid and that had been what prompted her to get her first job at thirteen. Of course, they'd never have taken the little money if she'd offered, so she'd leave money in her mom's purse, stuff it in the couch cushions or in their pants pockets sitting in the laundry basket. Not too much to raise suspicion, but enough that her parents believed they'd forgotten all about it, grateful to have discovered the money.

Or the time she'd told her mother that the school soccer team Jess had her heart set on didn't require any funds to join. Instead, Ava had paid for it out of pocket so Jess could get what she wanted without making her parents feel guilty that they didn't have enough to take care of their daughters' wishes and needs.

Since she was old enough, she'd carried that burden with her. It was the driving force behind every choice she'd made as a teenager and adult. It's how she'd achieved what she had and why she'd done it.

Like Jón had said, the pressure of it all could be too much to bear sometimes. She'd worked hard to keep the stress from causing her to lash out. She had always given the impression that she had everything handled. Covered. That she was reliable.

But there were moments when it was all too much. During those times, she ached to have someone to turn to, but she reminded herself that people were counting on her. That her *family* was counting on her. This reminder alone helped her get back up, dust off, and keep pushing forward no matter what.

Just like Brooks.

"His bark is worse than his bite." Jón winked.

The bell over the door tinkled as Brooks blew in, bringing a gust of cold air with him. His gorgeous husky followed him, her bright eyes searching the space. When her gaze landed on Jón, she did a happy dance.

"Okay, okay. One second and you can go to grandpa. Just hold still." Brooks unhooked her leash, and the dog bounded over to Jón and Ava. When Brooks lifted his gaze and spotted Ava, his eyes narrowed. "Having another one of your enlightening chats, I see."

"Hey, cowboy. I saw Ava passing by and invited her in for a coffee. Someone's gotta show her that not all the Jónssons are Neanderthals," Jón said, a playful smirk spreading across his face.

Brooks scowled.

After getting enough scratches from Jón, the dog took interest in Ava. Wandering over to her, she nudged Ava's hand. Ava laughed. "She's very sweet."

"That's Stella. She's my number one girl," Brooks said, his face full of adoration as he watched Stella lick Ava's hand. That glimpse of his softer side again humanized him in a way that tugged at her heart. Sure, she'd captured some moments of his caring side when they'd been out and about yesterday, but there was something about this open, unguarded moment that made her see past the snarky behavior and start to understand what Jón had been saying about his nature.

Ava's heart leaped in her chest. With that little insight, things clicked in place. His reaction wasn't so much about her, as much as it was what lingered from everything he'd been through. It was his defense mechanism, which Ava knew plenty about herself.

"So you're saying Stella is higher on the totem pole than Darlene?" She hoped the playful comment could serve as an olive branch.

Brooks's dark blue gaze lifted to hers. The skin around his eyes crinkled as a smile so powerful and brilliant filled his face, the air left her lungs. That smile was like seeing the first sunbreak after weeks of miserable rainy days.

The craziest part of it all was that he was smiling at *her*.

The tension between them faded as their gazes held. Ava returned his smile, a silent way to show him all was forgiven.

"Just don't let Darlene know," he said.

His eyes stayed locked on hers a moment longer before his smile faded and he shook his head, as if coming out of a daze. "I'll swing by later to get you. Okay? C'mon, Stella. Let's get you fed."

Stella gave Ava's hand one more kiss before she followed Brooks into the back of the store.

Ava turned to Jón. "Stella lives at the shop?"

"Yes and no. There's an apartment upstairs. Brooks lives there."

"Why did you call him cowboy? I heard Freyja say it too the other day."

Jón's eyes twinkled. "It's a term of endearment we have for him around here. Being from the States, he has the tendencies of the old Wild West cowboys."

Hm. The States? Interesting.

"Like shoot first and ask questions later?"

He barked out a laugh. "I like you, Ava. You've got spunk." Jón swiped away a tear from his eye. "More like when faced with a challenge or danger, he dives right in without hesitation. The name came about when he was visiting one winter break when he was a junior in high school. He was so reckless and determined to piss me off every chance he got." He shook his head, but a smile lifted his lips.

"What happened?"

"There was a farm down the road from our house. A neighbor had just gotten a stallion that needed to be tamed and broken in. That damn horse was just as wild as Brooks. Maybe he saw something in the horse, a kind of kindred spirit. Brooks decided to steal it and race off to the edge of town. By some stroke of luck, he happened to stumble upon a tourist who had lost his way while exploring the nearby forests to look for natural geothermal pools. He'd broken his ankle while hiking and had been stranded there for more than a day."

Ava gasped. "In the winter?"

Jón nodded. "Hypothermia was starting to set in. Frostbite had gotten a couple of his fingers. Brooks got the hiker onto the horse— no saddle, mind you—and galloped into town. I still remember the sight of him racing through the middle of the street on horseback like a bat out of hell, stopping traffic as he made his way to the emergency center. Brooks saved that man's life. I think that's when he discovered his calling for search and rescue."

"And his disdain for tourists, I'm sure."

They grinned at each other.

"The local newspapers had a photo of him racing through town on horseback with the headline 'Real American Cowboy Saves Injured Man.'" Jón laughed. "Brooks *hated* the attention brought on by that and how the nickname stuck. Eventually, he gave up trying to fight it."

The bell over the door tinkled again, and a woman walked in. "Hello. Are you available for tours?" she said in a thick Italian accent.

Jón stood. "Duty calls," he said to Ava. "Feel free to pour yourself another coffee and hang here for a while."

"I should get back," Ava said as she rose from the couch. "I have to finish packing before we head to Reykjavík."

"I'm sorry to see you go. Could you at least wait until tomorrow? The town's having its annual Christmas kickoff party tonight. We'd love to have you, if only to show you the true heart of our town instead of what you've experienced so far."

"I wish I could." Ava's gaze peeked at the stairs leading to Brooks's apartment. "But I think I might have overstayed my welcome."

He waved that off. "Nonsense."

"I should get going anyway. Somewhere I can get reliable internet and cell service at least." She shrugged. "Work stuff. You know how it is."

Jón's forehead crinkled. "At least try to enjoy yourself while you're visiting, will you? Iceland is a beautiful country. I'd hate for you to miss out on what makes it truly remarkable."

"I promise."

Jón held out his hand, and Ava shook it. "Although much too short, it was my pleasure to have gotten to know you."

"Likewise."

Ava left the shop all sorts of confused about the man who'd basically barreled into her life and invaded her thoughts since the moment she'd met him. Had she ever known someone as complex and interesting as that?

Lost in thought, Ava pushed through the front door of the inn and started to climb the stairs when she heard a woman crying. Pausing on the step, she listened to the voices coming from the dining area off to the side from the front desk.

"We'll figure this out," Helga's comforting voice floated from the room.

"This is bad, Helga. Very bad," the other woman said in between sobs.

Ava felt guilty eavesdropping, but the tortured words made it hard for her to step away.

"The government is overloaded with other things. It will be months before they can get here to investigate," the woman said more clearly. "We thought maybe some of the local research centers or nonprofits could help, but they don't have the funds to put toward it. One specialist said if we can raise the money, they'll make it a priority."

"So let's raise the money."

"We've tried, Helga, but we're not fundraisers. We're not able to get the awareness we need to secure the money fast enough. We had a good boost in the beginning, but it's nowhere near what we need. It's taking too long. By the time we raise the money—*if* we raise it—our fishing trade will be dead."

There was silence for a moment. "So we're out of options?" Helga asked quietly.

"If things continue the way they have been, our economy will take a massive hit. Worse than what we've seen so far." Another sob. "I talked to the other towns along the north coast who've dealt with this over the past year. The towns and their economies have suffered because of it. It's a ripple effect. We...we can't let that happen here. We can't let whatever this is destroy our home."

"Then we won't give up."

"I...just don't know what else we can do and how we can get it fixed quickly enough," the woman's voice wobbled.

Ava's heart clenched as she heard more about what the town was facing. Every tearful word. Every panicked thought. It stirred something within her.

She didn't know these people. She had no connection to Iceland. Yet as she learned more, she couldn't stop herself from being pulled further in.

Just as the thought came to her, so did the solution.

CHAPTER SEVEN

BROOKS

"You can't keep doing this, you know."

Brooks paused in his stealthy pursuit to the front door of his dad's business. With his dad's disappointed look from earlier that morning, Brooks had sensed a lecture was coming. To avoid it, he purposely timed his escape for when his father took his usual lunch.

No such luck.

Brooks exhaled a long, drawn-out breath and turned to face his father, who was relaxing on the lobby couch with a soup in hand. "What, Dad?"

"Ava's a nice woman."

He snorted. "She's pushy, opinionated, and doesn't know how to mind her own business." A little pang of guilt hit him in his gut. Maybe she'd come off that way at first—there was no denying they'd gotten off on the wrong foot—but Brooks had captured little glimpses of the woman behind that bullheaded exterior.

If he were being honest, he'd had a part in her prickly behavior. He hadn't been the easiest to deal with. It was a character flaw, but when his mind was focused on something, it was hard not to act a little grumpy when trivial things like playing tour guide stopped him from doing what mattered.

"She's a lot like you." Jón shared the casual remark as he blew on the heaping spoon to cool the soup.

Brooks knew to look beyond his aloofness though. Jón was winding up for something. "I doubt that."

Jón patted the seat next to him. "Let's talk, son."

Here comes the lecture.

Feeling like a disgruntled teen again, Brooks resisted the urge to roll his eyes. He crossed the threshold and sank down on the couch. "You were saying?"

"You can't keep punishing yourself, Brooks." Jón fixed him with a serious stare. Brooks's father was always a charming, happy-go-lucky guy who rolled with the punches with a smile on his face. Even when Brooks actively tortured him while growing up, Jón never lost his cool.

Which is why his serious expression made Brooks instinctively sit straighter and listen.

Brooks hesitated. "I don't know what you're talking about."

"What happened to your mother—"

Brooks sprung from his seat, his feet already pulling him to the door. Away from this conversation. Away from the memory. "I don't want to talk about this—"

"Sit. Down."

Brooks turned again, noting the flushing of his father's face and the narrowing of his eyes. He'd never heard his dad use that tone. Maybe if he had, Brooks would have learned better than to push the boundaries while growing up.

They stared at each other, his father's eyes a mirror reflection of Brooks's midnight blue ones, neither of them willing to back down. Finally, Brooks conceded and took a seat on the chair across from his father, needing a little bit of distance when they had this conversation. He'd known it would come eventually. His father had tried so many times since Brooks came to live here full-time more than two years ago.

With how his father was looking at him, Brooks knew he couldn't avoid it any longer.

"I let this go on for far too long." Jón placed his soup on the coffee table in front of him. He clasped his hands together and rested his elbows on his knees, his stare fixated on Brooks. "I understand everyone grieves differently. But over time, their lives go on. They get better." Jón shook his head. "You're stuck in a holding pattern."

"You don't know what you're talking about." Defensiveness rose in Brooks, fueled by the worry that his father could sense the pain he tried so hard to mask.

"I have eyes, son. I can see just fine. Although you're doing everything you can to keep the people you care about safe and happy, you've closed yourself off. Take Ava, for example. You shut her out for no reason. She doesn't deserve how you've been treating her."

"What's it matter if I get buddy-buddy with her? She's gone in a matter of days. I don't get the point you're trying to make." There was a bite in his tone, a reflection of how shitty he felt inside. Nothing about this statement or how he had treated her was right, but it was necessary, as much as he started to hate himself for it.

"Every person has a chance to leave a lasting impact on your life. Doesn't matter if you know them for one minute or a whole lifetime. I knew your mother was leaving after her semester abroad and that neither of us would budge on leaving our homes. Our relationship had an expiration date, even when we found out she was pregnant, but meeting your mother changed my whole life. Those few months we had together made me the man I am, even if I couldn't keep her."

"I'm not looking for a love affair. I'm not some cabana boy for a random woman to meet while traveling through Iceland."

Jón shook his head. "That's not the point I'm trying to make. You've closed yourself off, not only to other people, but to everything. You used to dive into things headfirst and now you hesitate. It might be for only a split second, but I sense that pause before you commit to something. You don't rise to the challenge anymore. Instead, you only seem open to what's safely within your control. You stopped living life, son. I know it's because of what happened to your mother. It wasn't your fault."

Brooks's gut clenched. He ground his teeth. "How could it not have been my fault? I should have noticed her weight loss. I should have pushed her to go to the doctor's sooner. Maybe if I'd taken better care of her, we would have caught the cancer before it was too late." He roughly shoved a hand into his hair. "Maybe if I'd done my job—my one fucking job as her son—and taken better care of her, she'd still be here."

Flashes of memories tore through his mind, eating at him. The way his mother cried in his arms when she found out she had cancer and how it had progressed far enough to be untreatable. She'd felt so frail.

"I was supposed to keep her safe, and I failed."

The echo of beeping heart monitors reverberated in his mind as a memory flashed of her lying in a hospital bed. Her cheeks had hollowed out, and her skin had lost its lively pink flush. It had all happened so fast. A matter of months, and she'd gone from the free-spirited, creative, loving mother he'd known all his life to a woman who didn't even have enough strength to squeeze his hand when he held hers.

It had just been the two of them. Because his mother had decided to stay in Atlanta, and his father had chosen to stay in Iceland, he'd spent his whole childhood and most of his adult life being the man she could count on. Even at a young age, he knew he'd do anything to protect his mom. He loved her. As he'd gotten older and went away to college, he made sure he was within driving distance so he could be there at a moment's notice.

He'd *hated* when she sent him to Iceland to spend time with his dad. Worry constantly ate at him, wondering if his mother was okay without him there to protect her.

From what? He didn't know. He just knew it was his duty to make sure his mother was taken care of the same way she'd taken care of him his whole life.

Those last few months with her wasting away in the hospital broke him. Every day, getting weaker and weaker.

And he couldn't do a damn thing. From that day on, he vowed never to be in a situation where he felt that helpless again.

As his father's words sank in, he started to realize that part of his vow had made him subconsciously shut people out. The realization sucked the air from his lungs.

He had enough people to worry about. His father. The people who'd become a second family to him here. Brooks couldn't be bothered with opening himself up to anyone else for fear he'd be spread too thin, making those who needed him slip through the cracks. Scared he'd trust the wrong person who would let him down when he needed them the most, leaving him weak, vulnerable, and useless.

He wouldn't let another person he cared about be hurt on his watch. He couldn't handle that sense of loss again. He refused to put himself in that helpless position where there was nothing he could do to change it.

He couldn't. Wouldn't. It was better to avoid that experience again.

"You didn't fail her." His father's soft, compassionate voice pulled Brooks out of his cycle of self-loathing. He focused on his son's face. "You might be a hero to many people, Brooks, but even superheroes have their limits. There was no way you could have stopped her cancer. All the money and treatments in the world couldn't have stopped it. And your mother didn't want to try."

Brooks's eyebrows furrowed. "What do you mean?"

"She called me with the news when she found out. She told me about the experimental treatments they'd offered her, but that none of them would cure the cancer. It would just extend her life by a few months. She didn't want to live her last days like that, son. Your mom had lived a good life. She had accepted that she needed to let go. This was her choice. You need to let go of that guilt."

"I want to. I don't know how." Brooks's voice was quiet. His eyes stung.

"You can start by living your life freely and bravely, like you used to, instead of living a life in fear and self-doubt. It's time you start connecting with others again."

"I can't be that man anymore, Dad." Losing his mother had changed him. The pain of it had eased as time went on, but he'd never truly get over it. It was part of him now.

"No. Maybe not. But you can be a new man. A better man." Jón gave him a pointed stare. "You just need to try. One small step at a time. Maybe start by apologizing to Ava. Convince her to stay one more night. Invite her to the party and show her what's so special about this town."

"I...I don't know, Dad."

"Just think about it. Can you do that?"

Brooks nodded. "I can try."

It felt like he'd had the shit beat out of him. As he walked the few yards from his dad's business to the inn, all the repressed feelings he'd kept locked up tight churned through him. He was raw, confused, and on edge.

Brooks had seen a lot of shit in his day as a search and rescue pilot. Somehow, even in the most dire of situations, not a single person had died in the ten years he'd been doing it. Lost a limb? Yes. Nearly drowned? Sure. Was in a three-month-long coma? Yup.

But no one had ever died on his watch.

Until his mom.

She was his person, and she was gone. Two years later, he still hadn't recovered from it. Now, his dad had pointed out how it was affecting his life. He'd become a coward. Scared of loss. He might put himself out there to help those who needed it, but he'd become more cautious. More of a calculated risk-taker.

When push came to shove, would that split second of hesitation be the reason he lost another person?

Lost in his thoughts, he ended up at the inn, climbing the stairs to Ava's room and knocking on her door.

Maybe what his dad had said about needing to connect with others had some merit, but that wouldn't be today, and that wouldn't be with her. He just needed to get her on the plane back to the city and see her off. Once she was gone, maybe he could make some sense of his life again. Maybe connect with someone who wasn't about to leave Iceland, never to return again.

Ava swung open the door. Her cheeks were flushed pink. "You ready to go?" he asked as he glanced toward her feet, expecting to see a packed suitcase sitting next to her.

"No."

Brooks's gaze rose to meet her dark brown eyes, seeing a spark of something behind it. Excitement? Nervousness? He wasn't sure. But something was different. "I can come back when you're ready."

Her chin lifted in defiance, a slight movement, but one that confirmed that whatever was going on with her wasn't all in his head. "I mean I'm not going to Reykjavík."

"Okay..." He rubbed his hand along his chin, his fingers running along the rough stubble that had grown in since yesterday morning. "So where am I taking you?"

"Nowhere. I'm staying here." She crossed her arms. "I'm going to help."

The muscle in his jaw ticked. "Not this again, Ava. I told you—"

"And I'm telling *you*," she said as she took a step forward and poked him in the chest. He winced and rubbed at it. How did such a delicate finger hurt so much? "I'm not taking no for an answer."

"You don't know what you're talking about." Panic bubbled up inside of him as he deflected. Instantly, guilt washed over him as the conversation with his father from a few moments ago came rushing back. Yet he wasn't ready to budge.

She raised her hand to poke him again, but he gently grabbed her wrist. In unison, they looked to where he clutched her, his fingers engulfing her tiny wrist. His rough, calloused hands contrasting with her butter-soft skin.

For a second, he had the urge to reach up and stroke her face just to find out if her skin was silky smooth everywhere. Touching her was testing the limits of his willpower, which is exactly why he needed to get her on that damn plane.

He dropped her wrist, and Ava took a slight step back, her brown eyes wider than usual. "Anyway," she said, her voice breathy. "I know enough. I know there's something going on with the water and it's affecting your tourism and trades. I know the town has tried to get help, but they've been deprioritized or can't get enough funding to speed it up. I know everyone is worried that by the time help arrives, it will be too late." Her shoulders rose and fell with her deep breaths. "Is what we saw flying here the other day part of this? And don't even think about dodging the question again. If you don't tell me, someone else will."

There was a pregnant pause as Brooks grappled with what to tell her. She already knew enough, so there was no point in lying. But if he confirmed all this, it meant she'd try to stay, which was a whole other problem.

What could a woman who was leaving by the weekend, who has no ties to Iceland, be capable of doing? It would be a waste of time and energy getting her up to speed just for her to go back home, leaving them no better off than they were. Making them believe things could change for the better, only to disappear from their lives, taking their last shred of hope with her.

"Brooks." Her pleading voice pulled him from his internal debate. Her face softened, making him believe she meant well.

"Maybe. We're not sure. It's something I planned to investigate after you were gone."

She nodded and bit her lip as she absorbed the new information. Pushing open her door, she let him in her room. "I overheard a woman talking to Helga saying there are a few nonprofit organizations they think can help, but the issue is they can't raise enough funds in time." Ava followed him inside and paced back and forth, tapping at her chin. "How much do we need?"

He hated to admit how much he liked the way she said "we" as if she'd gladly be a committed member of the community if they'd welcome her. Normally, the presumptuousness would irritate him, with her being an outsider and all, but the determined set of her jaw and how she was reaching for one of her notebooks, a pen in hand for notes, somehow made it endearing. Excitement radiated from her, showing just how much she genuinely wanted to support them.

It was that genuineness that made him second-guess his initial judgment of her. Made him want to believe in her. Made him *just* reckless enough to share more with her.

"They're thinking around a million dollars. But that depends on what we find. This issue seems to be affecting the other northern towns. We're not sure if it's all connected or coincidence."

"Okay." Her pen paused from scribbling notes. "And if we got this million, how soon can these organizations get out here and do work?"

"Our cause is a priority, but without the capital, their hands are tied. They've done what they could to raise money, but they're smaller organizations, and fundraising can take a long time. It's a slow trickle. The capital they had has already been committed to other needs. If left up to them, it could take over a year to get the funds we need."

"And we don't have that time."

"No. At the rate this is going, we might have a few months tops before our economy and the wildlife are completely destroyed. Even if we fixed the issue after the fact, the damage would be done. It would take years to recover and rehabilitate it. At that point—"

"Örugg Höfn wouldn't survive."

"I don't see how it could." They stared at each other for a long moment as the weight of his words hung between them.

"Okay," Ava said, letting out a big breath and pacing again. "So what if I was able to get you the money in two weeks?"

That wasn't possible. Was it?

Brooks reached out and tugged her elbow, spinning her to face him. He rested his hands on her shoulders to hold her in place. "How?" He tried to keep the hopefulness out of his voice. They'd already tried so many things and failed time after time.

He knew nothing about Ava. She could be one of those toxic-positivity people who lived in la-la land, making promises based on undeserved optimism rather than realities.

"I'm a marketing executive. I've helped a startup back home scale from a pipe dream into a multimillion-dollar leader in the marketplace."

His heart thumped hard in his chest. "So that means..." He needed to hear the words.

"It means I know how to build awareness and make money. What we need is to put together a campaign asking for help, and we need to go wide." A look of concentration crossed her face again. "You may hate tourists, but they might be your saving grace. Iceland is on so many people's bucket lists. Those who've visited have fallen in love with the island and hope to come back someday. Maybe by letting them know there's a threat, they'll do what they can to preserve this little piece of heaven."

It seemed too good to be true. Yet what she was saying made it seem possible. He dropped his hands from her shoulders and shoved a hand in his hair. "You really think you could pull this off?"

"I think it's possible, but it's going to be all hands on deck."

"We'll do anything."

"So...you'll let me stay and help?"

"Yes." Brooks was shocked by his lack of hesitation. Only minutes ago, he'd convinced himself it was for the best to let her go. Now, his heart thrummed at the thought of spending more time with her. It both scared him and made him feel more alive than he'd felt in a long time.

A slow, radiant smile filled her face. One that made him feel like he'd just given her the greatest gift in the world.

That smile could out-dazzle the Northern Lights. It could provide more peace than the flowing waterfalls. It could create a sense of awe and wonderment more than the vast landscapes of volcanoes, mountains, glaciers, and beaches.

That smile changed his world.

Ava let out a little squeal as she jumped up and wrapped her arms around his neck. "Thank you, thank you, thank you."

He wasn't sure why this meant so much to her or why she'd go out of her way to help them, but he wouldn't question it.

Instinctively, Brooks wrapped his arms around her waist and squeezed her tightly. She felt good against him. Soft and feminine. Her scent swirled around, filling his senses and releasing the tension in his shoulders.

She slowly released her grip, but they didn't let go of each other just yet. A piece of her hair had fallen across her cheek. Brooks reached up to tuck it behind her ear, his fingertips circling behind her lobe, down her jawline, and along the line of her neck. Her pulse pounded under his fingertips.

He smiled, knowing it matched his own.

He was mesmerized by Ava Espinosa. Maybe he'd been since the moment he'd met her but had been too bitter and closed off to recognize all the qualities she'd shown were things worth admiring.

Even after how he'd treated her, she still was offering to help. She was big-hearted, just like the people of Örugg Höfn. They deserved to have someone like her on their side, and he'd be damned if he was the one who prevented it from happening.

"So now what?" His voice was hoarse. The air between them seemed to disappear as their gazes stayed locked on one another.

Ava's pupils dilated. She licked her lips. "Now, we—" Her cell phone blared from her pants pocket, breaking the trance. She shook her head and pulled it out. "It's work."

Reality set in. He took a step back and shoved his hands in his pockets. "Right. How are you going to help us? Don't you need to be back at work?"

"I'll figure something out. Let me take care of it."

Wariness filled him. He wanted to put the walls back up. Wanted to give her an easy out. Wanted to push her away.

But he couldn't.

It would be stupid to put all his faith in her when it was clear she didn't have the freedom. But when his father's words came rushing back, he fought the urge to write her off and go it alone.

There had to be a happy medium, right? Maybe he wouldn't go rushing in to trust her until there was some proof that it was worth the risk. Maybe the best route was to ease her into it before he got the town all riled up with excitement. He could show her the realities of what they were facing and what the commitment would be from her if she did want to help.

She'd make the decision if this was something she could do, especially if she had a high-profile job back home to deal with. He doubted Ava could get the extra time to stay here and fundraise without sacrificing a lot to do so. Even if her boss agreed, how helpful would she be if she's being pulled in two directions?

He guessed he'd find out. It was time to see if Ava was the real deal before he let her into the fold.

"There's a town meeting about it later around dinnertime. Can you make it?"

"Of course."

He nodded. "All right. You need to promise me you'll be a fly on the wall. Listen before you make promises. These people will cling to any shred of hope offered to them. What you're saying you can do is a big commitment. I want you to really understand what you're signing yourself up for before you say a peep. Got it?"

She pursed her lips and raised an eyebrow. "You're not very good at accepting help, are you?"

"About as good as you are minding your own business."

Instead of her normal retort, she simply smiled a genuine smile that gut-punched him again. "I'll see you tonight, Brooks."

"See you tonight." He paused in the doorway and turned back to her. "There's a thing tonight after the meeting. An annual Christmas party." He tried to find the nerve to finish what he'd started to say. "You're more than welcome to come."

Nervous excitement rolled through him, as though he was asking out the most popular girl to prom. The anticipation of her answer could make his day or crush him. That worried him, but not enough to dull his racing heart when her eyes sparkled.

"Your father mentioned that earlier. I'd love to, but are you sure? I don't want to intrude on your town's tradition."

"Everyone would be more than happy to have you."

He was direct, sometimes to a fault. Yet he wasn't quite ready to say what he actually felt: *he* wanted her to be there.

He couldn't remember the last time he'd felt like that. With how shut off he'd been lately, he'd expected it to be a lot more worrisome. She should be the last woman in the world to stir any of these emotions, and he sure as hell shouldn't be entertaining them...but he didn't hate it.

CHAPTER EIGHT

AVA

THE CURSOR on Ava's screen blinked. It had been taunting her for the last forty-five minutes. After Brooks left the inn with a promise to pick her up for the meeting at The Chantey later that evening, she got to work on a campaign plan for the ZettaBytes product launch. A realistic one she'd planned to share with Benson to help him see the light, if she ever got in touch with him.

How she'd approach it was going to be tricky, especially because she still had to talk to Benson and her team about extending her trip. In theory, it shouldn't have been a problem. Half of her marketing team was scattered around the country, and the C-suite could be found across the globe. Despite being distributed, they'd worked together just fine.

Her track record *should* ease any cause of concern. She had pulled together huge campaigns with tight deadlines while on the road before. Plus, she'd be back in Boston well before the launch went live. But those ones had been straightforward. Something about this campaign made her stomach churn.

Even all the logical reasoning in the world still wasn't enough to help her calm down. She worried how her feedback would be received. Oddly enough, she was less worried about her job being on the line and more worried that Benson would pull her home before she was ready to leave Iceland.

Funny how that worked. She'd only been here a few days, and yet the feeling she got when she thought of leaving was strikingly similar to homesickness.

Her eyes focused on the stupid blinking cursor. After poring over the countless emails and documents sent to her, she'd hoped to have some spark of inspiration to drive the campaign strategy. But as she read more and more about the product launch goals, she became queasier and queasier.

A bit agitated too.

As if she wasn't already in a time crunch, her mind kept wandering back to her conversation with Brooks a couple hours earlier. His walls had been firmly up when he first showed up at her door. Miraculously, she'd convinced him to take a chance on her. His face had been hard to read as he'd considered it. He had a good poker face, she'd give him that, but it was the little flash that lit up his dark blue eyes that gave him away.

Like something had clicked for him.

Brooks was always a little rough around the edges. Gruff. This afternoon he was even worse for the wear. However, when she told him what she could offer, his shoulders relaxed. The hard edges of his face eased. He'd even invited her to the party tonight. A way into the fold, even if it was just for a few hours.

Would it be ridiculous to think that maybe Ava had restored a bit of his lost faith? With what he'd seen in his life, Brooks was likely jaded. Cynical. When he'd left her room, though, the dark cloud that followed him around dissipated just enough to make Ava feel like she'd gotten a foothold. Maybe with time, she'd get enough leverage to lob herself over those walls he'd erected. Hopefully.

They were making a turn. Maybe he didn't completely open himself up, but it was progress. That was a victory worth celebrating, no matter how small.

The opportunity to help this town and do a little good had sparked the inspiration she'd lost along the way. The outcome of what she could deliver was important. This wasn't about selling a product. This wasn't about beating the competition. This was about people's livelihoods.

There were plenty of businesses struggling—some that had been passed down from generation to generation and others that were new, first-time owners. The hardships that hit the fishing trade and marine tourism had a ripple effect. Fewer tourists meant local shops and restaurants would see a downtick. The drop in income meant less taxes. Less taxes meant less funds to improve their school system, fix potholes, and ensure roads were taken care of after a big snow.

A lot was riding on their ability to raise money to investigate the mysterious issue and, hopefully, mitigate it. She had the skills and know-how to support their cause. It felt meaningful to be giving back with no expectations of receiving anything in return. This could be the one and only time she would ever visit Iceland. If she helped the town, she may never get to reap the benefits of creating a healthy ecosystem.

It didn't matter though. What they needed was bigger than her and her wants.

As if her fingers had a mind of their own, she clicked out of the blank document and pulled up her Slack, pinging one of her go-to engineers, Marissa.

Ava: Hey, Marissa. Quick question. If I were to use our databases to look up information about trends...say, climate or geological or whatever, how easy is it to cross-reference other databases?

Marissa: Depends on if the information is publicly available. We've got a lot of scientists who are using it to fight climate change, so I suspect they'll have their research out there to collaborate with others.

Ava: Cool. Thanks.

Marissa: LOL such a random question. What's going on?
Ava: Long story. I'll fill you in when I get back?
Marissa: Fineeee. Let me know if you need anything else.
Ava: Sounds good. Appreciate it.

If there was one thing she learned while working at ZettaBytes, it was that people had used their database products for extraordinary things. Earlier in her career, she'd often sit in on customer interviews to learn how they were using the product, and it astounded her. The flexibility of their databases really helped people make their big dreams come true, no matter what it was. The databases had only gotten stronger since then. The use cases were boundless.

Part of that had to do with the open-source community. With their contributions, those using the product had collaborated in fascinating ways, helping them to achieve things quicker and more effectively.

Although she hadn't poked around in that depth, she wondered if there were ways she could connect with the open-source community and put feelers out, explain the situation in Örugg Höfn and see if there were certain things they should be searching for in the public databases.

Maybe there was a trend they were missing that could help them get a head start on what was happening to their ecosystem.

It was almost three in the afternoon. She had a few hours to start digging into this option before Brooks picked her up for the town meeting. If Ava was anything, it was prepared. She'd use her time wisely so that when she finally was let into the inner circle, she could gain their trust.

And hopefully, his too.

Three hours later, Ava swung open her door. Brooks stood on the other side with his hands stuffed into his jeans pockets, looking slightly unsure of himself. Despite being more on the casual side, he looked nice.

Okay. Nice wasn't a strong enough word for it. Ava had always found him attractive. However, tonight his good looks only seemed even more amplified.

His snow boots were replaced with stylish ones, and his jeans were crisply pressed. Rather than a hoodie or a flannel, he wore a button-up that molded to his fit physique. Beanie gone, his dark hair was pushed back. She was almost tempted to run her hand through it. Right then, with the look of uncertainty filling those captivating eyes, he was disarming.

Again, she got the sense that he wanted to believe in her, but something was holding him back.

That small hint of vulnerability made him that much more endearing.

When Brooks's gaze lifted to meet hers, she felt that pang in her heart again. Probably like how the Grinch felt when his heart grew a few sizes bigger at the end of the story. It was a hard thumping that made her all too aware she was alive.

He made her feel alive.

In the midst of all that thumping, she realized she liked this pattern of him showing up at her door. Even if it was temporary.

"You look beautiful," he said, his gravelly voice rumbling in the space between them.

Thump. Thump.

She turned away to grab her jacket, unsure if she could handle a second more of her erratic heartbeat when he looked at her like that. "Thanks. I hadn't planned for a party, but I hope this is okay."

She'd thrown on a red wrap-top and black slacks, showcasing her hourglass shape. With dangling black earrings and a sparkly black bracelet, she'd hoped she'd looked nice enough. She wasn't sure what to expect.

"You're perfect. Ready?"

"Yup." Her voice sounded wobbly. Almost as wobbly as her knees.

Even when he was dead set on pushing her away and practically begging her to ask for a refund, something about him drew her in. She could push all she wanted. She could reason with herself high and low. But the moment they'd met, she'd felt tethered to him. Each moment, it tightened, pulling her closer.

Not knowing what to make of it, she shoved those feelings deep down. It was no time to fantasize about a guy who lived across the ocean. A guy she barely knew. A guy determined to keep her at arm's length.

That was probably for the best.

All that mattered was getting him and the people of this town to open up to her so she could help.

Grabbing her bag and closing the door behind her, she followed him on the short walk to The Chantey. They navigated the sidewalks, now clear of snow but still icy in some spots. Side by side, she could sense that tether again. Tugging. Making her aware.

Her chest went tight, and the urge to grab his hand was hard to ignore. It was the weirdest urge. Made absolutely no sense. Yet something inside her ached to be closer to him.

It wasn't like Ava hadn't had her fair share of dating. Most of them were short stints though. In a city full of successful people, she found it shocking how many men were intimidated by her work ethic and success. The ones who weren't had way too much ego for her to handle. Of course, she'd had the occasional fling—but it had been years since anyone had made her feel like this.

A little out of control. Every cell in her being on alert. Primal.

The feeling consumed her. Confused her. Hit her like a speeding train. Unexpected. Intense. Mindless.

And likely, very, *very* stupid to give it another thought.

"Are you okay?" Brooks asked, pulling her from her thoughts.

Light snowflakes drifted lazily around them. She zipped her jacket as far as it could go as bouts of wind stung her cheeks. "Sure. Why wouldn't I be?"

"You're quiet. You're never quiet. It's unnerving."

She grinned. "What's wrong? Miss the sound of my angelic voice?" Ava batted her eyelashes, trying to make light of the situation so he wouldn't catch on to the awkward change in her feelings toward him.

"You've caught me." Brooks glanced at her from the corner of his eye, a slight grin lifting his lips.

Whatever cold she'd thought she'd felt instantly disappeared. She didn't know him well enough to gauge his sense of humor, but something about how he said it made her believe he'd meant it.

Or maybe it was wishful thinking.

They stopped in front of the bar. Ava suddenly wished they weren't already there and walking in. Once they slipped through those doors, their private time together would be done. She wasn't ready for that.

"Remember, you're a silent spectator tonight," he said.

"Why?" Her smile transformed into a frown. "I thought you wanted to let them know I could help if I felt I could handle it."

A distressed look crossed his face. "We talked about this. I don't want to get their hopes up. You need to use this time to really listen and understand what we're up against before you come riding in on your white horse."

"Well, first off, I love that you're progressive enough to insinuate that a woman can also be a white knight." She smirked. "But okay. I'll do my best."

"Ava." He shot her a warning look.

She tossed up her hands in surrender. "Okay, okay. I'll simply be a spectator tonight. But if I listen and feel that I'm up for the challenge at the end, I'm going to run my idea by them. Deal?" She held out her mittened hand.

He hesitated and blew out a breath. "Fine. Deal." He grabbed her outstretched hand and shook.

Even though both of them had gloves on, something about the contact zapped through her. She could have sworn he sucked in a breath as he held her hand long after the deal had been shook on. Their eyes locked, and the wind and the flurries seemed to have slowed down, enveloping them in their own private world where only they existed. The warm light and jolly chatter from the bar created peaceful white noise. Heat radiated from his body as he stepped closer.

"Ava." It was a whisper on his lips. His hand squeezed hers lightly as he took another step forward, suspending them in time.

"There you are," Jón said as he pushed the bar door open. The warmth and noises from the bar spilled out loudly, breaking their spell. "We're waiting on you, cowboy."

Brooks gave her one last lingering, private look. "Come on." He held the door open so Ava could go in first.

The Chantey was packed. Groups of people mingled among each other, deep in discussion. Ava recognized a few faces from the last time she'd been here, plus a few people she'd met during the tour of the town the last few days.

Freyja balanced a tray of beers and served them to a group of women nearby. "Ava!" she said as she finished handing out the beers. "It's so nice to see you again." Freyja tucked the empty tray under her arm and squeezed Ava in a quick hug. "There are a couple seats at the bar, if you'd like to sit there."

"Thanks."

Brooks followed as Ava wove through the crowd toward the bar. Helga spotted them and patted two empty seats next to her and Jón.

Despite the friendly and welcoming greetings, worry fluttered in Ava's stomach. She felt like an intruder and wondered how people would take her being there.

A few people sent her curious stares. However, for the most part, people either smiled at her and raised a drink or were too involved in their own conversations to even notice.

Maybe Brooks was right in telling her to keep quiet this first meeting. Although everyone had been nice to her, they might not take too kindly to her injecting herself into their business. She may be able to help them, but she wasn't Icelandic. How would they feel having a stranger coming in and imposing her thoughts on their problem?

As if sensing the flurry of anxiety rushing through her, Brooks handed her a beer. His eyebrows lifted. "Is this okay?"

"I'm fine. Don't worry."

His lips twitched. "I was actually questioning your tolerance for beer. Can you handle one or am I going to have to carry you home again?"

She narrowed her eyes and took a healthy gulp. "Unless this beer is infused with secret liquor, I think I'll be just fine."

A short, middle-aged woman with pale blonde hair and a round face with ruddy cheeks clapped as she made her way to the front of the bar. "Okay, everyone. Let's settle down so we can get down to business. I know we have our annual party tonight, and although I don't want to put a damper on it, time is of the essence in our situation."

Brooks leaned closer. "That's Lotte. She's the mayor," he whispered, the warmth from his breath fanning across her neck. If she turned her head even slightly toward him, his lips would be millimeters from hers.

Those full, expressive lips. The ones that were typically in a tight, distrusting scowl whenever she was in sight.

Except today. Today, he'd actually acted in ways other than annoyance toward her.

Lotte clasped her hands in front of her. A grim look filled her features. "As you know, our town has been suffering these last few months. It's aligning with the trends our neighbors in the north have seen this past year, but the root cause is still unknown." She shook her head. "Although their towns have suffered, the devastation here has been much worse and came on much quicker. What we're experiencing now is at a level well beyond what they've dealt with. If it keeps going down this path, the damage to the marine ecosystem could be irreversible."

A few gasps filled the space. Quiet whispers among the group filled the air. Ava scanned the crowd, noticing the range of emotion across their faces. Some looked numb. Tears filled a few women's eyes. A handful of men looked pissed.

This is even worse than I thought.

Lotte held up her hands to quiet the crowd again. "We've put in a distress call to the government asking for aid. Unfortunately, our request was denied due to the issue not being catastrophic enough to use disaster funds to support us. We're low on their priority list. We've turned to scientific organizations and nonprofits to help us, but their financial resources are strapped too. We're waiting on one last organization to respond—"

A woman in the crowd stood from her chair. "I'm sorry, Lotte. I just received an email from them right before the meeting. They can't help either."

Lotte held her stomach as if she'd just been stabbed. She took a slow breath with her eyes closed. Dropping her hand, she looked at the crowd again. "Okay. We're out of immediate options then. These organizations want to help, but they need money to do it. The grants they've received are dedicated to specific projects. Whatever donations and fundraising they've gotten isn't enough for the amount of work needed to be done."

Helga stood. "We've been trying to raise money, but it's been slow going. At this rate, it could be years before we can ever come close to raising as much as is needed."

"And we don't have years," Lotte said. "We need a new plan of action. Do any of you have any ideas?"

Ava turned to Brooks and shot him a pleading look. He shook his head. His eyes held a warning.

She leaned closer to him. "I understand you're worried, Brooks, but you're not in a place to deny help. *Any* help at this point will make a difference. Maybe I won't be here long enough to see it through, but I can at least get the town in a place to make traction. It can make a real difference." Butterflies fluttered inside her stomach, making her mission to help feel that much more important. "*Please* let me do this for you. For all of you."

His chest rose and fell with his steady breathing as he paused to consider it. Brooks might have been willing enough to bring her here tonight, but he'd mostly fought her tooth and nail the entire time she'd known him. She understood that it was his way of protecting the people he cared about. He didn't know her well enough to trust her with something this big.

As the seconds stretched on, she was almost certain he would shut her down. Instead, his gaze locked on hers and he gave a tight nod.

"Don't let them down, Ava."

His words lingered between them. They were weighty and held more meaning than what was said. If she offered to help, if she spoke up, this meant he was letting her in and it was up to her to show him it wasn't a mistake.

Their dynamic would change. She'd no longer be the pesky tourist just passing through. How they interacted with each other from now on would be deeper. Real.

This would change everything.

"I promise."

He exhaled like he'd been holding his breath the whole time. "Then do your thing."

Ava stood and raised an arm, feeling like Katniss in *The Hunger Games* volunteering for tribute. "May I speak?" she asked Lotte.

Lotte gave her a curious look but nodded, waving for Ava to take the stage.

She weaved through the tables, every set of eyes burning a hole in her back. Turning to face them, she looked to Brooks, giving him one last chance to change his mind. Instead, he offered an encouraging smile.

Well, a smile in Brooks's standards. Small. Subtle. Easy to miss if you weren't paying close attention.

"My name is Ava Espinosa. I'm just a visitor here, but I've learned about your struggles in the last few days, and I want to help."

"Are you independently wealthy? Have a small team of marine biologists and specialists in your back pocket. How can *you* help us?" A gruff man Ava recognized from the coffee shop the other morning spoke up. He crossed his arms and leaned back in his chair, his distrustful stare just waiting for her to shrivel under its scrutiny.

She hadn't made it this far in life by shying away from challenges. Every day, she'd been tested and doubted.

She proved them wrong every time.

"I'm a chief marketing officer for a successful technology company in Boston."

The man let out an acidic laugh.

Brooks looked like he was ready to murder him.

"And what good is that to us?"

Ava raised an eyebrow and stood straighter as a silent way to tell him she wasn't going to take his shit. He wouldn't scare her away. "You need to raise awareness and money, don't you? I just so happen to be really fucking good at that."

The man looked at her but said nothing.

Okay. He's not goading me anymore. That means I've got his attention.

A few others had leaned forward in their chairs, interested in what she had to say. More confident now, she continued.

"When I started at that company, I was their first and only marketing person. They were a startup in an incredibly competitive field in a market that would swallow them whole in a second if they didn't produce. With my expertise, I not only helped them secure funding to continue to grow and build, I helped them beat the competition because we could secure enough brand awareness and trust to do it. We had a lot going against us these last ten years, but we survived and thrived because of the strategies myself and my team put in place."

"A technology company is different than what we're facing though," a young woman stated. "I don't see the connection."

"You're right. It's very different. However, the contacts and strategies I've used in the past will help you expedite fundraising. We need to go global with this to get more funds. I have contacts for major media outlets and reporters that can share the story."

Lotte smiled, a look of hope filling her face. "You think this could work?"

"That's just one part of a larger strategy to boost fundraising, but it's a good start."

"What else can we do?" the mayor asked.

Now energized, a spark of creative ideas flooded Ava's mind. "Let me show you." She turned to Freyja and pointed to the oversized chalkboard hanging on the wall. "Mind if I erase your menu?"

CHAPTER NINE

BROOKS

HE COULDN'T DO anything other than stand back and watch as the creative genius formerly known as Ava Espinosa went to work. It was both fascinating and admirable to see how her mind worked as she dove right in and took charge.

After pushing the tables aside and pulling out a short stepladder, Ava stood at the helm near the freshly erased chalkboard and started asking questions. Smart, thoughtful, interesting questions. Questions no one had even thought to ask. He figured she was brilliant and organized, if that ridiculous binder from the first day he'd met her was any indication, but watching it unfold in front of him was eye-opening.

The townspeople became more animated as the night went on, their forlorn expressions now changed to bright eyes and smiles. This was more like the people he knew, not the beaten down and worried lot that they've been these last few weeks. Ava's high energy was sparking life in all of them again.

He couldn't help but succumb to the pull too.

It was as if her mere presence and willingness to commit to this had eased the burden that had been weighing on him. Not much, but it was something. It gave him a little more room to breathe and consider beyond the here and now. She scribbled frantically on the board, helping him see the big picture again.

Maybe they *could* pull it off.

"Okay, so this is just a rough idea," Ava said as she filled up the last empty spot on the chalkboard.

Brooks barely could suppress a grin. She wrote off her strategy as a rough idea—meanwhile, it looked like Albert Einstein had used the board for coming up with the theory of relativity. There were arrows and flowcharts. Calculations and mock-up drawings of advertisements. There were timelines and costs. There were even assignments for people to divide and conquer.

Ava's forehead creased as she stared at the to-do list. She tapped her chin with the chalk. "We need to talk to the neighboring towns about what they've seen."

"We've talked to them before. Lengthy phone calls," Lotte said.

Ava shook her head. "In this case, it might be better to go in person. We need to see if what happened to their marine life is the same as what we're seeing here." She turned to face the crowd. "Viktor, can you give us some of your fish? I want to show the other towns what you're pulling out of the water to compare it to what they've had."

A little twinge of pride tugged at Brooks's chest. Viktor had been an asshole when Ava first stood up there, grilling her with his questions. But she didn't back down, and she didn't take his shit. That alone won Viktor's respect.

Kind of like how she'd pushed back when Brooks had done the same. The grin he'd been trying to suppress won out. A huge smile spread across his face.

That's my girl. She can roll with the punches like the rest of us.

His smile faded as quickly as the thought came. Ava was *definitely* not his girl.

So maybe they were spending a bit more time together than he'd normally spend with tourists. Maybe he found the mix of her fiery personality with her soft compassion endearing. Maybe the moments when she smiled at him—truly smiled that unguarded smile—he felt like he could take on the world.

And he guessed the fact that she made him laugh was another thing that made him enjoy his time with her. She didn't mean it half the time. It was just her way. Yeah, she occasionally had her quiet, pensive moments, but it was the moments when she set her mind to something that really got him. She'd verbally spar with him, possessing wits that ran circles around him, and she wasn't afraid to get her way.

He liked that about her. He wasn't above admitting that he sometimes unnecessarily pushed her buttons just to see how she'd react. She was lively, always keeping him on his toes. Leading a life in which he needed to predict every outcome, he felt now that there was something undeniably addicting about the anticipation of their interactions. He never knew what to expect.

Maybe his dad had been right when he'd said he'd been playing it safe for too long, but Brooks only recognized that when someone fiery like Ava came along and turned his world upside down, challenging everything he thought he knew.

Brooks loved the way her cheeks turned pink when she was passionate about something and the way she pursed those full lips, popped a hip, and hitched up an eyebrow when she was winding up for an argument. And the way her dark brown eyes sparkled when she talked about something that mattered to her.

She was the most beautiful during those times. So beautiful, it made it hard to breathe.

One or two times, he may have been tempted to pull her in and kiss that bossy mouth senseless. He wanted to know if that same passion translated to other areas in her life.

Like, maybe as a lover.

Those thoughts aside, she wasn't his girl. The thought was ridiculous. She deserved more than a vacation fling, especially with a guy who was emotionally unavailable.

"Brooks," Ava's voice broke through his thoughts. "Can we fly in a couple days? With the number of towns scattered along the north coast, we'd cover more ground by taking your plane."

He nodded. "Of course."

"Great!" She wrote their names together near the task. It reminded him of a high school girl writing it on her notebook with little hearts. Was it weird that he liked seeing their names next to each other like that?

Maybe he was no better off than a lovesick teenager.

"Okay. That does it for now. We have everything covered," Ava said. "Try to enjoy the party, because we're going to hit the ground running first thing." She threw a smile at Freyja. "And maybe take it easy on the mulled wine tonight." The crowd laughed knowingly.

It warmed him to see how they'd welcomed her in on their inside joke, almost like she's been one of them all along.

Many people in the crowd raised their half-empty beer mugs. A few came to chat with Ava, giving her hugs and pats on the back. She was a natural born leader, her charisma easily inspiring and influencing people to get on board. Brooks had assumed it would take a lot more to convince the town that someone with no history here could have a good plan. Not for Ava though.

Just another thing about her he was coming to admire.

Brooks made his way to Ava as the crowd around her thinned out so they could get refills or head home. "Pretty interesting strategy."

A sheepish smile filled her face as she shrugged. "Sorry. I know you wanted me to ease into this, but once I got going, I was on a roll." She helped him move the tables back into place. "I hope that's okay?"

"The town's on board with it, so I think it's fine."

That seemed to satisfy her. "Good." Her stomach growled so loud he could hear it over the boisterous chatter of the bar.

"Hungry?"

She flung her head back and mock-wailed, "Staaaarving." Ava

peered at the bar where Freyja was fielding a bunch of orders. "Doesn't look like I'll get something to eat here anytime soon."

"I wouldn't count on it. When we have meetings like this, the kitchen tends to get backed up. Most places will have closed up early for the party. There will be some appetizers tonight, but nothing substantial enough for dinner."

Ava hoisted her oversized purse onto a nearby chair and dug around. "I'm sure I have a granola bar somewhere. Might be a little smushed though." She continued to dig around to the point where Brooks was almost concerned she'd be swallowed whole by the bag. "It's probably expired too, but I don't think granola will be bad after a few months, do you?"

Brooks grazed her shoulder with his hand to stop her from disappearing into the black hole of her purse. "We've got a little more than an hour until the party starts. I'll cook you something. C'mon."

"You cook?" She slipped on her jacket, looking at him with guarded curiosity. "What? Like baked beans and hot dogs?"

He barked out a laugh. "Do I come off like that much of a caveman?"

She circled her scarf around her neck. "Not sure what's the right answer here. Plus, I've tasted your version of coffee." She shuddered and made a gagging face. "I just figured you're like the wilderness guy out here in Iceland, flying around, saving people from treacherous situations. I could picture you pitching a tent in the woods somewhere and cooking a squirrel you caught with your bare hands."

"Have you been watching too much *Man vs. Wild?*" He pushed through the bar door. They made their way down the sidewalk toward his apartment. "I've been known to camp, but I wasn't always in the wilderness like this. I grew up in Atlanta."

"Your dad mentioned you were from the States." Ava nudged him with her elbow. "I knew you had some other accent than Icelandic, I just couldn't put my finger on it." She shook her head, a look of awe on her face. "Wow. That's so confusing. So your accent is a mix of Southerner and Icelandic?"

He shrugged. "Apparently, the Icelandic embedded its way into my speaking patterns, even though I barely spent a few months a year here growing up until recently. I guess when you're around it enough, it just kinda catches on."

Unlocking the tourism storefront, Brooks led them through the back room to the stairs leading to his second-story apartment. Stella scratched and whined at the door at the top of the stairs.

"Brace yourself," he warned. "Stella gets a little crazy whenever I come home."

He pushed open the door. Stella danced like a lunatic, her little nails tapping on the hardwood floor. After a quick kiss attack, she sprinted around the open floor plan, zooming through the kitchen and sliding on the floors as she turned corners, before barreling up and over the couch and stopping on the throw rug to roll around.

"Wow. She's got a serious case of the zoomies." Ava closed the door behind her and hung her jacket and purse on the coat hanger in the foyer.

"That's why I don't bother with nice things. I can't tell you how many things she's slid into and broken." He nodded his head at Stella, who was still rolling around happily. "And that's why I can't have a coffee table there. Whenever I move it in its place, she pouts until I move it out of the way again."

Ava cocked her head and raised an eyebrow. "You know, for a guy who doesn't take anyone's shit, you sure let Stella boss you around."

At the sound of her name, Stella trotted over and plopped in front of Brooks, leaning hard into his legs as he leaned down to scratch her. "There are just some women you can't say no to." Brooks gave Stella one last scratch, and she sighed with contentment. "Make yourself at home while I whip something up. Any food allergies or special diets?"

She followed him to the open kitchen and took a seat on the island's barstool. "Nope. I'm open to whatever."

"Great. Beans and fresh-caught squirrels it is." Brooks pulled a few pans down from where they hung above the island.

"Ha ha. Very funny." She rolled her eyes and settled into the chair, looking more than comfortable in his apartment.

Had he ever had a woman over here? It was an unusual sight to get used to, but he couldn't deny he liked her company. Something about it made the space feel a little warmer. A little more like home.

It reminded him of growing up with his mom. It was just the two of them, and she'd often pull him into the kitchen while she cooked dinner to ask him about his day or just to talk. She'd also pull him from his designated seat at the small breakfast nook to teach him how to cook Southern staples. Collard greens and okra. Biscuits and gravy. Fried chicken. Macaroni and cheese. Of course, being in Georgia, he learned how to finish off dinner with a decadent peach cobbler.

As he moved around the kitchen the same way she used to, he realized how much he missed it and how badly he wanted that again. The smells of a home-cooked meal. The easy conversation. It felt natural.

"Do you want any help?" she asked as he moved on autopilot.

"It's fine."

From the corner of his eye, he saw Ava chewing on her lip as her gaze tracked him. Her head tilted as she watched him with curiosity. "When you said you were going to whip something up, I thought maybe something simple. Microwavable. Or a sandwich. I wasn't expecting a five-course meal."

He smiled and flipped a towel over his shoulder as he seasoned some meat. "Not quite five-course. More like a main and a side."

"Where'd you learn how to cook like this? You look like an expert."

He paused a fraction of a second as he thought about his response and how much he wanted to share with Ava. They might be turning a corner in their tumultuous start, but was he ready to open up about something so personal?

"My mom taught me," he said, bracing himself. He'd expected it to hurt more. To punch him right in the gut like it had those first few months after she'd passed. Oddly, that breath-sucking reaction never came.

"I'm so sorry to hear about her, Brooks. Your father mentioned it."

The pain he'd kept buried for far too long ached to get out. Begged for sweet release. To confide in her. "Thanks." He coughed, riding a wave of emotion as memories swarmed him.

Not the heartbreaking kind this time though. Instead, they were the good times. Memories he'd thought had been replaced by the harsh ones from her last few months on earth. "My mom had a retro radio that sat near the bread box," he started to say, getting a feel for whether he was ready to talk about this. When his words didn't get caught in his throat as they used to, he continued. "She'd always put on the oldies, which of course I'd vehemently complain about, but after a while it became our thing."

It was better to remember her like that. Young. Happy. Full of life.

Brooks had moved back into his childhood home those final months to take care of her. He'd cook and clean, take her to the doctors, and sit on the porch with her. At first, everything seemed normal. She might have been a little more tired, but she'd still make her way to the kitchen to help him make dinner and talk about his day, refusing to rest no matter how much Brooks had protested.

As the months went on, she'd help less and less, opting to do little things like fix a salad and set the table. Eventually, Brooks would cook alone and bring dinner to her in bed, where she finished out her final weeks before passing away in the hospital.

Ella Fitzgerald filled the air, replacing those painful memories with ones of better times. As if sensing the heartache he was internalizing, Ava had gone and given him a small gift. A reminder that he could keep the best part of his mom's legacy alive by embracing her traditions.

He'd avoided those traditions for far too long.

"I hope you don't mind me putting on this station." Ava's soft voice was filled with empathy, something he hadn't known he needed.

He peered over his shoulder, his gaze locking on her brown eyes that were filled with compassion.

There she went, surprising him again.

For just a second, he'd almost crossed the room and wrapped his arms around her in a tight embrace. He thought holding her would ground him.

He shook his head, not daring to need someone like that. Not wanting to rely on someone who would leave any day now.

He had no business wanting this from Ava, no matter how much she'd managed to weave her way into his heart with her generosity tonight or how she listened—really listened—as he recalled some of his treasured memories.

"It's perfect." He cleared his throat, trying to get rid of the sudden tightness. "Want a drink? Water? Wine? Something else?" Brooks asked, falling back into the role of host before things got a little too real between them.

"Water would be fine." She bit her bottom lip. Another wave of appreciation filled him when he realized she wasn't going to push for more. Apparently, there were rare moments where she wouldn't test the boundaries. He was thankful for it.

"Maybe a little wine too, to take the edge off," she said. "I hate speaking in front of crowds." Ava lifted her hand, and it shook a bit. "See that? That's my adrenaline going. Every time I have to present or speak to a crowd, I feel all jittery. Sometimes it takes a few hours to go away."

Brooks was surprised by that. In the few days he'd known her, she'd commanded attention. Tonight was no different. "You were a natural."

She shrugged, an unsure smile filling her face. "That's thanks to the public speaking coaching I got a few years ago. It was expensive but worth it. Unfortunately, no matter how poised and professional I appear, it can't get rid of the nerves."

He searched the fridge for the white wine he usually used for cooking and remembered he'd finished the last of it over the weekend. Closing the door, he leaned against the counter and rubbed his hand on the back of his neck. "Guess I should have checked before I offered. All out of wine."

She feigned shock. Her hand flew to her heart. "Are you saying that you don't have a hidden wine cellar stocked with the best vintages?"

Another rush of appreciation filled him. She was steering their conversation into something lighter. Something he'd gladly play along with.

"Must have cleared it out with one of my elaborate soirees this weekend. Jay Gatsby style."

Ava perked up at that, her eyes sparkling with interest. "A reader of the classics? I wouldn't have pegged you for it." Brooks nodded to the living room behind her as he tended to the steak on the stovetop. She swiveled around on the barstool and stood, making her way across the apartment. One of the squeaky floorboards groaned under her. "Wow. A library wall?"

"I wasn't always a reader, but it's a pretty big thing here in Iceland. Did you know Iceland has one of the highest literacy rates in the world? It also has more writers, readers, and books published than anywhere else." He switched off the burner and transferred the meat to the plate to let it rest. "Makes sense," he said as he followed her into the living room and took stock of his growing collection. "The winters can be long and brutal. It's a good way to kill time."

Ava trailed a finger along the spines, taking stock of his random collection. There were the classics, of course, but also murder mystery, sci-fi, self-help, cookbooks, and even a romance or two. Her finger stopped on one of the Regency romances and pulled it out. She turned to him with a sly smile on her face. "Well, well, well. What do we have here? Are you a closet bodice-ripper romance lover, Mr. Jónsson?"

He took the well-worn paperback from her hands and put it back in its place. "It was one of my mom's." Of course, he'd never admit to her that he had read it too. And liked it.

"She had good taste."

"C'mon. Dinner's done." Brooks led them back to the kitchen. Opening the cupboard above the stove, he pulled out a bottle of bourbon and two crystal tumblers. "I don't have wine, but I have something even better. Whiskey. Will that help tame the jitters?"

"That should do it. Just a little," Ava warned as he pulled out the cork and began to pour. "I'd like to be conscious during the party tonight. I can't have a repeat of Freyja's mulled wine incident and completely lose the faith of everyone I talked to tonight."

"Yeah. It'd be nice to not have to worry about you cracking your head open on the walk back."

"Because of the insurance paperwork and not that you care about my precious skull, right?"

"Exactly. That paperwork is a nightmare." He slid a tumbler with a light pour to her and raised his. "Cheers."

She lifted hers before taking a dainty sip. "Woah." She coughed. "Good, but strong."

"Warms you up. If you're going to stick around here a little longer, you'll take all the sources of warmth you can get."

Walking back to the counter, Brooks put the finishing touches on their plates and placed them on the island.

"So I have an idea," Ava said as she took a seat and draped her napkin on her lap. "The company I work for has this database technology. I was talking to one of the engineers, and there might be a chance that scientists and some of these nonprofit organizations have made their research public using the databases."

He grunted a response and forked a piece of steak into his mouth. Although he was pretty savvy when it came to aviation technology, whatever Ava was saying was over his head.

"What I'm thinking is we can start gathering specific details from the town and the neighboring towns and do a Boolean search through the public databases to see if there's a close match. Maybe we'll get lucky and discover what we're experiencing was something that happened elsewhere and there's a fix."

The woman was resourceful. He might not know much about this database technology, but what she was proposing sounded like a step in the right direction. It could give them an advantage they hadn't had before. If he'd allowed himself to act on his misjudgments and had convinced her to leave, he might have screwed his town out of this insight and help.

"You're impressive." The words tumbled from his mouth before he could stop them. The space between them grew quiet.

Almost scared to look up and see her reaction, he reluctantly peeked at her from the corner of his eye. Ava froze, the glass of bourbon halfway to her mouth. Carefully, she placed it on the granite countertop. "Did you just...*compliment* me?"

"Don't let it go to your head. Darlene has a weight limit." He nudged her plate closer to her. "Eat before it gets cold."

He made the joke in an attempt to hide the awkward feeling of honesty. Even though the words he'd said were true and simple, something about it made him feel vulnerable.

As if he were treading on an icy cliff, just one slippery step from careening off the edge.

But when he looked at her and the satisfactory smile she had on her face as she took a bite of the steak, that edge didn't seem so bad. Warmth flooded through him as a sense of safety enveloped him.

A woman like Ava was hard to come by. In the few days he'd known her, and in these last few hours especially, he felt it in his gut. Knew if he'd opened himself up to her, she'd be impossible to walk away from.

Trouble was, she'd be the one walking. Her life was an ocean away.

"So..." He took a sip of his bourbon, savoring the sweetness and spice. "You talk to your boss about extending your trip yet?"

It was a normal question, given the extensive plan Ava had written on the chalkboard earlier. For some reason, though, Brooks involuntarily held his breath waiting for her answer.

She glanced at him and placed down her fork. "I have a call scheduled with him tomorrow, but I'm confident he'll let me do it."

"That so?"

She nodded. "I've got a plan."

"Always got everything figured out, huh?"

Ava held his gaze a beat too long. The air between them grew thick with tension. The few inches between them suddenly felt too close, but also too far.

"Not everything," she said quietly and turned away. "Oh crap." She pointed at the clock on the stove. "Is that the time? We're going to be late for my very first Örugg Höfn party."

"We can't have that," he said drily, secretly adoring her excitement. He took their empty plates to the sink and rinsed them. "Think you'll be able to save me a dance?" he asked with an air of casualness.

"You might have to fight for a spot on my dance card." Ava winked.

A deep laugh bubbled out of Brooks, earning him a look of delight from her.

She may have been joking, but he couldn't deny that she'd be worth a black eye if it meant holding her, even for just the length of a slow song. The thought should have scared him. Instead, he found himself thoroughly looking forward to spending the evening with her.

CHAPTER TEN

AVA

THIS WASN'T the vacation she'd set out to have, but she wasn't exactly hating it. Brooks pulled open the solid wood door leading into the town's community center. Butterflies filled her stomach.

Dinner with him had been...nice. The curiosity that had been eating away at her had only been piqued more as she gained glimpses of his life tonight and what made him the man he was today. Those rough edges had softened enough to allow her to dip her toes in and dig deeper. To find out what made him tick. To discover all the complicated facets to him.

She swallowed, wondering if maybe she should have declined coming tonight. If she'd just left him after dinner, she had a fighting chance to keep things professional. Surface level. She had no business knowing Brooks more intimately, but damn if she wasn't dying to.

Every look. Every smile. Every slight touch made her pulse skyrocket. It woke her up in ways that were foreign to her, but undeniably good. She wanted more of that feeling, which was exactly why she needed to make sure she stayed busy tonight so they didn't have a chance to dance together.

Ava knew that if he held her close as they swayed to some romantic song, she'd get sucked further into this fantasy.

And that's all it really was, right? A fantasy. They barely knew each other. She'd be leaving before they ever really could know each other. There was no point in getting turned inside out for a man who probably was nothing like she'd dreamed up, filling all the empty pages of his life story with ideas of being heroic and compassionate and caring.

For all she knew, he could have a temper. Seemed that way in the beginning at least. Or maybe he left dirty plates in the sink until they stunk up the kitchen. Or he sucked in bed.

Ava closed her eyes and drew in a breath, annoyed with herself for even imagining him in bed. Something about the fluid way he moved, his passion, and his intensity made her believe that last thought wouldn't be true in the slightest.

"Are you going in?" Brooks's asked.

She blinked as if waking up from a dream and focused on the concerned look across his face. "Sorry."

Stepping through the door, a festive Christmas display greeted them. Twinkle lights filled the area, offering a dim, welcoming space. Live spruces lined the sides with red and green ornaments. A hot chocolate and mulled wine station sat to the side where people lingered, laughing as they sipped their preferred drinks. A makeshift stage with a Winter Wonderland theme was lit up with a small band playing Christmas classics, sung in Icelandic. It was quaint and charming, just like the town itself.

"This is lovely," Ava said.

Brooks stepped beside her, evaluating the space. "It's nice. It's not as festive as normal. With all the issues we've been facing, we've struggled to get into the holiday spirit. Too distracted. Normally, the town would be decked out for all of December. You could probably see it from space with the amount of lights they use." A small smile lifted one side of his lips. "They're always trying to outdo themselves, and they usually succeed."

"Even if it isn't the usual setup, I love it all the same." She scanned the crowd. "That's so cute that they do an Ugly Sweater party too."

"Ava," Brooks said, looking at her with a serious face. "We don't have Ugly Sweater parties in Iceland. That's just how they dress."

Ava's face flamed. "Oh my God. I'm such an idiot."

Brooks's shoulders shook, and she realized he was holding in a laugh.

She swatted at him, a laugh escaping her lips too. "I hate you. You're a jerk."

"You're cute when you're flustered." Their eyes locked, and the laughing died.

Did he just say I'm cute?

Brooks rubbed the back of his neck, looking like he'd wished the floor would swallow him whole. "I...uh. I better make the rounds. You okay?"

"Sure, sure." She shooed him awkwardly. "Go ahead. I'll be fine."

"There's the woman of the hour." Lotte came over with outstretched arms, saving Ava from doing something stupid, like asking Brooks what he meant by that comment. "We were just talking about you. I'm so glad you could make it. Come join us."

Lotte hooked her arm through Ava's and pulled her away. Ava stole a last look at Brooks over her shoulder and could have sworn a flash of disappointment crossed his features before he walked off in the opposite direction.

For the next hour, Lotte introduced her to other townspeople who hadn't been at the meeting. All of them were warm, friendly, and genuine like the rest of the people she'd met so far. Normally, Ava hated those initial meet and greets, especially back home where everyone tried to make themselves seem more important than they actually were. Always filled with strained small talk. Yet that wasn't the case here. Conversation flowed effortlessly, and she found herself enjoying learning about them and their culture.

The whole time, she sensed Brooks's eyes on her. She'd turned and caught him watching her as he made his rounds. When he wasn't, she couldn't stop herself from seeking him out. Wanting to know his attention was on her.

It was ridiculous. And yet it made her a little giddy inside.

Giddy. *Giddy!* Who was she turning into?

"Care for a dance, young lady?" Jón offered his hand, his white eyebrows wagging with amusement.

"I'd love to." Ava slipped her hand into his, and they made their way to the dance floor. "Are you sure this is okay for your knee?"

"Nonsense. I'm not going to let a little pain stop me from enjoying a dance with a beautiful, intelligent woman like yourself." He looked back to the group she'd just been part of. "Plus, I figured you needed a break. Love those people, but they will talk your ear off if you let them." His gaze lingered a moment longer on one particular woman.

"So...Jón. Maybe I'm off base here, but do you have a thing for Lotte?"

His eyebrows shot up. "Oh. No, no. We're just old friends."

"You sure?"

He looked away. "Ah, even if I did have feelings for her, who would want an old man like me? If this surgery showed me anything, it's that I'm past my prime. I'll be lucky if I can do the tourism business much longer. It gets harder each year that passes. Then what? What would I have to offer her?"

"Companionship. Love. Someone to laugh with. Cry with. Enjoy the small things in life with."

"Wouldn't have taken you for much of a sap," he teased.

"I guess we're all full of surprises." She nodded her head toward Lotte. "Go on. Why don't you take a small step and ask her to dance? This song is about to end anyway."

"All right." He sucked in a breath and puffed up his chest as if finding the courage. "I'll go ask her." He gave Ava's hand a squeeze. "Thanks for that little boost. I needed it."

"Of course. Go get your girl."

Jón ambled off to Lotte and asked her.

Ava was pleased to see the pure joy in her face when she took his hand. Maybe this was the start of something amazing for them.

"Happen to have a spot open in your dance card?" Brooks's deep voice rolled down her spine and made her shiver with awareness.

She turned to him, overwhelmed by his proximity. It was more than his broad build and the fact that he stood more than a head taller than her that struck her in the moment. It was the way he was looking at her. His dark eyes were sensual in the dim light, focused only on her. That zing of aching want hit her again.

It should have been a warning. A flashing sign that she shouldn't take his outstretched hand.

But she did, and she loved the warmth and steadiness of it. The roughness of his skin against hers. How it pulled her close enough that their chests only brushed against each other when they inhaled.

She breathed him in. That woodsy smoke scent that lingered on his skin with a slight hint of dinner's aroma clinging to his button-up. A touch of spicy whiskey on his breath.

Resting her arms around his shoulders, she tried to ignore the way she felt with his arms wrapped around her waist.

They swayed to the music in sync, as if they'd done this a million times before.

"It's been longer than I'd like to admit to see them like this," Brooks said. His voice was low, making their conversation intimate. Only for them to share. A little bubble in the sea of people.

"Like what?" She lifted her gaze to meet his. His eyebrows were slightly furrowed, like he was trying to make sense of something.

"Happy." The tension in his forehead eased, and his features softened. "I've been talking to a few of them tonight. Word about the meeting at The Chantey is spreading like wildfire. There's hope in their voices again."

"I'm glad—"

"It's because of you, Ava." Something about the way he said it filled her with a sense of pride she'd long missed. Her insides warmed, and her heart swelled.

She broke their eye lock and let out a small laugh. "I doubt it's because of me."

He took her chin gently between his index and thumb, reconnecting them again. "It is...I shouldn't have misjudged you when we first met. I'm starting to realize how wrong I was about you."

All the air escaped her lungs. It was a simple statement, one she'd heard plenty of times before. But the words wrapped around her, warming her through, carrying so much more weight than they ever had before. Because Brooks had said them.

His gaze dropped to her lips. He moved his fingers from her chin, stroking her jawline before cupping the side of her face.

There was so much want in his expression. That raw emotion did things to her. As if her body had a mind of her own, she lifted to her tiptoes, desperate to feel his lips on hers.

Just a few more inches, and she'd know exactly how it felt to be kissed by Brooks Jónsson.

CHAPTER ELEVEN

BROOKS

"Okay, everyone. I hope you had an amazing time tonight," the emcee announced from the stage, startling Ava and breaking their moment. "It's that time. Grab that special someone for the final dance of the evening."

Brooks could have killed the emcee, even if he was the nicest guy on the planet.

If they'd had one more minute, would he have known what Ava tasted like? Would she have wrapped her arms tighter around him, as desperate to feel him as he was for her, or would she have turned away and given him some line about keeping things platonic?

If that was her choice, he would accept it as much as he'd hate it.

He prayed that wouldn't be the case.

"Is it already almost eleven?" Ava stepped out from his arms and scrambled to pull her phone from her pocket.

Brooks shoved his hands in his pockets and rocked on his feet. "Are you going to turn into a pumpkin at the stroke of midnight?"

"No, but I'll probably piss off a lot of people. I have a meeting with my product team in a few minutes."

He crossed his arms as a wave of protectiveness and concern washed over him. "Aren't you on vacation?"

"Remember when I said I had to convince my CEO to allow me to stay longer despite it being crunch time for a major product launch?" she asked over her shoulder as she walked to the coat check.

Brooks followed. "Mmhmm."

"Well, this is part of it." She thanked the woman at the coat check and slipped on her jacket. "Mind walking me back? I'm a little turned around and can't afford to be late."

"Sure." He'd have done anything for one more minute with her.

He led them out to the quiet road, the first to leave the party. Although it was set to end in a few minutes, he was sure the rest of the town would linger well past midnight as usual. Brooks flexed and unflexed his hand, trying to release the tension coursing through him. Trying to stop himself from reaching out and taking her hand.

What the hell was he doing? How was she twisting him up like this?

It had been a while since he'd dated seriously. He tended to keep things casual, especially when he'd moved to Iceland full-time to watch over his father—not that Brooks would admit that to anyone. Jón would get huffy if he knew the real reason why Brooks had made Iceland his new home. After losing his mother, his dad was all he had left. He wanted to be there to take care of him. He wasn't getting any younger, after all.

Brooks wasn't looking for anything serious, so his arrangements suited him. They were easy. Light.

No woman—serious or not—had ever made his heart race at the mere sight of her like Ava did or turn his thoughts to useless mush.

Made him want so damn much. It wasn't just sexual. There was something else there.

Ava did that. A woman he'd known for mere days made him think all kinds of thoughts he hadn't entertained in years. Made him want to slip out from the tough armor he'd wrapped around himself—

around his heart—and see if there was more to life than playing it safe.

It was the way her dark eyes seemed to look right into his soul. How their little mischievous twinkle made him want to rise to the challenge. How the empathy and compassion within them made him want to trust her.

Made him want to let everything go.

"Thank you for letting me be a part of this really big thing." Ava stopped outside her door, oblivious to the overwhelming thoughts swirling through his mind. "And for dinner. Your mom taught you well."

There was that urge to hold her again. The way she was looking at him right now in the soft light of the hallway. Hopeful. Grateful.

"You're welcome."

His body instinctively leaned closer to her, eager to finish what they'd might have started while dancing tonight. He forced himself to stop leaning closer, to stop getting intoxicated by her flowery, fresh perfume. To stop his gaze from landing on those inviting lips that seemed to be moving closer and closer.

Because they were. Because she was rising on her toes to move toward him too.

It was a mistake to go down this path, but damn if he didn't want to throw caution to the wind. To close that gap and kiss her with everything in his soul.

Her eyes fluttered closed. All she had to do was lift a couple more inches and his mouth would be on hers, putting him out of his misery.

"Ah, Miss Espinosa. I didn't realize anyone was back from the party yet." Helga's voice broke their moment. "I came back early to get a late check-in settled in their room."

Twice in one night. Did the universe have it out for him, or was it doing him a solid and saving him from embarrassing himself?

Ava's eyes popped open. She looked stunned, her breath coming out shallow. "Call me Ava."

Helga smiled at her warmly. "Of course. Ava. Thank you so much for your help. The town couldn't stop talking about it tonight."

"It's my pleasure."

Helga handed her a pile of fluffy white towels. "These are for you. I was just coming to refresh them when I saw you here." She looked between Brooks and Ava, her smile transforming from motherly to looking like she stumbled upon a juicy secret. "Well...goodnight, you two."

They murmured their goodnights as Helga walked down the stairs again.

Ava tucked a thick lock of dark hair behind her ear. "Um...I should get going. The call is about to start."

Brooks wanted to curse. "Sure."

"Thank you again, Brooks. I'll see you tomorrow?"

"I'll be here. On time," he promised as he reluctantly left her at her door.

He wasn't sure what was changing between them. All he knew was he wasn't ready to write it off just yet.

CHAPTER TWELVE

AVA

"Okay. Now you're just doing this on purpose," Ava said through gritted teeth as she grabbed onto the sides of her seat to keep steady.

Brooks smirked. "I thought you were glad we weren't taking Darlene."

Earlier that morning when they arrived at the hangar, Brooks had rolled up a garage door to unveil a practically new Bell 505 helicopter. As in, it didn't have parts Duct-taped together like Darlene did.

Brooks explained he'd named this aircraft Hank the Tank because it was sturdy and dependable even in the most extreme situations. Hank had been an upgrade purchase when he moved to Iceland, allowing him to navigate search and rescue missions with ease.

He'd given Hank a pat as he talked about how it could land on any terrain, but instead of the look of affection as he'd had for Darlene, this one was full of pride.

Ava had assumed this newer model meant the flight would be safer and smoother. That was her first mistake.

Her second mistake was not taking Dramamine.

Brooks had told her they needed to take Hank because some of the towns they were visiting were remote and didn't have an airstrip to land. Hank would make it easier for them to get in and out so they could cover more ground. What Brooks hadn't told her was how nimble the aircraft was. She could have sworn he took sharper turns than necessary to pay her back for talking shit about Darlene.

Ava shrieked as he swooped around to find a clear landing spot in Ísafjörður. Images flashed before her eyes of the helicopter door sliding open and dumping her out the side to fall to her death.

At least the views would be beautiful. They were the only things keeping her from having a nervous breakdown. Ava had never feared flying, but flying with Brooks was in a whole different category. There was no friendly pilot talking over the intercom about the weather and promising a smooth ride. Nope. With Brooks, he flew like he owned the sky. No fear. No regard for sharp turns, clouds that made it impossible to see, or gusty wind. He was at ease with it all.

Brooks righted the helicopter again, and Ava stared out the front window, taking in the scenery and several deep breaths. Ava found the small harbor town of less than three thousand inhabitants picturesque, nestled in breathtaking landscapes of the Westfjords peninsula. The blue water contrasted against the bright, white layer of snow sparkling under the afternoon sunlight.

Ísafjörður, another big fishing area, had been the first town to report the issue. They'd been hit hard when it first started happening more than a year ago. Thankfully, whatever had caused their fish to suffer seemed to have disappeared as soon as it had come, and they recovered quickly.

Brooks lowered the helicopter with a grace and ease that sharply contrasted with his twists and turns in the air. Ava let out a breath when they touched solid ground, and he went through the procedures to shut the helicopter down.

"So it's just about three o'clock now," she said, checking her phone. She slipped it back into her purse and dug out a binder. "We'll be meeting with Olav while here. Ideally, we'll get everything wrapped up around four so we can fly back while there's still light."

Brooks slipped off his beanie and ran a hand through his hair.

"Normally, I would give you a hard time about your rigid schedule and the stupid binder." He flicked the binder with his index finger. "But you've done good. If you hadn't kept us on track, we might not have been able to cover as much ground as we have."

Ava beamed. Things between them had definitely shifted, although she wasn't quite sure how or why. There had been moments during the party that Ava had sensed his gaze on her. Assessing. Reevaluating.

Then there were those near-miss kisses and the obvious disappointment in his eyes when Helga interrupted him seconds before his lips met hers.

They had a day between the party and their trek to the neighboring towns. Other than a few texts to coordinate for today, Ava was left alone with her own thoughts. It was one thing to harbor attraction for him knowing she was in it alone. It was something else knowing Brooks might feel the same way.

If she thought the temptation was bad before, this made it unbearable. She spent yesterday trying to think rationally. It would do them no good if they acted on their attraction. Her time was limited in Iceland, and she needed all her focus—when she wasn't dealing with her own work things—to help these people.

Like she'd promised.

Ava had willpower of steel. By that evening, she was certain she'd push down those lust-filled emotions and keep it professional.

But then she saw him this morning. Her willpower slipped from her control when he helped her into the helicopter. She may have pretended to slip just so she could be caught by him. To feel his strong arms holding her body steady.

Even she wanted to roll her eyes at her ridiculous behavior, which is what helped her regain some semblance of willpower again. She needed to keep it together. There were so many kind, caring people counting on them to get this right.

It wasn't *only* about them though. Over the last few days, inspiration flowed from her like water breaking through a dam. She'd forgotten what a rush the feeling was and how it sparked creativity she'd thought was dead. She was using her brain in new ways. Curiosity was making her dream of new options.

She didn't want to lose that, and that's why she needed to push aside those thoughts about kissing Brooks. There was too much at stake.

This next week was about their mission. That had to be enough.

Despite the harrowing helicopter ride, they'd managed to work in sync. Like a team that had practiced together for years. Every moment had gone smoothly as they'd traveled from town to town.

Brooks had led the questioning, showing the townspeople the fish they'd kept on ice. Ava took notes, interjecting here and there when it made sense. As they flew, Ava cleaned up the notes and started looking for trends, highlighting common occurrences from the information they'd gathered.

It had been a long day, and even though they were traveling the northern section of the island for a different reason than what she'd originally booked for her tour, she appreciated everything she'd seen so far. From up above and on the ground in the thick of it, Iceland was stunning beyond words. It amazed her to see so many natural wonders—volcanoes, glaciers, forests, waterfalls—all in a short flight up and down the island.

They'd even caught a glimpse of a whale pod swimming in the nearby harbor of one of the recovering towns. The look on Brooks's face hit her right in the gut. It was a mix of awe and hope. If this town could recover, maybe his would too.

What these towns were going through was hard and heartbreaking. Their landscapes and marine ecosystem were their lifeblood. Ava couldn't recall ever being in a place where everything seemed so clean and natural. Rather than bulldozing all the beautiful landscapes the country had to offer, towns built around them, respecting nature. And rather than overpopulating each area to the point where it was congested and polluted, the towns appeared to know when to stop growing and leave things as they were.

Every place they'd been only made Iceland grow on her more. Or maybe that was thanks to Brooks, who claimed he hated playing tour guide but had managed to be the perfect one. As they flew to the locations, he'd share insights and interesting stories about each place, weaving in Icelandic superstition and folklore.

She could listen to him for hours. That deep, smooth voice was low, hitting all the right notes and giving her a sense of calm as if she were listening to spa music.

Whenever there was a lull, she'd ask more questions just to hear it again.

What would it sound like if he whispered to me while we were alone, tangled up with each other?

Ava shook her head. It was exactly what she was trying *not* to think about. Maybe it was the fact that they were with each other, mere inches away in the cockpit. The awareness shot through her every second they sat there.

His scent filled the air, wrapping its way around her like a warm cocoon. The sunlight highlighted his face, showing off his defined jawline and strong nose and making the stubble on his face shine like gold.

And when he lifted his sunglasses from his face and turned those dark-blue eyes in her direction, her mouth went dry, and her insides clenched.

She never had a fighting chance, did she?

Each moment that ticked by, she found there was so much more to him than she would have thought. He was selfless and strong. He had an unrivaled passion for things that had meaning. He cared about the people in his life.

There was something refreshing about his outlook on life. About what he valued.

He wasn't driven by the things she had been surrounded by. The people she rubbed elbows with in Boston were driven by status, money, and career growth. They collected awards, degrees, and certifications and built personal brands that made them a celebrity in their fields.

They were always reaching for more, never satisfied with where they were at.

She hated that. As she spent more time with the people of Iceland, and with Brooks especially, she worried she'd become just like the people back home.

Yes, moving up in her career was important to her, as was the financial security that came with it. But it wasn't because she wanted to keep spending her money on ridiculous luxuries or to be a quasi-industry celebrity with her own TED Talk. It was about making sure her family was never left wanting again.

The work ethic they'd instilled in her was why she made it as far as she had. Sometimes that meant missing their regular family dinners or being distracted while celebrating the holidays together because her email was blowing up. Sometimes it meant not being fully present because her mind was thinking through a complex problem or depleted from a long day of work.

Being out of her comfort zone and spending time somewhere different was showing her a new perspective to life. In pursuing her career goals to give her family security, she'd traded off something more important: quality time with them.

Ava thought of how the townspeople interacted with each other. They were fully invested and present every moment they were together. They went out of their way to help one another, whether it be lending a hand or lending an ear. They had banded together to try and fix their town's issue, putting the community first rather than their own individual needs. They still found time to enjoy their company and celebrate, even when facing something impossible.

She wondered if her parents' reluctance to accept her financial help wasn't a pride thing but because they saw something she didn't. Maybe they worried she was running herself into the ground to provide. Or maybe they wanted something more important. Something that money couldn't buy: her time.

"Are you okay?" He took her hand and gave it a gentle squeeze before letting go.

"Just processing everything we've learned so far today. I wonder if Olav will have anything new to share." She wasn't ready to unpack whatever thoughts were coursing through her mind. She had enough on her plate and didn't need to be flipping her life upside-down by focusing on it too much.

By the time they were due to get back to Örugg Höfn, the East Coast would be well started on its day. She had a slew of media contacts she planned to call. She'd accumulated a lot of "no questions asked" favors over the years. Now she was going to cash in on every single one of them.

Brooks helped her out of the helicopter and led them through town to the pub by the harbor where Olav was waiting. Just as they'd done for the other four people they'd met that day, Brooks asked the questions and Ava joined in the discussion when needed. Olav was a friendly man with a boisterous personality. Even with the struggles his town had faced last year, he was optimistic.

Then again, the economy and marine life had nearly recovered already, so he had made it over the hump.

As they left their final meeting an hour later and settled in the helicopter for takeoff, Ava's phone chirped with a message. Clicking a few buttons, she opened an email from HR. Relief washed over her. "Good news."

"What's that?" Brooks asked distractedly as he did the pre-flight check.

"My CEO approved my request to work remotely in Iceland a little longer. As long as I'm back before the holidays with an official campaign plan."

Brooks grunted a response. He pressed his lips into a thin line of disapproval.

"What?"

He shrugged. "Although I'm happy you'll be staying longer, it didn't seem like you had much time to enjoy your vacation."

"That's expected for someone in my position. It's not realistic to think I can just go without responding to people. I'm a decision maker. People need to be able to reach me."

"Thought I overheard you telling Lotte the other night that your new position didn't officially start until the new year."

"Maybe not, but I'm transitioning. I still have a job to do." She bit her bottom lip, not wanting to get defensive about it, especially with how unsettled she was feeling after her revelation today. "I'm glad I can stay longer, but I'll have to check with Helga to see if the room will be open for that long," she said, changing the subject.

"Even if it's not, we'll figure something out. If worse comes to worst, I have a guest bedroom." Ava's pulse spiked at the suggestion.

Sleeping at Brooks's place? It was like the devil himself was doing everything in his power to make her act on her temptations.

"Or anyone else in the town would be glad to put you up," he added quickly. "We'll find a place for you, don't worry."

Ava took the headset Brooks held out to her and tried to ignore the rush of awareness that hit her when he reached over to double-check her seatbelt. "A little overkill?" Her voice shook as she pushed away sexy thoughts of them playing roommates.

She doubted she'd last more than twenty-four hours before she caved and knocked on his bedroom in the dark of night.

"Figured if I double and triple-checked your safety, maybe you'd stop squealing every time Hank takes the slightest turn."

"Okay. First off," she said, lifting up her index finger, "those turns aren't *slight*." She lifted another finger. "Second off—"

"You realize that when you scream into the mic, you nearly make me deaf."

She narrowed her eyes at him. "Noted."

He smirked in return.

My, how much has changed between us.

To ignore the influx of nerves she always had during takeoff and landing, Ava busied herself with the notes from the day. "Hmm." She tapped the highlighter to her chin as she sorted through her scribbles.

Brooks slipped on his sunglasses to ward off blindness from the setting sun. As he lifted the chopper into the air and steadied it, he glanced at her. "What's up?"

Ava highlighted a few trending comments and made notes in the margin of her notebook. "I'm no expert, but it sounds like every town faced a similar situation. However, it all varied in level of severity and duration." She flipped through a few pages and trailed her finger across the paper as she read. "It also almost seems like the problem has been migrating."

Brooks turned to her for a moment, a look of confusion crossing his face. "What do you mean?"

"It kinda followed a path, almost like it was traveling from town to town."

"You think the marine life had gotten infected and migrated to the neighboring towns, infecting the other animals in the area?"

"I'm not sure, but maybe once my engineer helps me plug this into the database, we'll get a clearer picture. All I know is that it appears Örugg Höfn has not only had the worst case of it, but that it's already surpassed the typical time the other towns have seen before things started turning around again. Based on the timelines, we should have seen some of the problems ease up. Instead, it's only getting worse."

Brooks said nothing, but by the way his jaw ticked, she knew he was lost in thought. Although talking to the towns had given her some sense of hope that there was a light at the end of the tunnel, the fact that Örugg Höfn was still in the thick of it after months only made it even more worrisome.

Static from the radio sounded in her headset, and a deep voice speaking Icelandic started rattling off a bunch of words Ava couldn't even begin to comprehend. She turned to Brooks hoping for some clue. In a matter of seconds, his whole demeanor changed. Determination and concentration filled his face as he listened to the voice on the radio.

Brooks responded back in Icelandic. Despite speaking slower, since it wasn't his native tongue, Ava still couldn't pick up a single word. All she knew was that whatever it was, it was something serious.

After clicking a few buttons, he took a sharp turn, the unexpected turn making her stomach lurch to her throat.

"Is everything okay?"

Brooks steadied the aircraft and barreled through the open sky. "We got a SAR call."

"SAR?"

"Search and rescue. One of the nearby towns got an SOS call from a hysterical woman. There's been an accident off one of the rural roads. The driver appears to be bleeding out and not responding. None of the emergency units can get to them in time. We'll get to them sooner."

"We're…we're going to *save* someone?"

"Let's hope we get there in time to be able to."

Ava clasped her hands together, squeezing tight. She'd never been good with blood or injuries. Once, Jess had dislocated her shoulder from doing a slide kick during one of her soccer games, and Ava nearly fainted. Jess barely flinched even when a medic popped it back in.

How was she ever going to deal with a situation like *this*?

Thankfully, Brooks slowed the craft before Ava could have a mini panic attack, as she went through all the horrible scenarios they could possibly face when they found the injured people.

The remains of daylight retreated, making it difficult to see in the remote area without a single house light or lamppost in sight to break through the darkness. Flipping on a spotlight, Brooks hovered over the coordinates the emergency personnel radioed in. He adjusted the light, illuminating the empty road engulfed by towering mountains.

Ava shivered as she looked at the open expanse covered with ice and snow. What she'd admired only hours before now seemed cold and desolate. She couldn't imagine how scary it must be for the couple stranded out there, desperate for help but so far from anyone or anything.

Something glinted a few miles ahead as the spotlight swept over the area. He positioned the light again to linger on the area in question. From their vantage point, Ava could make out what looked like a badly damaged Jeep that had veered off the side of the road. With nothing around for miles, what could have even caused that level of destruction?

"Hold on, okay?" Before Ava could respond, the helicopter was moving again. "This might be a bumpy landing," he warned as he descended to the ground. The sudden drop caused her stomach to lurch in her throat.

The landing was rough. Ava's teeth chattered upon impact. As soon as he stabilized the helicopter, Brooks was unhooking his seatbelt and rummaging through the back for medical supplies. He located what he needed and jumped out of the chopper.

Unsure of what to do, Ava fumbled with her seatbelt and hopped out of the aircraft. Her hair blew wildly from the wind generated by the rotors. Even over the helicopter's deafening noise, she could hear the faint screams of a woman.

Ava swallowed, not ready to face the bloodshed, but also feeling it was only right to help Brooks. She might have no medical experience aside from basic first aid, but there had to be *something* she could do.

Forcing her feet forward, she made it to the smashed SUV and yanked open the passenger door. A woman in her early thirties spun in her seat to face her. Her eyes were wide, and mascara had left black streams down her cheeks. Dried blood was caked to her forehead and hands.

Brooks was on the driver's side, hacking away at the seatbelt holding up an unconscious man.

"Please! Please. Save him," the woman pleaded, her voice hoarse from screaming. "He...he hasn't woken up. He hasn't woken up!"

"There's a faint pulse. He's lost a lot of blood," Brooks said as he freed the man and held him in place to keep the body stable. "Oh, fuck." A fresh patch of blood saturated the man's shirt.

"Stop! You're killing him!" The woman swiped at Brooks's arms.

He dodged the blows but took an unruly one to the cheek, leaving a streak of blood across his jaw. "You have to stop! If you don't let me help him, he'll die."

Ava grabbed the woman around the waist and pulled her from the car. Her ears felt like they might rupture from the hysterical screams.

"What's your name?"

The woman looked bewildered as turned her focus from the car to Ava. "Leah."

"Leah. Leah," Ava said, grabbing the woman's hands to stop her from going back to the car. "Are you from Iceland?"

"No. My boyfriend and I were visiting from Virginia."

"How old are you?"

"Thirty-two."

"When's your birthday?"

"June 1."

"What's your phone number?"

Ava continued asking Leah questions, not missing a beat. With each question, Leah's breathing steadied and the flowing tears slowed down.

Brooks secured the man onto a backboard and called out for her. "Ava, I need you to help me get him into the chopper. We have to keep him steady. I've slowed the blood for now, but there's no doubt there's internal injuries. I just don't know how bad."

"Rob!" Leah reached out to him, but Ava held her back.

"Leah, I need you to stay put for just a moment while we take care of Rob. We'll get you both to the nearest emergency center. You have to work with us, okay?"

The woman nodded as a loud sob escaped her. She held her breath, trying to keep it together, her eyes never leaving Rob's lifeless body stretched out on the backboard.

After a few adjustments, Ava and Brooks slid the backboard into the back of the helicopter. Brooks jumped in to secure it.

"You can sit there with him, but you can't touch him," Brooks said. "We don't know how bad his injuries are. His chances of survival are dwindling. We can't risk it."

Leah nodded again. "Okay, okay." Brooks helped her into the back and secured her seatbelt as Ava got situated in the passenger seat.

Seconds later, Brooks lifted them in the air, rattling off something in his headset in Icelandic as he flew forward, doing his best to keep the aircraft smooth and steady.

"We're about fifty kilometers from the nearest emergency center," he said.

"How long will that take?" Leah asked.

"Roughly fifteen minutes."

"Do we have enough time?" Ava asked.

Brooks shot her a worried look but said nothing. Instead, he kept his eyes ahead of him as he flew through the black evening.

CHAPTER THIRTEEN

BROOKS

THREE MINUTES. Three minutes could change a whole life.

Brooks had pushed the helicopter to its limit, shooting through the clear, inky sky toward the hospital. Those fifteen minutes felt like a flash and yet seemed to drag on forever, stalling them in place.

They'd made it to the emergency center in time for the doctors to slow the internal bleeding.

Brooks had waited with Leah in Rob's hospital room as the doctors performed emergency surgery down the hall. For the entire two hours, they'd said nothing. Ava had checked in once or twice to ask if they needed anything, but otherwise she stayed in the waiting area, following hospital rules.

Rob's blood had dried on Leah and Brooks's clothes, leaving dark, angry stains on their shirts, pants, and bare skin. Brooks had managed to scrub most of it off his hands, face, and wrists. Leah was too shellshocked to even think of it.

Finally, the doctor had come in to let them know they'd stabilized Rob and stopped him from hemorrhaging. Had they arrived three minutes later, Rob would have died.

Brooks was in a daze when he left the hospital room, thinking of the stark difference between the traumatic experience Rob had faced and the long, drawn-out months his mother had. Brooks had seen a lot in his life as a SAR pilot. As part of his training, he learned how to compartmentalize his empathy and grief in those moments, otherwise he'd be rendered useless when people needed him most.

This was the first situation since his mother's passing that he'd faced losing someone again. The majority of his rescue missions had been helping stranded or lost people, treating frostbite or hypothermia, or helping tourists from a stupid situation they'd caused by trying to get the perfect photo.

None of them had been as dire as Rob's situation, and the weight of it punched Brooks straight in the gut and gripped his throat. After losing his mother, he was having a hard time separating his feelings. As he watched Leah's hysterical outbursts and saw the numbness in her eyes while she waited helplessly in the hospital for news on Rob's condition, all the memories of his last few months with his mother came rushing back.

Maybe her death wasn't nearly as dramatic as Rob's situation, but that feeling of not having any control over the outcome was all too familiar.

Brooks had never known pain like that of being a helpless bystander while a loved one teetered between life and death.

The fluorescent lights of the waiting area nearly blinded Brooks as he turned the corner from the dimmed hallways. Ava sat in the far corner alone, her elbows resting on her knees. Her legs bounced up and down, and she wrung her hands—also stained with blood—as she stared blankly at the wall across from her.

She was the reason they'd made it to the hospital in time. She was the reason they had three minutes to spare. She was the reason Rob was alive.

Brooks hadn't expected her to leave the chopper or to pull Leah from the car and distract her. If Ava hadn't been there to keep Leah calm and out of the way, he wouldn't have had any shot of pulling Rob from the Jeep long enough to stop the bleeding.

He'd done this job alone for most of his career. Had faced things on his own. But he knew damn well that letting Ava help was the only reason why Leah wasn't making funeral arrangements.

His father was right. He'd been keeping people at arm's length for a long time now, and for what? To protect them? To protect himself? He wasn't sure anymore.

All he knew was that he was thankful Ava wasn't the type to let him get away with it. She did what she was in her nature—charged right through any obstacle to get things done. To help.

That was the kind of person she was. Courageous. Selfless. Kind.

He paused mid-step a few yards away to watch her. To appreciate her. He needed a moment to take it all in, to make sense of the messy emotions jumbled up inside of him.

The sight of her made him feel whole. The world could be falling down around him, but it felt like as long as she was around, he'd be okay.

He'd been wrong to think it was only simply attraction this whole time. It was more than that.

The truth both scared the shit out of him and somehow brought him a sense of relief. It was as if he'd been waiting his entire life to find the right piece to fill a void he didn't realize existed.

Ava was it.

She turned, spotting him frozen there. Once her big brown eyes met his, he found the strength to move again, closing the distance between them in a few long strides.

She stood. "Brooks—"

Before she could get out whatever she had to say, Brooks pulled her into his arms, bending down to rest his forehead against hers. He closed his eyes and breathed her in, warmth and light filling his tired body as they held each other.

"You're a brave man, Brooks." Her voice was soft and soothing as she rubbed her hands up and down his back. "I could never do the things you do. To keep calm under that amount of pressure. Is he...going to be okay?"

"Yes." His answer came out gravelly and hoarse. "And you can do what I do, because you just did it. He's alive because of your quick thinking."

Brooks pulled away to look into those eyes he wanted to get lost in. He cupped her cheek, stroking her soft skin with his thumb, thinking how perfect and right it felt to touch her.

He realized he'd never felt as connected to a person as he did now.

"I couldn't have done this without you," he whispered right before he dipped his head to close the distance between their lips, pausing just a fraction away from kissing her.

Ava wrapped her arms around his neck, pulling him down to her and pressing her lips to his. Her fingertips ran through his hair as she rose to her toes to deepen the kiss.

It wasn't soft. Wasn't tentative. It was packed with emotion and need and understanding. With each stroke of his tongue, he felt as if he was giving a piece of himself away to her and receiving pieces of her in return.

Her lips were softer than he'd imagined. He loved the hungry way they pressed against his, moving in sync, demanding so much.

In a perfect world, he wouldn't have kissed her for the first time in a quiet emergency center waiting room, exhausted from traveling all day, covered in someone else's blood.

He would have asked her on a date. Would have made her laugh and smile. She'd look at him in that way that made him believe he could handle anything the world threw at him.

He would have taken his time with her.

But the world was far from perfect, and sometimes moments called for action. Brooks couldn't last another second without kissing her. Claiming her. Showing her how much she was coming to mean to him.

Ava broke their kiss and dragged her hands from his neck to cup his face. He loved knowing he was the one who caused her breathlessness, her eyes to go dark, and that look of want and affection on her face.

He wanted to blame the adrenaline for this rush, but it ran much deeper. There was a spark between them from the first few moments they'd met each other. Even though they'd been set to not cross that invisible line, something had been drawing him to her from the very start.

Brooks was done keeping her at a distance.

He tucked a lock of hair behind her ear, loving the way her cheeks turned pink and her pulse thrummed in her neck. "Let's go home."

"Okay."

The flight back to Örugg Höfn was quiet. Intimate. Both of them were lost in their thoughts. Toward the end of the flight, Brooks found the courage to reach over and take her hand. He squeezed it and ran his thumb in soft circles along her palm before taking the controls again.

"I should have asked you before I kissed you," he said, breaking the silence.

Ava let out a soft laugh. "How chivalrous." She turned in her seat to face him. "Can I ask you something?"

"Hmm?"

"Was that kiss because of what happened or because you truly wanted to kiss me?"

Brooks couldn't stop himself from smiling. "You never mince words, do you?" Always straight to the point. He liked that.

"I find it better to make sure I'm on the same page with someone before..."

"Before?"

She huffed out a sigh as if he'd forced some hidden truth from her. "Before I let myself get carried away."

He pulled his gaze from the star-speckled sky and looked at her directly. "Ava Espinosa, I've wanted to kiss you for days now. That kiss had nothing to do with anything other than me wanting you."

She grinned and turned back in her seat to look straight ahead. "Well, okay then. That's that," she said, all business-like.

"Since we're on the subject of ensuring we're on the same page as one another, I have a question for you now." He turned to look ahead too.

"And that is?"

"If I wanted to kiss you again, would you be open to that?"

"Yes!" Her enthusiastic answer shocked them both. Ava's hand flew to her mouth, and Brooks barked out a laugh. She cleared her throat and folded her hands in her lap primly. "I mean, yes. I would enjoy that very much," she said in an even, professional tone.

"Good."

"Great."

The town's lights came into view. As Brooks prepared for landing, a sense of regret washed over him knowing that in a few moments they'd part ways for the night. He wasn't ready to let her go.

"Have dinner with me tonight."

"Is this a demand or a request?" He grunted. "Ask nicely," she said with saccharine sweetness.

"Ava, would you kindly accompany me to dinner at my apartment?" he asked, matching her sarcasm.

Ava's stomach growled, making them both laugh again. "I guess that answers that." She bit her bottom lip. "Let me take a shower and change."

"Works for me."

An hour later, Ava stood at his door, fresh-faced and smelling florally and citrusy, like a tropical paradise.

He'd showered too, opting to toss his clothes out since they were far too gone to save. The memories of the day came flashing back as streams of red had rushed down the drain while he'd showered. That same heaviness he'd been feeling for a long time threatened to come back, but as soon as he saw Ava's face, it retreated.

"Perfect timing. Dinner was delivered a couple minutes ago." Brooks pushed open the door to let Ava in.

Stella zoomed around the house at the sight of her.

"Seems like someone's happy to see me." She laughed.

Brooks planted a chaste kiss on her cheek. "We both are." He slipped her oversized purse from her shoulder and nearly dropped it from the unexpected weight. "It's no wonder why women have such bad back issues. What do you have in here? Boulders?"

"My notebook from today and my laptop," she said as she slipped off her boots and hung her jacket on the coat rack.

"Do you ever stop working?" He placed her purse near her boots.

"I made the town a promise. I don't take that lightly."

"Fair enough." He led them into the kitchen and pushed her shoulders lightly so she'd sit on the barstool. "First you eat, then you work," he said as he passed her the container of food.

He wasn't sure if she inhaled her food because she was hungry or if it was because she was eager to get to work, but Brooks watched her wolf down her dinner in five minutes flat.

"Impressive," he said as he took slow enough bites to allow his brain to register that he was actually eating.

"Yeah. Well, apparently, a person can't be sustained on smushed bottom-of-the-purse granola bars for eight hours. I would have gotten something at the hospital cafeteria, but it was late and all I saw was Jell-O and pudding." She made a face. "Do you mind if I work while you finish up? I have a lot going through my head, and I want to get it down before I forget."

"Go for it."

As much as he'd loved to linger over dinner and talk to her all night, he'd simply take being around her. He loved that she felt comfortable enough to come by in lounge clothes, complete with fluffy socks, no makeup, and her hair in a messy bun. Something about seeing her natural and cozy in his apartment gave him tingles.

"Okay. This is awesome," Ava said a half hour later.

"What's up?" Brooks leaned back in his barstool and took a sip of his bourbon.

She turned the computer so they both could see. "Remember that engineering friend I have at work?"

"Mmhmm."

"She was able to use the information we gathered to cross-reference the open databases throughout the world. Look at this." She pointed to a section on her screen.

Brooks pulled the computer closer and scrolled through the information, confusion setting in as rows and rows of data filled the screen. "Mining? Drilling?" He looked at Ava. "That can't be right."

"Everything she's pulled up keeps pointing to these reports."

He shook his head. "Iceland is very serious about protecting the environment. If there's any drilling, it would have to follow certain rules and regulations. This would never happen."

"Unless..." Ava swiveled the computer back to her and punched a few keys and clicked the mouse. She turned it back to him. "They're doing it illegally. Look here," she said, highlighting a section on the screen. "If they're doing it illegally, they're likely not following the regulations. This means whatever they're doing might be polluting the water sources that stream out to the ocean—"

"Putting marine life in danger." Brooks ran a hand through his hair. "If that's true, how could they get away with it? It's not like people would miss massive machines drilling into the earth."

"Iceland has plenty of remote areas where no one's around for miles. They might miss it if it's a small enough operation and if they're constantly moving around."

A flashback to the day Brooks first picked up Ava hit him like a freight train. "Fuck. Ava, I think that's what we were seeing when we first flew to Örugg Höfn. Remember? I wanted to investigate it, but we had to make it back before the storm came through." He pulled up a map on the computer and zoomed in on the area they'd roughly seen it. "You see here," he said, moving the cursor along a river. "If they were drilling close enough to this, the fluid might be getting dumped in the rivers leading to the harbor towns. Maybe we're on to something."

Stella padded into the room and barked. "Looks like Stella's demanding her bedtime walk. Do you want to come?"

She shook her head. "You guys go on without me. I want to dive into this a little more."

"Okay. I'll make some calls while I'm walking her. Call my cell if you need me. We shouldn't be gone for more than thirty minutes."

Ava waved them off, her gaze glued to the screen.

Nearly a half hour and several phone calls later, Brooks and Stella climbed the stairs to the apartment, finding her slumped on the kitchen island. He unhooked Stella and quietly walked into the kitchen, careful not to disturb her. Her laptop rested next to her. A presentation filled the screen.

Brooks leaned against the island and scrolled through the slides. Somehow, in a matter of minutes, Ava had pulled together an impressive campaign. The presentation was still in rough form visually, but the strategy and ideas she'd laid out were impressive.

Seeing her genius only made him believe that maybe, just maybe, it wasn't a foolish hope to put his faith in her. He wanted to believe she could help the town raise the money. Now, seeing this, he was confident she would.

A new email popped up.

Ava,

Done. No problem. We'll take this national tomorrow. Send me the link ASAP once it's live.

Rosita Santiago

Brooks stared at the logo in Rosita's signature. She worked for *the* biggest national news station in the United States. Its viewership far outranked any other news station by far.

And Ava was able to get promo for their fundraising campaign.

He had half a mind to scoop her in his arms and kiss her senseless, but as her soft snores sounded next to him, he decided to wait to follow through on that. They'd both had an incredibly long, harrowing day. It was only right to let her sleep.

He gently picked her up and carried her down the hall to the guest bedroom. She rustled in his arms. "Brooks?" Her sleep-laced voice was barely audible.

"Shhh. Get some sleep." He placed her on the queen-sized bed and pulled the covers around her. The moment her head hit the pillow, she was asleep once again.

He placed a kiss on her forehead before leaving the room. He paused at the door to look at her as she settled into bed. The tension and guard she normally kept up were gone as she snuggled deeper into the blankets and let out a content, sleepy sigh.

At that moment, he wondered if Ava coming into his life was a happy accident. Not just because of all she was doing to help the town, but because being with her eased the dark cloud that had lingered over him these last couple of years. It felt as if the broken pieces of him that had been haphazardly glued together piece by piece were now fusing together into something stronger. Resilient.

He would have kicked himself in the ass if she'd actually left any of the times he'd tried to push her away. Thank God for her stubborn determination.

He wouldn't make the mistake of pushing her away again. Every second that passed showed him how much he needed a woman like her in his life.

CHAPTER FOURTEEN

AVA

"That's really something, Ava." Lotte pointed at the presentation displayed on one of the TV screens at The Chantey. "And you've managed to do all of this in just a day?"

"Yes. Thankfully, I had some people follow through on the favors they owed me over the years." She clicked to the next slide to show a timeline. "I know it's important to get as much money raised as soon as possible, but we don't want the story to fizzle out by flooding the world with our message all at once. Based on what I could work with my media contacts' scheduling, we'll stagger our promotion."

Lotte nodded and tapped her chin. "Makes sense. Judging by this, it looks like the first round of promotion will go out in two days."

"Right." She highlighted a few marks on her timeline. "And you can see we'll have mixed media promotions going out every other day for the first two weeks. After that, we'll spread it out a little more."

Freyja passed by and handed Ava a beer, giving her a smile and wink as she tended to the other nearby patrons.

"Where's all this promotion going to go?" Jón asked. "We don't have a website or anything."

Ava grinned and clicked to the next slides that featured screen grabs of the site she'd been working on the last few hours. "We don't yet, but we will soon. This website will allow us to accept donations and tell more about the story."

Lotte's jaw nearly dropped to the floor. "Again...you've managed this in a day?"

Laughing, Ava's gaze scanned the room and met Brooks's. A proud smile had been plastered on his face for the last twenty minutes as she presented.

"Ava?"

Ava shook her head and focused on Jón, who was squinting at her.

"Everything okay? You just zoned out for a moment and look a little flushed."

She caught Brooks's stare again. He was watching her intently, and his lips twitched as he raised an eyebrow.

"Sorry about that. It's been a long few days." She clicked to the next slide to show more mockups of the site. "I think I have decent bones for the site, but I need your help to tell the story of this town and its people and what you're all facing. It's those things that will pull on people's heartstrings and convince them to open their wallets." She turned to Lotte. "As the mayor, I'm also going to need you to speak on some of the news segments I have slated in the upcoming days."

"Whatever you need."

"I know Brooks has filled you all in on what we *think* is happening to the ecosystem. That's what hooked our media people. Shocking headlines get people's interest—now it's time to connect in a humanized way. We need to show them what makes this town special and what we're bound to lose if we don't get the resources needed to fix the issue. In a sense, we want them rooting for the underdog." She scanned the room and pointed at a few members of the town who were getting hit the hardest. "They'll likely want to bring in field reporters to talk to you about what we're seeing. To make the direness of the situation more tangible. Are you up for it?"

Viktor gave a tight nod. "Of course." Although he'd warmed to her a bit, he was still a tough nut to crack. This was the best she could hope for.

"Lotte and I can work with you on telling our story. We're about as old as the town itself," Jón said.

"Speak for yourself. I'm still in my prime." Lotte nudged him playfully, causing him to laugh.

"I can help too," Freyja said. "My great-grandmother used to tell me stories about my family's history. It doesn't go back quite as far as the first settlers in 860, but she has a few hundred years documented in some of her journals. My ancestors helped establish Örugg Höfn into the town it is today."

"Can she share some of these stories?"

Freyja shook her head. "She died a few years ago, but she made sure I knew the stories of Örugg Höfn and our family as if I'd lived through it myself. While most children were told bedtime stories about the fairies and elves, she was telling me these stories instead. If I dig through her old albums, I'm sure I'll find some letters and photographs too."

Ava's face lit up. "Yes! We should put that on the site. Maybe add a tab about the history and people of Örugg Höfn." She grabbed her notebook resting on the table nearby and scribbled a note to herself.

"Mind if we start brainstorming the key points of our story now? We can flesh it out more tomorrow," Lotte said.

"I'd love that."

For the next hour, Ava sat with Lotte and Jón at the bar, allowing Freyja to chime in whenever she had a moment to spare. With each sentence she typed in their working document, Ava got more excited. There was a sense of fulfillment and purpose that overwhelmed her—in a good way.

She embraced how alive she felt as she put together the campaign strategy and website. It was as if her ideas flowed freely and effortlessly. With the stories Jón, Lotte, and Freyja shared, her strategy now had heart.

In fact, she no longer looked at it as a "strategy." That word was too tactical and cold. It felt more like a mission. It connected them all to a bigger purpose.

If only she'd felt this way about the campaign her CEO was pressuring her on. She'd managed to scribble down some ideas, but it had been nearly impossible to come up with anything that was going to impress him the way he expected.

It had been that way for the last few years. She thought maybe she'd just burned herself out and lost her mojo. That was part of the reason for this trip: to give her mind a little rest to recharge before she stepped into her new role.

But as she dove into the mission to help the town with ease and inspiration, and still struggled to come up with anything useful for her company, she started to worry that maybe the problem ran deeper.

A problem for another day. Right now, Lotte, Jón, Brooks, and Freyja were giving her so many ideas she could barely contain her excitement.

The hour flew by in a blink. When she looked at the time on her laptop, she couldn't believe it. Meanwhile, the minutes dragged on like days when she worked on the ZettaBytes campaign.

It felt like she was checking the clock every few seconds. In reality, it was about every three minutes, but that still was a little concerning.

Even more telling was the fact that in the few days she'd been in Iceland, she barely paid attention to the time. She wasn't counting down the minutes. She wasn't checking her phone obsessively. She wasn't bound by a rigid schedule that left no time for spontaneity.

She wasn't even getting those low-grade anxiety attacks when she saw the number of unread emails ticking up each day.

It was nice. *Really* nice.

She suspected that had to do with the fact that she didn't *want* the time to pass. Every moment that ticked by only brought her closer to her flight back home. In Iceland, with these people, doing what she was doing, she felt fulfilled.

How could she stay suspended in time so she never had to leave?

She looked up from her laptop, catching Brooks's gaze once again. All evening, he'd been there to support her with a simple look. A whisper of a touch. Words of affirmation and encouragement.

Butterflies filled her stomach as she remembered how it felt to wake in the early hours at his apartment. She thought she'd had it bad before, but now that she knew how his lips felt—hot, soft, demanding, and made perfectly for her own—it was hard for her to be logical about things.

He lived in Iceland. She lived in Boston. What good would it do to cross that line? If he was someone else, someone she looked at as a casual fling, then the question wouldn't even be there. But getting to know Brooks these last few days made it impossible for her to see him as some guy who'd scratch the itch.

As soon as he'd kissed her, the unclear feelings she'd been having became clear as day. It was electric. It was fire. More importantly, it was intimate. Despite standing in the middle of a hospital that smelled like cleaner and crappy cafeteria food, tired and dirty from a harrowing experience, under the harsh fluorescent lights, the moment had been magical. It should have been anything but, and yet it only burned its memory in her mind as one of the best moments of her life.

He was something special, and he was someone she'd be scared to lose if they moved too fast and burned too bright.

Maybe she was overthinking this. It wouldn't be the first time. For all she knew, they could have weeks of mind-blowing sex and she could walk away without breaking whatever trust and bond they'd established.

They couldn't have each other forever, but maybe that was okay.

Didn't her sister tell her to embrace living in the moment for once? Would it be so wrong for her to stop fighting it and give in, no matter how short-lived? At least she knew it would be with a decent man with a good heart.

Just see how it goes. What's the worst that can happen?

As far as she could tell, nothing. The only thoughts filling her mind right now were racy ones of her and Brooks tangled up in the sheets, holding each other. His broad, bare chest pressed against her skin as he devoured her mouth in another searing kiss.

Would he kiss even better if we'd been in a private setting?

Tingles ran through her. She definitely wanted to find out.

"You want to get out of here?" Brooks asked, the rumble of his voice sending shockwaves of desire through her. His proximity was making it hard to breathe.

She let out a breath and tucked her hair behind her ears in a jerky motion. "Sure." Standing on wobbly legs, Ave packed her notebook and laptop into her oversized purse. "I was hoping to get something to eat. I was so into getting this presentation polished for tonight, I forgot to have lunch."

Brooks held up a to-go bag. "I've got it covered. Figured the kitchen would be backed up once the meeting ended, so I put in an order early."

"Wow. Did you just admit to planning ahead?"

He shrugged and looked away. "Possibly."

Her stomach growled. She salivated at the scent floating from the bag. "My stomach and I thank you."

A mischievous grin filled his face. "Truth be told, I had other plans for you tonight. If you'd like to spend the evening with me, that is."

The swirl of X-rated thoughts from earlier hit her like a Mack truck, and her mouth started salivating for other reasons than food. "I'd be open to it." She tried to play it cool, but the embarrassing pitch of her voice gave her away.

Judging by his smirk, he didn't miss it. "Great. Bundle up then."

Okay. What I had in mind involved less clothes, not more.

"Don't worry, you're going to like this," he said, revealing she hadn't been successful in hiding the disappointment from her face.

Moments later, Brooks led her down a dock in the harbor. The boats bobbed rhythmically in the water as they made their way to a small boat at the very end. The salty air mingled with the scent of their dinner from The Chantey.

"I've watched enough Lifetime movies to know the woman always ends up dead when a guy takes her out to some remote place in the middle of the night."

"If I told you that you can trust me, would you?" Brooks asked as he held out his hand to help her onto the boat. She could feel his nerves radiating from him, and it was clear this meant something important to him.

As soon as he said the words, a zing hit her in her gut. An instinct that told her she *could* trust him. That he would take care of her.

Was that reaction purely her confidence that he'd keep her physically safe? Did that care extend to her heart too?

"I trust you." She meant it. Reaching for his hand, she allowed him to pull her effortlessly into the boat. "How about a hint though?"

"Let's just say...it's an experience of a lifetime."

Are we going to have boat sex?

Before Ava could decide whether she'd puke from the rocking of the boat during sex, Brooks untied the ropes and hopped in, handing her the food and a blanket. "You might want to bundle up. It gets a little cold on the water."

"Where are we going? It's pitch black out there." She eyed the nonexistent horizon as she settled onto a wooden bench near the steering wheel.

"Fulfilling one of many things you hired my dad's company for."

"I'd say we've gone completely off-script when it comes to the itinerary."

Brooks laughed. "I told you this was Iceland time. We make it up as we go along."

He started the engine and eased away from the dock. Even moving at a slow pace, the breeze blew through Ava's hair and stung her cheeks. She dug a beanie out of her purse and shoved it on her head before wrapping herself snuggly in the thick, fleece-lined blanket.

"I guess we've technically followed some of it. We did explore the northern island, even if you put me to work." She was teasing, of course. Maybe they hadn't done what she'd signed up for, but she was finding it to be so much better. It wasn't the superficial tourist experience, only breezing through the sights, rushing from one place to the next without a moment to truly appreciate any of it.

Instead, she was thrust into their world. Understanding their hopes and fears. Seeing what made their towns and this country truly remarkable. Every moment she spent there showed her a new side to this beautiful place. It was turning out to be more than she could have ever dreamed of.

Ava studied Brooks's profile. His features were strong and steady, highlighted by the light coming from the fading town, drifting farther away as they ventured out from the harbor into the depths of the Greenland Sea.

It's funny how much had changed between them in such a short amount of time. Sometimes life was like that. At least, that's what her mother had told her whenever she shared the story of how she and Ava's father had met.

How had she put it? Like a dormant volcano coming alive. They'd met in high school. Her father had transferred to her mother's school. On that first day he'd been running late, lost in the winding hallways of the new school. Her mother had left class to retrieve a book she'd forgotten. Just as she turned the corner, they collided.

As soon as he had reached out to steady her, she'd felt it. A new phase of her life: life before him and life with him.

Instant. In that instant, she'd known this was her person.

Ava used to love that story as a child, but as she'd grown older, and become more aware about life, she'd pushed that thought aside. To her, it was a fairytale. Unrealistic.

With that belief in mind, Ava had approached dating with the same efficiency as she'd approached everything in life. There were checks and balances. Milestones. It was something she paid close attention to so she could protect her time, heart, and trust until she was *really* sure they were worth it.

Her high standards meant no one ever made it through. There were a couple who had some real potential, but in the end it never worked out.

Now here she was, admiring the man only a couple feet from her. A man who had no potential for the long haul. A man who she'd hadn't put through the rigorous system she'd put in place for any other person she'd dated.

As luck would have it, he was the very man who was making her believe in the stories her mother had told her.

There was just something about him that felt different. Like two pieces clicking into place. Like waking up from a fog.

It had to be him. The guy I have to leave behind sooner than I'd like.

The boat slowed, jerking her from her thoughts.

"I forgot something." Brooks handed her a blindfold. "Before we go any farther, I need you to put this on."

"Okay. I was joking about the Lifetime movies, but now I'm starting to get concerned."

He kneeled in front of her and ran the pad of his thumb along her jaw. Every muscle in her body quivered at his touch. Her pulse beat in tandem with the pulse between her thighs. How could one simple touch affect her so much?

"Please. Do this for me, Ava?"

How could she ever say no to that? At this point, she'd do anything if it meant feeling his hands on her, especially with the way his dark stare held hers, flitting to her lips and back again.

Please kiss me. Please kiss me. Please kiss me.

"Fine." Her answer came out in a breathless whisper as her insides clenched with anticipation. He leaned in closer, still focused on her mouth.

Leaning forward too, she closed her eyes. Waiting with as much patience as she could muster for his lips to devour hers again like she'd been imagining for the last day. Instead of his lips, his hands pressed the cloth to her eyes and tied it securely to her head.

You have to be freaking kidding me.

"What was that?" Brooks asked.

Even blindfolded, she could hear the grin in his voice. "I just said that out loud, didn't I?"

Brooks laughed. "Yes. You did. Have you been hitting Freyja's wine tonight?"

"Nope. I'm just naturally embarrassing," she said drily.

"It's cute." Brooks pressed a featherlight kiss to her lips, and she all but whimpered when he disappeared. Thankfully, she didn't haul him back to her for another kiss like she'd wanted to. She needed to retain some form of dignity tonight.

She slid in her seat as the boat lurched forward again, going at a much faster clip than before. The choppy waves splashed against the sides. She held onto whatever she could as they bumped along, the wind whistling past them.

Before she could fall overboard or turn into an icicle, Brooks slowed the boat again and turned off the motor. Just as she was going to ask how much longer until they got to their destination, the blanket disappeared and his large hands took hers, lifting her to her feet.

Behind her, with his hands on her hips, he slowly guided her to what she assumed was the front of the boat. Her legs were unsteady, but Brooks held her close, righting her when her knees went all wobbly.

"Are you ready?" His warm breath tickled her cheek. For a moment, she almost wanted to say screw it to whatever crazy plan he had up his sleeve and beg him to keep holding her tight.

"Yes." Her voice shook.

Brooks untied her blindfold.

She couldn't contain the gasp when her eyes adjusted. Was she breathing? She couldn't tell at this point.

Everything in her being was fixated on what was in front of her.

Swirling greens and purples danced across the sky like pure magic. It was the most beautiful thing she'd ever seen in her life. She was certain that it might be the most beautiful thing she'd ever see even to her dying day. "Beautiful" wasn't even a good enough word.

They stood on the bobbing boat in the middle of nowhere. Not a single person or thing obstructed the Northern Lights filling the sky. As if the colorful sky wasn't enough, the lights reflected in the water, surrounding them in their glow everywhere.

"I've been tracking the solar flares since you arrived. It finally had all the right conditions. Is it everything you thought it would be?"

Ava turned, lost in the way the lights lit up his eyes. The look on his face—like he wanted to make her happy—filled her heart in a way she couldn't describe. If she thought the moment seconds ago was perfect, she'd been wrong.

This moment was. With him.

She couldn't imagine a single person she'd rather be standing here with. Ava swallowed the lump in her throat. It was all too much. The surprise. Him. Everything.

"It's perfect." She reached up and touched his face. "Thank you, Brooks."

He pushed the hair gently from her face. She loved when he touched her like that. Intimate and natural, like something they've done a thousand times before. "You've given up your vacation—one you really need—to help our town. I wanted to share my appreciation and show you what you're fighting for." His gaze lifted to the swirling lights before looking at her again. "*This* is worth fighting for."

The words hung heavy between them. A flash of hope filled her, wondering if his words held deeper meaning.

Does he think we're worth fighting for too?

She rose to her toes and kissed him soft and slow, feeling his smile against her lips. He gripped her hips, pulling her flush against him, warming her with his body heat. Lowering his head, he deepened the kiss, taking his time to discover what she liked.

A soft moan escaped her when his tongue eased into her mouth and stroked against hers. As he wrapped his arm tighter around her body and grazed her jaw and neck with his fingertips, his kisses became more drugging. Addictive. With each swipe of his tongue and the trail of his fingers on her exposed skin, her body broke out in goosebumps, yet was on fire.

She shoved her hands in his thick hair, scraping her nails against his scalp, drawing him closer so there wasn't even a breath of air between them. She kissed him harder. More desperate. Brooks groaned against her lips, the rumble traveling from him through her.

A gust of wind convinced her not to strip off their jackets, even though she was dying to. All the bulkiness of their winter gear was confining. A tease. She could feel the heat from him and the solidness of his body, but she wanted to know what it was like to be pressed against him. All the hard edges and ridges of his body.

She *needed* it.

But you know this isn't purely sexual.

The realization made her pause.

Reluctantly, she broke the kiss. Brooks's eyes slowly opened. He looked dazed and turned on and as desperate for her as she was for him.

"Brooks." His name came out on a breath. "What does this all mean?"

She hated being that woman pushing to define something so new. Putting pressure on the relationship. Normally, she was the one going into things slowly. Cautiously. Using the checks and balances system.

The checks and balances were a lost cause when it came to Brooks. She didn't want to put him through her scrutiny, nor did she want to put up those protective barriers with him.

Truth was, she was already losing her heart to him.

Ava didn't think she could bear going any further with him if it meant nothing but a casual hook-up. It was best to be up-front than dive into it and pretend she was okay, only to know deep down it would crush her to get closer to him and realize he didn't hold the same level of care and respect for her.

Brooks let out a breath and rested his forehead against hers. "I'm not sure, Ava." He paused a moment, still holding her, before he continued. "What I *do* know is that it feels like you bring out the best in me. And there's something about you that makes me want to see where this goes. See this through." He pulled away and looked into her eyes. "That's got to mean something, right?"

Her heart swelled at his answer. It may not be ideal, but neither was this gray area they were in. "Yeah. I feel the same about you too."

"So what do you want to do about it?" His voice was a low rumble that made every atom in her body perk up.

She wanted to hear that voice say all kinds of things to her while he was wrapped around her, but she also wanted to be smart.

"Maybe we take things slow? See what happens?"

"You're okay with that?" He tilted his head, looking like her answer could make or break him. "You'll be leaving soon. Would going down this path make things harder than it needs to be?"

"Brooks Jónsson, are you trying to talk me out of this?" A smile lifted her lips.

He hugged her tight and kissed her jaw. "Wouldn't dream of it." Pulling back, he held her gaze again. "But really, Ava, is this what you want?"

Jess's words came rushing back to her. *Maybe by being open, you'll find exactly what you need.*

Jess had been right. Nothing about this trip had gone according to plan, but she'd risen to the challenges. Because of it, she was finding inspiration and joy that she'd long forgotten about.

Maybe if she leaned into the messy uncertainty of being with Brooks—no matter how short-lived—she'd find something worthwhile too. Maybe, sometimes, the moments and people who matter in life don't need to be around forever. Just the memory and lessons do. Just because the end was in sight, didn't mean she needed to write it off.

Why not bask in the good of it while she could instead of fighting it? It might feel like shit when she boarded the plane to Boston, but she wasn't about to deny herself another couple of weeks of adventure, happiness, and affection because she knew without a doubt this would end.

"Yes." The unshakable confidence in her answer made Brooks light up.

As the swirling greens and purples of the Northern Lights continued to dance above them, creating the most romantic backdrop she was sure ever existed, he cupped her face and kissed her with unguarded passion.

This was the right choice. Definitely the right choice.

CHAPTER FIFTEEN

AVA

AVA LET OUT A LONG, sullen sigh as she stared at the blinking cursor on the screen. Her campaign strategy for ZettaBytes had pretty much gone nowhere, even though she'd dedicated the whole morning to work on it. Benson was still MIA. Until she talked to him, it was pointless anyway.

She checked the clock and noted it had been four minutes since she'd pulled up the document again after checking the fundraising site incessantly the last hour.

The town's story had gained momentum that afternoon as more news stations around the world picked it up for syndication. She'd have to send very big thank you baskets to her media contacts for helping her pull this off. It had only been a couple of days since they launched, and it finally caught on like she'd hoped.

Yet the donations left a lot to be desired. Small ones trickled in consistently. Ten dollars here, fifty dollars there. Chewing her fingernail, she wondered if she'd been too optimistic about her abilities, and she worried she'd get the town's hopes up.

A text lit up her phone. She couldn't contain her smile when she saw it was from Brooks.

He'd gotten caught up carting around a tourist for a half-day tour and then had flown to Reykjavík for supplies, so she hadn't seen him at all yesterday. A little space was good to focus on the work she'd put off.

That had been the plan anyway. Instead, she was distracted by fantasies and memories of him.

There was something exhilarating knowing he could show up at her door any minute or bump into her in town when she went for a coffee run. Maybe it was the anticipation. Maybe it was the connected feeling she'd gotten since arriving in town. Maybe it was that after living in a city where a person can feel lost and forgotten in the overwhelming sea of people, it was nice to be somewhere she was starting to know everyone. She almost felt like she'd stepped onto the set of *Cheers*, but better.

Just yesterday, she'd gotten caught up chatting with a few people in town as she ran errands and stopped by Lotte's office to finalize the fundraising site. The community was special, and she was happy to have gotten the chance to experience it. To be part of it.

But it didn't feel right without Brooks. She found herself missing him a lot more than she would have expected.

She pulled up his text message.

Brooks: Heading to Chantey to grab a bite in a bit. Care to join me?
Ava: I wish. I really need to get some work done.
Brooks: I can bring you something to eat. I can't have you surviving on bottom-of-the-purse granola bars.
Ava: As if you would be any less of a distraction.

He sent her a devil emoji, and she laughed—truly laughed out loud. After their night on the boat, things had been good between them. Yes, they were going slow, but she couldn't deny the sexual tension simmering between them now that everything was out in the open. Getting on the same page broke down the last barrier holding her back, making it tough to stick to their plan to take it one day at a time.

He was a constant temptation, especially since she didn't get her fix of him for a full day. It took all her willpower to ease into this without knocking him to the ground and having her way with him.

He was so damn sweet, which also made her laugh. If someone had told her he'd be like this the day he almost mowed her over at the Blue Lagoon, she would have said they were insane. As the days went on and they learned more about each other, she couldn't think of him any other way than as a thoughtful man with a big heart.

She saw the things he did when he didn't realize she was paying attention. Most of them were small, but every one of them had the intention of making someone's day or life a little better. He took care of this town and the people in it, and if that wasn't endearing as hell, she didn't know what was.

If anything, his awareness of the needs of others only made her check herself. Back home, she'd get so wrapped up in her work and her day-to-day responsibilities, she rarely took notice of what was around her. Yes, she paid attention to her family and did what she could to support them. And of course, she was there for her friends.

Everyone else though? Not so much.

Brooks wasn't limited to helping only those he knew, he also went out of his way to help strangers. Perhaps it was something ingrained in him as a search and rescue pilot. Maybe you had to have that level of empathy and service to do your job well, so much so that it bled into your everyday life. Whatever it was, it inspired her to do better. To take stock of her life and what really mattered to her.

What *should* matter to her.

Maybe if she hadn't been so self-absorbed or trapped in her own life, she would see that there was so much more out there she could be doing.

She could take part in things for the good of it, not for raising profit margins.

Mindlessly, she clicked out of the document she was working on, pulled up the fundraising site again, and frowned. Still nothing of note. What would she do if she let everyone down?

A message from Benson popped up on her screen, distracting her from the slow trickle of donations.

She let out a breath. *Finally.*

Benson Whitlock: Updates on the campaign?
Ava Espinosa: It's coming together, but I think we should connect first. There are some details I want to iron out.
Benson Whitlock: Mind giving me access to the doc? I want to get a sense of where your head's at.

Panic filled her as she clicked back to the document. It was bare-bones. Benson wasn't one of those asshole CEOs. He was fair and generally positive...if you kept up with his expectations. He was ambitious, and to succeed in the world of tech, you couldn't be complacent. They might not be a startup anymore, but they still functioned at that fast-paced, nimble clip as they always had.

If Benson had any idea how little progress she had made in the last week—despite her logical reason for stalling on the campaign until they talked—she'd likely fall from his good graces. She didn't think she could handle her credibility and capabilities being questioned. She'd worked so hard to get to this point in her career. The last thing she'd want is to make him and the other leaders second-guess if she was the right person for the CMO job.

Was her first act as a CMO to push back on her CEO's directive? It felt right, but she had no idea how that conversation would go.

Benson Whitlock: ???
Ava Espinosa: It's still in a very rough state. Not ready for consumption. I'd rather talk about this live. Do you have a few minutes for a call?
Benson Whitlock: Heading into a meeting. Connect with my assistant to get on my schedule.

Ava Espinosa: Will do.

A rush of anxiety tore through her. She minimized the chat and gave herself a pep talk on how she should approach the conversation with Benson. As she was about to close out the fundraising site, something caught her eye.

A $5,000 donation had come through a few minutes ago.

Before she could even process her excitement, another donation for $10,000 popped up.

Ava switched screens and checked the news, finding more global news sites had picked up the story and it was trending. She pulled up her social media accounts. The posts had gone viral. #SaveIceland was in the number two trending spot on Twitter.

"Holy shit," she whispered.

It was happening. It was finally happening. She only hoped they could keep up the virality of the story long enough to make a difference. They were nowhere near the million-dollar goal, but if larger donations like these started to pick up, maybe they had a shot.

She checked the fundraising site again, seeing more small donations again, but this time much quicker.

And then it happened. A $100,000 donation.

Ava jumped from her seat and let out a triumphant squeal. This...*this* was what she was hoping for. She could kiss the generous person who'd donated, but unfortunately, they'd chosen to remain anonymous.

Grabbing her jacket, she raced out of her room and down the stairs, making it to The Chantey in record time. She pushed open the door, her chest heaving from the sudden burst of exertion, and scanned the busy dining area to find Brooks in the lunch hour crowd. His tall frame leaned against the bar as he chatted with Freyja and his father.

She beelined straight for him and squeezed him tight, unable to contain her excitement.

"Woah. You okay? You're hyperventilating." Brooks grabbed her face and looked her over with concern, ignoring the curious, Cheshire Cat smiles from Jón and Lotte nearby.

"Look." She shoved her phone in his face, practically knocking him out in the process.

He pushed the phone out of his way to get a better look at her. She probably looked like a lunatic, but she couldn't fight the adrenaline fueling her lunacy. "Back up a second and tell me what's going on."

She lifted her phone again and held it at a reasonable distance, before shaking it. "Have you guys been checking the website?"

"No. What's going on, Ava?" Jón pulled his phone from his pocket and clicked a few buttons. His eyebrows practically disappeared into his thick, white hair. "Wow. Is this right?"

Ava nodded like a bobblehead on speed. "Just came through a few minutes ago."

"Would you look at that?" Jón let out a whistle. "Over $170,000."

"Wait, what?" Ava looked at her phone screen to find another large donation for $50,000 had come through in the short time it took for her to run from the inn to the restaurant.

In a matter of minutes, the worries she had about letting down the town had started to ease. They'd pull this off after all. If she could keep the momentum going, and if the story continued to trend, they had a serious shot at raising enough money.

Tears misted her eyes.

Brooks's forehead creased as he dipped lower to meet her at eye level. "Hey," he said in a soothing tone. He rested his hands on her shoulders and rubbed them up and down. "This is a good thing."

"I know." Ava sniffed. "These are happy tears. I think?"

It had been a while since she'd felt this sense of pride. Sure, she'd always had some satisfaction with the work she produced over the years, but this was different. It was as if this was a reflection of what she was capable of. The outcome mattered. She could see her impact. It was so much more tangible than anything she'd ever experienced before.

Could work always feel this way?

The answer came in an instant: *Not down the path you've been going.*

Before she could dissect that epiphany, Kristofer burst through the door in a panic.

"We need help! Come down to the harbor. Quick!"

No one had time to ask questions. He had already raced out the door and past the front windows toward the water.

"What the hell was that about?" Jón stood and threw down money near his half-eaten sandwich.

"Whatever it is, it can't be good." A hard expression filled Brooks's face, one Ava had come to recognize as the expression he made when he went into protector mode. Whatever had Kristofer spooked was a cause for concern.

Fueled by his drive to protect and help, Brooks peeled away from the bar and stalked through the dining room, the first of the pack to follow Kristofer to the harbor.

The whole restaurant had gone quiet. Worried looks passed between patrons. After a few seconds of stunned silence, more people pulled out their money and placed it by their uneaten meals as they left The Chantey in droves.

Jón followed the crowd, moving slower than usual. "This damn knee," he said, frustration lacing his voice. "I missed a day of physical therapy, and it's already stiffened up!"

Ava wrapped an arm around his waist. "Let me help you."

"No." He shook his head. "You go on. If they need all the people they can get, I can't be holding you back."

She nodded and let him go.

"Ava," Freyja called out as she reached the door. "Be careful."

"I will."

The bright sunlight nearly blinded her as her eyes adjusted from being inside. Getting her bearings, she turned right and made a left at the corner where a crowd was forming in the distance.

A man held a woman who was weeping uncontrollably. As Ava got closer, she saw a range of emotions filling people's faces. Anger. Heartbreak. Disbelief.

What the hell happened?

She navigated along a thinned side of the crowd, looking for answers. Looking for Brooks. Finally, she spotted him.

The breath left Ava's lungs. Her hand flew to her mouth. What had been tears of pride only moments ago transformed into tears of sadness.

Brooks was crouched down, shaking his head. In front of him was a beached whale. It was massive and majestic.

And suffering.

At first, Ava thought it was dead. On closer inspection, she could see the subtle movements of its body. It was still breathing.

"Excuse me!" The crowd made a path so a middle-aged woman could come through. A stethoscope was wrapped around her neck, and she carried a massive case in her hand.

"Thank God. The vet is here," a woman next to her whispered.

The vet wasted no time getting down to business. She checked the whale's vitals and took a few instant samples to test. After a few more tests, she took a step back and shook her head.

"She's been poisoned," the vet said.

"How do we fix it?" Kristofer asked, panic still in his voice. "We have to do something!"

The woman took his hands, a tender look filling her face. "I'm sorry, Kristofer, she's too far gone. With the toxicity levels I see in the instant test, she likely won't survive the night. I'll take the blood samples back to my clinic for more thorough testing, but tests showing levels that high are rarely wrong. The bloodwork might come back and show she has a little more time, maybe a day or two more. But she's not coming out of this alive. I'm so sorry."

Kristofer swiped angrily at his eyes and pulled away, looking out to the open water. "If she's poisoned, that means—"

"There's something in the water. And it's likely going to poison any remaining marine life too," the vet finished.

Brooks stood and searched the crowd, his gaze locking on Ava's in a moment of solidarity.

In a matter of minutes, the progress they'd made now seemed pointless. Seeing this whale set them back twenty steps. It was a ticking clock that was almost out of time.

They needed to solve this problem now more than ever. She only hoped that by the time they raised the money, it wouldn't be too late.

CHAPTER SIXTEEN

AVA

"W HAT THE HELL is going on out there?" Jess asked.

Pushing through the door to Emilia's cafe, Ava switched the call to her earbuds and slipped her phone into her pocket. The somber tension in the air hit her immediately. The few patrons there stared off into space, looking numb, as the daily newspaper they typically read sat untouched on the table next to them.

It had been a bad day for them all. Earlier, she had stayed behind with the rest of the crowd, trying to make the gentle whale comfortable as they waited for the toxicology report to come back. She stood with them in solidarity, offering Helga a shoulder to cry on, lending an ear to Jón, and holding Brooks's hand to let him know she was there for him.

Word had eventually gotten out. Ava's phone had rung off the hook as her contacts looked for more information to share on their networks. Reluctantly, Ava had left Brooks's side to speak to the reporters about the events of the day.

She'd hated exploiting such a sad situation, but with how desensitized people were to the news, this was an opportunity to show how dire the situation was. Seeing the beached whale would make the gravity of it more tangible. Maybe the footage would help them reach more people so they could raise the money they needed.

"It's been a mess, Jess." Ava sighed as she waited by the breakfast bar to place an order for a triple shot. She needed all the caffeine she could get.

"How much longer are you staying there?"

"A little over a week. I hope it's enough time to make a difference."

A couple seats down the breakfast bar, two unfamiliar men sat with their coffees, hunched over a laptop. They didn't seem happy, but they didn't have the same lost expression everyone else in the cafe had.

Must be tourists.

The larger of the men clicked the mouse and pulled up a new browser tab. Ava tilted her head, recognizing the interface for the ZettaBytes database dashboard. How funny was it that even all the way across the ocean, she got a chance to see her company's product in the wild?

Emilia stopped by to get her order. When Ava turned back to the breakfast bar, the men had already left.

"Huh," Jess said, her usual tell for when she was about to say something Ava might not like.

"What?"

"I know you've been keeping us in the loop about everything through text, but this is the first time I'm actually hearing it out loud."

"Okay. And?"

"And it seems like you *really* care about what's happening to this town. I haven't heard that passion in your voice in a very long time."

"If you were here, you'd understand. I might have only been here for a short time, but the people draw you in and make you feel like you're a part of something. There's no pretense here. Everyone wears their heart on their sleeve and genuinely wants to find good in the world. How could I not care about helping them?"

Deep down, she had recognized this the first couple days she had been there. She might not be one of them officially, but their openness and compassion made her want to be.

"I can't believe this is still happening. You'd think with all the awareness about climate change, the government or some of these environmentalist groups would be doing something. I thought Iceland was known for their clean energy and all that."

"It is," Ava said. "But these groups can only do so much. The resources are finite, and somehow our problem isn't big enough to be on their radars. They're focused on other issues."

"I've been sharing the story with everyone I know. Even if people don't want to hear about it, I'll shove it down their throats. I'll do whatever I can to support you."

Ava's lips twitched "Thanks, Jess."

"I miss you. Can I stop by when you get back?"

"Of course."

Jess squealed, her happiness lightening Ava's dark mood. "Great. I'm going to bring a bunch of wine and get you saucy so you'll *finally* share all the dirty details about this Brooks guy. What's going on with you two? Anything new besides that romantic boat ride to see the Northern Lights?"

She sighed, wishing so badly there was more to share. "Nothing yet, unfortunately."

"How are you not about to explode? I don't even know the guy and I'm swooning for him. Maybe this time when you get him alone, you'll find out if he's the package deal?" Ava could almost feel Jess's pervy eyebrow wagging across the line. She couldn't help but smile.

"We're taking things slow."

"How much slower can you go? If you go any slower, you might miss the opportunity before you leave."

Didn't Ava know it. The last few days, she'd battled her desire to get to know him more with the desire to give in to her urges and let him strip her down and devour every inch of her body. "I know, I know."

"So go and get yours. It's just sex. The world won't end if you decide to have it sooner than whatever this going slow plan dictates."

"The thing is...it wouldn't be just sex with us."

Jess sucked in a breath. "Oh wow. I thought you just had the hots for him and were going to have a little vacation fun." Her voice turned serious. "It's more than that. Isn't it?"

Ava said nothing.

"Wow. Wow. Wow." Jess paused. "You've caught some real feelings for him then?"

"Yes." It felt so real now that she'd admitted it to someone. Sure, this realization had been swirling around her for days, but saying it to Jess meant she was finally accepting it.

"And if you cross that line, leaving will be that much harder," Jess said, voicing Ava's worries.

She grabbed her to-go coffee and slipped out of the quiet cafe to walk to the inn. "Exactly. Will it be worth it when I'm sure it's only going to make it hurt when I go?"

"Here's how I see it. Nothing in life is certain. You could try to be proactive by protecting yourself from heartache. But is that heartache inevitable? You don't *actually* know. Right now, it's all a theory."

"How did I get such a philosopher of a little sister?"

Jess laughed. "You were always the practical one, watching out for me and Mom and Dad. That gave me the freedom to go after my heart and learn from my mistakes."

"Ah. Yes. A true enlightened one," Ava teased.

"Exactly, which is why you should listen to me," Jess said. "Seriously, I want you to think about this. You might lose a little by trusting your gut and your heart, but what you gain may outweigh it all. Is it worth stopping yourself from finding out?"

Ava stopped midstride as Jess's words reached deep inside of her, encouraging her heart to stop being so scared. She was right.

Taking it slow wasn't about being practical. It was about protecting herself. If this was the only time she had with Brooks, wouldn't she want to make the most of it? He was the first person in a long time to make her feel like this. She should be embracing it, not keeping it at arm's length.

Before she could answer, another call buzzed through. "Listen, Jess. I have to go. I'm getting another call."

"Okay," she singsonged. "But you'll tell me all the details, right?"

"You're the worst."

Jess laughed and hung up.

"This tragic story is just one of many the northern Icelandic towns have faced these past few months. We urgently ask for your support to help us stop this from continuing to destroy our beautiful country and the hardworking, kind people who call Iceland their home. Please go to the website at the bottom of your screen to donate today."

Ava watched the evening news segment as a shot of the whale panned back to the reporter's serious expression. With her help, Ava was able to syndicate the message and get more reach.

In a few short hours, more donations had come in. Refreshing the fundraising site again, Ava saw they had finally hit a quarter of a million dollars. It was a small win. A bright spot in this mess.

She switched off the TV and sat on the edge of her bed, resting her face in her hands. It had been a hell of a day, and she hadn't had to deal with anything nearly as devastating as Brooks and the rest of the townspeople had dealt with. She couldn't imagine what they must be feeling right now.

A knock on her door pulled her from her anxious thoughts. Checking her reflection in the mirror by the desk, Ava wiped away the smudged makeup under her eyes and fluffed her hair before answering.

Brooks stood on the other side, leaning against the doorframe with his head hung low.

Her heart squeezed. She was going to miss him showing up at her door like this once she left.

"Brooks." Her voice came out breathless, both grateful for his unexpected visit and heartbroken over how worn he looked.

"It's been a day." He let out a long, harsh breath. "We got to the point where it was more humane to put the whale down. It wasn't kind to watch her suffer anymore."

The ground fell out from under her. "Oh, Brooks. I'm so sorry." With shaky hands, she pulled him inside and closed the door behind them. She wrapped her arms around his torso and held him tight.

"How can I help?" Ava asked, cupping his cheek as she looked into his midnight blue eyes. Dark purple shadows had formed underneath them, making his eyes look more doom and gloom. Thick scruff covered his jawline.

He closed his eyes and shook his head, placing his forehead against hers. "You've done so much for us already, Ava."

"I could do more," she whispered. "Just say the word."

He lifted his head and placed his hand behind the crook of her neck, rubbing the pad of his thumb along her sensitive skin as he looked at her with appreciation. "Right now, I just...*need* you. Just be here with me for a moment."

"I'm here, Brooks. I'm here."

"Since you've come into my life, it seems like I'm always reaching for you when I'm facing something impossible. You make me believe things will be okay." His voice was rough and raw, reaching into her soul. The words making a home inside her heart.

They held each other's gaze, a million unspoken emotions passing between them.

Her heart almost beat out of her chest as he dipped his head low and took possession of her lips. Deep and hard. Soft and urgent. His hands were all over her, moving slowly down her arms, gripping her hips, holding her closer.

She fisted his shirt and bit his bottom lip as she trailed her mouth along his jaw, the coarse hair tickling her skin.

Brooks's breath was ragged in her ear as she nipped at his neck and earlobe. Her name quietly spilled from his lips as he pulled her closer. His hand snaked up the back of her shirt and ran along her skin. His fingertips were chilled from the outside air, causing goosebumps to prick her skin in their wake.

"I need you too," she said quietly against his lips as she pulled him in for another scorching kiss.

Any lingering thoughts about taking things slowly vanished from her mind as his hands moved around the front of her, pushing underneath the edge of her bra and palming her breast.

A harsh gasp came from her, her brain losing all sense of reality while he took her nipple between his index finger and thumb.

She wanted him. Every bit of him. The thoughtful and the frustrating. The caring and the skeptical. The affectionate and whatever this erotic side of him was. Brooks was a blend of all the interesting. All the good. He kept her on her toes. He made her *want*.

Truly. Deeply. Want.

He made her let her guard down and just *be*.

Ava pushed his unzipped jacket from his shoulders. It slipped to the floor as she grabbed the hem of his Henley shirt and lifted it over his head.

She paused, taking in the view of his bare torso. It was beautiful. Stunning. All the peaks and valleys. Hard muscles. Warm skin.

And it was there for her to touch.

Brooks titled his head back and closed his eyes while Ava's hands worshiped the hard lines of his body. A ragged breath escaped from his lips.

She was overwhelmed by him. The sight of him. "I need to feel you. More. I need...I need..."

She couldn't form a coherent sentence. All her nerves and anticipation made her a little dizzy.

She pulled off her shirt and loved how Brooks's gaze devoured the sight of her. Is this how she'd looked at him? Hooded eyes, full of lust.

His dark gaze went even darker as he lifted his hands and traced the swell of her breast with his index finger.

"You're beautiful. So damn beautiful. Ava Espinosa, you drive me insane."

He kissed her again and pulled her close. Skin against skin. Warm and smooth. She moaned at the sensation. Every nerve in her body electrified.

Her hands reached for his belt eagerly. Before she could unhook it, he broke the kiss and grabbed her wrists, stopping her in the act.

She lifted her gaze, confused by the tortured expression crossing his face. "What's wrong?"

He closed his eyes and pressed his lips in a thin line. "I can't believe I'm saying this, but we should stop."

Ava dropped her hands, wrapping her arms around her body. "I thought—"

He reached for her again. "You thought right. I want you, Ava. So damn bad. But not like this. Not when emotions are raw from what happened today." He cupped her face, stroking her cheek with his thumb. "When this finally happens, it's going to be because we're all in. It will be only about you and me, not about finding a release to distract and numb a painful situation."

She rested her hand on top of his and squeezed. "Is this what this is? A way to forget for a moment?"

"I want to say no, but I can't be sure. Everything's so fresh. When I finally have you the way I've wanted, I'll show you exactly how much you matter to me."

Her knees almost buckled. "I hate that you turned out to be a decent guy." She grinned.

He smiled back. "The thoughts I have about you are far from decent."

She tilted back her head and groaned. "You're killing me."

"I promise, it will be worth the wait." He kissed her exposed throat and nipped at her ear.

"This isn't helping." She pushed him back and grabbed his clothes, tossing his shirt at him. "If you want me to behave myself, you need to hide all of that." She waved her hand around his muscular torso.

She turned to pick up her shirt and slipped it over her head. Brooks took her elbow and gently turned her around. "In all seriousness, I meant it when I said I need to be with you tonight. Can I stay a while longer?"

Ava's insides melted. "Of course." She took his hand and pulled him to her bed, settling next to him.

His eyes shined in the dim light of the room as he ran his hand down her arm and intertwined their fingers. They stayed like that for a long while, holding each other. It was right then that Ava accepted Brooks had buried himself in her heart.

CHAPTER SEVENTEEN

AVA

AVA RUSHED through Brooks's front door, her laptop in hand and her oversized purse slung over her shoulder. "I'm sorry! I know I'm late—"

At the sight of her, Brooks tossed the dishrag he was holding onto the counter and crossed the kitchen in two long strides, meeting her at the front door. He pulled her close and stroked the soft skin of her cheek. Desire and warmth filled his eyes before he dipped his head low and captured her mouth.

After an early morning SAR call pulled him from her arms the other night and kept him gone for more than a day, she'd felt the effects of not being around him those twenty-four hours.

She hated it. And judging by the way his fingers lightly pressed into her hips, pushing his body closer to her, his hands in her hair to give him better access to her lips, it was safe to say he'd felt the same way.

He pulled away and pressed his forehead against her. Their breaths came out ragged. "Hi."

Ava suppressed a smile. "Well, hello there. That was quite a greeting."

A timer buzzed from the kitchen. Brooks sighed, gave her a quick kiss on the lips, and pulled away to go check what was cooking in the oven.

With the moment of space to come back to earth, she was suddenly hit with the most delicious smell. "Oh my God," she moaned. "Now I'm *really* sorry I'm late. What is that?"

He looked over his shoulder and smirked. "So it's the food that got that reaction."

"You're okay too." She grinned back. "Don't take it personally. With you being gone, I've had no one to remind me that crushed granola bars are not a proper meal replacement. Chalk it up to Maslow's pyramid of needs. Maybe when I get some food in me, I can reconsider my reaction to that kiss." She came further into the kitchen and tried to peek over his large frame. "Whatcha cooking?"

"Braised beef cheek, scalloped potatoes, and asparagus." He rolled up his sleeves, showing off his toned forearms speckled with dark hair. "I became obsessed with it when I first tried it at the Old Iceland restaurant in the city. I've tried to replicate it over the years but never quite mastered it. It's still great though. I hope you like it."

He pulled the meat from the oven to let it rest before he served it. "Figured I had to pull out all the stops so you'd choose to eat here instead of The Chantey."

"Jealous of my sudden popularity?" She rested her chin on her hand and batted her eyelashes.

"Exactly. It has nothing to do with me wanting to be alone with you without someone constantly interrupting."

"Can't help that I've got the it factor." She frowned. "Where's Stella? I was expecting to be knocked on my ass from her excitement by now."

"Dad's got her. He had to put down his dog last year, so sometimes he steals Stella for the night to get his fix. He's always had animals, so I'm sure it won't be too long until he's ready to get another dog."

"That's sad and sweet."

Brooks rolled his eyes and grinned. "Dad likes to spoil her and teach her bad habits. I'm pretty sure that's his passive-aggressive way of getting back at me for being such a little asshole to him while growing up."

She bit her lip, holding in her laugh. She could picture playfully mischievous Jón doing exactly that.

"Oh! I completely forgot! I want to show you something," Ava said as she went to grab her laptop from her purse by the door.

"Ava." Brooks placed his hands on her shoulders and dipped lower to look into her eyes. "You can take a break for a few minutes, right?"

"Ummm..." She eyed her laptop beckoning her, excited by the headway she'd made with Marissa, but also wanting to enjoy a semi-normal evening with a man she found herself thinking about *way* too much.

Brooks stepped away, his hand to his heart. "Woman, you wound me. After I slaved over the stove for this beautiful meal, you still had to think about it?" His eyes twinkled with mischief.

"Judging by the timer, we still have a few minutes. Humor me? When the timer goes off, I promise to be one hundred percent all yours."

"Such an honor." He pulled out her seat and handed her the laptop.

"Marissa emailed me about an hour ago with some interesting info." She opened her email and searched for Marissa's email, already buried under nearly a hundred unread messages. "Here it is," she said as she pulled it up and opened the attachments. "Oh, wow."

Brooks cocked his head and squinted. "What are we looking at?"

"Okay. So you know how my company has this huge database that has access to an insane amount of data?"

"Kinda."

"Well, Marissa was able to cross-reference some of the notes and themes we've seen here with public-facing data. These are satellite maps."

"I can see that."

Ava pulled up another, similar map. "You see these dark spots here?" She pointed to small spots in Iceland's northern interior.

"Barely, but yes." She pulled up another map, this time with two more spots closer to the northwestern shore. Another showed three more dots in a line moving northeast. "What are they?"

"From what we've learned, they're consistent with mining. Although very, *very* small mining sites. If we hadn't already suspected this, it would have gone undetected. Marissa was able to find satellite images with a different contrast so we can see these better." She highlighted the dates on each of the maps.

"Holy shit." Brooks ran a hand down his face. "These dates are around the time we were starting to see the issues with our marine life emerge."

"And look at this," she said while zooming in. "It looks like almost all of these sites are close enough to a water source. So—"

"They might have done illegal dumping and it would have flowed down the rivers and into our oceans," he finished. He pushed back, let out a breath, and shook his head as if trying to absorb all the information and the fact that they might have been right. "Your company's product can find all this information?"

"It's insane the way people use our product. Some of them are simple databases, and others are more complex. We have some of the most important agencies in the world using it. I could only imagine what places like NASA and the FBI use it for."

"And that information is public?"

Ava shook her head. "No. They use it privately. However, we do have an open source side that allows people to access and collaborate on things. Some people use it for silly things, like a database for every movie or TV show filmed in Iceland. Others, like scientists and doctors, use it to share information and try to partner with others to find cures for things. I only have access to this because it's public."

"Judging by these satellite images, it looks like the people mining are moving every few weeks along the northern coast to the east."

"That's what it seems like."

"So how can we guess where they'll be next so we catch these fucking bastards?"

"Working on it. We're trying to gather a list of all the natural resources Iceland has that might be valuable enough for these people to go through this trouble. Maybe that will help us pinpoint where they'll go next so we can get ahead of it. Marissa should have something in the next few hours."

"So now, we sit and wait."

"Unfortunately."

Brooks turned the computer toward him and studied the maps before looking at Ava again. "We might actually get to the bottom of this. Once things are back to normal, Darlene and I are going to show you the real Iceland. On the house." He winked.

Although he was smiling as if to make light of it, she could sense his hidden meaning underneath the humor. Brooks was clearly selective about who he let in his life, and even more so when it came to giving them his trust. A sense of pride stirred in her knowing that he'd let her into that small, exclusive circle.

She refused to let him down.

"Maybe we should fly out tomorrow and check out some of the areas we think they'll head to next. Once we get the report from Marissa, we can select a few places to look at."

"That's a good idea," Brooks said just as the timer dinged. "Guess you're all mine now." He walked to the oven and started plating their food.

"Oh wow. Even brought out the nice dishes this time too."

"Only the finest for you. Truth be told, I didn't think I'd ever see these dishes again."

She cocked her head. "Why's that?"

"They were my mom's. I hadn't unpacked them since moving here. Didn't really see a point." He rubbed the back of his neck and let out a quiet laugh. "I guess her lessons of Southern hospitality must have stuck with me. She always said that the most special guests deserved the good china."

Her heart melted a bit. "Sounds like she raised you right. I'm honored that you thought I deserved the good china."

Brooks held her gaze for a moment before he turned back to the counter and held up a wine bottle, eyebrows raised in question.

"Sure."

After he poured them both a glass and took his seat, Ava dug in. She barely needed the knife, because as soon as her fork hit the meat, it all but fell apart. "Brooks, wow. Oh wow." She took a second bite, her eyes closing in pure satisfaction.

"I take it that you like it?"

Ava held up a hand. "Please, I need a moment of silence."

He laughed and shook his head as he continued to eat his meal like a civilized adult. The opposite of Ava, who had to actively remind herself not to tear into it like a deranged animal.

Brooks, bless his heart, allowed her to eat in silence. It was only after she started to slow down that he ventured to speak. "So...I know you seem very fond of PowerPoint and all, but what do you normally do for fun when, ya know, you aren't trying to save a small Icelandic fishing town?"

Ava rested her fork on her empty plate and quirked an eyebrow. "First a fancy dinner and now personal questions? This feels oddly like a date. Have I accidentally stumbled into a date, Brooks?" She smirked.

"You want it to be a date?"

She held his gaze in a staring contest, not ready to back down from this game.

Brooks wiped his mouth and tossed his napkin onto the counter. He leaned back on the barstool. "We've spent all this time together here, so you've been able to learn a lot about me and this town, but I've only gotten to know bits and pieces about your life in Boston. I just want to know you. Can you blame a guy?" he asked with a bashful shrug.

"Hmmm. What to tell? What to tell?" She tapped her finger on her chin. "I mean, you know a lot more than you realize, as sad as that is."

He squinted at her in disbelief. "I hardly doubt your whole life orbits around work. There's much more to you, Ava Espinosa. From what I've seen of your character, that much is clear."

"Okay. Fine." She rested her wine glass on the countertop and swirled the liquid around. "Work aside, I like to get dinner and drinks with my friends...although those occasions are becoming far and few between now that they've either moved out of Massachusetts or started families. I'm happy for them, even if I miss them."

"I get that. I had a few close friends I left behind when I moved here. Thankfully, Iceland is a place they've been more than happy to visit."

Ava lifted an eyebrow. "And here I thought you hated tourists."

His shrugged. "I can make a few exceptions. What else?"

"I torture myself with jogging when I can. Absolutely hate it, but I do it for the views of the Charles River. I *love* the water, so it makes it a little more worth it."

"Even in the winters?"

"Even in the winters." Ava took a sip of her wine as she thought more. "I've tried taking up hobbies, but my work can be demanding—as you know—so I never have enough time to actually master something." She smiled to herself. "I actually have a closet full of half-started attempts, swearing I'll get to it one day. I know I never will though. At least not while I'm working the way I do."

His face filled with concern. "So what *do* you have time for then?"

She titled her head as she considered his question. "I guess not much. I'm pretty boring."

"I highly doubt anything about you is boring."

"I used to travel, except now most of my travel is work-related. This was my first personal trip I've taken in years—"

"And we still put you to work." His full lips pulled into a boyish grin, contrasting against the hard edges of his face—now covered in a dark five o'clock shadow—and the usual determined glint in his dark, assessing eyes.

Ava pushed away a wayward lock of thick dark hair from his forehead. "This isn't work. This matters. Other than that, my family is one of the few things I make time for. They mean everything to me."

"Seems like they raised an amazing woman."

Ava put her face in her hands and shook her head. Compliments like that always made her feel awkward. "Don't be a cheeseball. That's not on brand for you."

Brooks pulled her hands from her face. "I mean it. Ava, I see *you*... every moment I'm with you. I didn't need to know your life story or daily habits to know you're one of the good ones." His thumb made soft circles on the sensitive skin of her wrist. "It can be hard for me to...let people in sometimes."

Ava snorted at that. "Wouldn't have guessed."

He grinned. "In all seriousness. I know our circumstances are unconventional, but what I've seen reminded me that sometimes it's worth opening up to someone," he said with a pointed stare, all joking now gone. "You're not a woman who needs saving—"

"If you're trying to woo me, you're a little rusty."

"Ava."

"Okay, okay. Sorry. Continue."

"I'm trying to tell you that you're strong, smart, and inspirational. Stubborn as hell, yes, but you also remind me that it's okay to rely on someone. To be a partner with someone. In my life, I've had to be the one who makes everything okay. I could never let my guard down. People relied on me to be that steady person they could count on. It's both scary and a relief to know that I don't have to take it all on alone. There are so many things about you that make you special, but the one that matters to me most is the trust I have for you."

Ava's heart lurched in her throat. The way his voice shook just a little only showed her how scary, but important, it must have been for him to tell her that.

As if she needed any more reasons to fall for this man, he had to go and put his heart out there and make her feel all kinds of special, seen, and appreciated.

"Here I was thinking I was crazy to feel so connected to someone I'd only met. Crazy to miss you so deeply when I didn't see you for one day. *One* day. You help me live in the moment. When I'm with you, there aren't to-do lists swirling through my head. I don't check my watch every five minutes. Where there used to be everything that kept me busy but left me hollow, now there's you, and I don't feel hollow at all." She looked away, trying to calm her racing pulse enough to share a coherent thought.

"I don't know what's going to happen once I leave Iceland," she said quietly before looking at him again. "I just know that I've never felt this way about anyone. I don't care if that's coming on too strong—"

Before she could finish her thought, Brooks closed the gap between them with a searing kiss. She could feel the heat of his skin, the thrumming of his heartbeat as his hands let go of her wrists and he shoved them into her hair, gently holding her there, letting her know he didn't want this to end.

Each time they kissed, it was like exploring something new with him. Exciting and adventurous, just like the man himself. Heart-stopping and heart-pounding. A mix of nervous anticipation and sweet relief every time she gave in.

What would it be like if I gave myself completely to him?

She was ready to find out.

CHAPTER EIGHTEEN

AVA

"Ava." Brooks's rough whisper rumbled in her ear as he kissed her jawline.

He pulled her from the barstool, lifting her so she could wrap her legs around his hips. Their kisses were fevered and hot as he walked them down the hall to his room.

She broke the kiss long enough to strip off her shirt over her head. Brooks stopped and pressed her against the wall, his eyes devouring her body before dipping his head to trail his lips along the swell of her breasts.

"I need you, Brooks. *Now*," she said as she arched against him, her body humming and aching to be touched by him.

He pulled her away from the wall and carried her to his bedroom in a frenzied mess of kisses and moans.

Faint light from a streetlamp filtered through the bedroom windows, giving just enough light to make out the outline of his furniture. As he led her through the doorway, Ava felt like this was one of the last barriers between her and Brooks. This symbolized he was letting her in completely.

He placed her on the edge of the bed and grabbed the back of his shirt to remove it before leaning over her again. His hands were everywhere. In her hair, running down her body, pushing her legs apart.

His hard cock strained against his pants as he rocked his body into hers. She sucked in a breath, her body shaking at how badly she needed to feel him. Skin to skin. Inside of her. Wrapped around her.

This was it. This was the moment when it will all change between them.

It was like pouring gasoline on a fire. It would go up in brilliant, hypnotizing flames. With his mouth on hers again, Ava knew right then that she didn't care about getting burned. She'd set this whole damn thing on fire if it meant having him.

Their groans mingled as he twisted his hips, rubbing the length of him in perfect circles against her sensitive nub. It was all too much— and at the same time, not enough.

She broke the kiss. "Take off your clothes."

A sensual smile lifted his lips. "Now this is the kind of bossy I can get behind." Without hesitation, Brooks had them both naked. If she wasn't so distracted by how turned on she was, she would have been impressed by the sheer speed in which he got it done.

But there wasn't much time for thinking. Not with how his hand dipped between her thighs, touching her like his life depended on it.

Nothing else existed outside of this bedroom. Maybe this was the first time in her life that she'd ever been so focused on one thing. Not planning ahead. Not checking the time. Not focused on her to-do list.

Right now, all she could see was him. All she could feel was how he made her nerve endings light up.

She lifted her head to capture his mouth again and traced her tongue against his, loving the taste of his lips. "Tell me you want me."

"I want you more than anything, Ava, and I'll show you."

Brooks lowered his head and took a nipple in his mouth. She gripped his shoulders and dropped her head back, letting out a mix of a moan and whimper. She was in agony, both wanting to have everything—feel all of him—right this second and wanting to savor the moment.

"Oh God," she breathed out, slightly lightheaded from the adrenaline and anticipation. He gave her one last kiss before getting up.

"Where are you going?" Panic collided with her insatiable lust as Brooks walked away.

His deep laugh rumbled through the quiet room. "Relax. I'm getting a condom."

Watching him cross the room to the nightstand, Ava couldn't help but admire the way the dim light highlighted the peaks and valleys of his torso and the deep V displaying his perfect cock that made her insides pulsate at the sight of it. She took a deep, shuddering breath, a new wave of lust hitting her with the force of an asteroid crashing down to earth.

Brooks came back to her side and stood by the bed for a moment, his naked, perfect body on full display. She reached for him, nearly pulling him down on top of her, eager to have him buried inside of her.

Brooks stopped her before she had the chance. He lowered to his knees and pushed her down on the bed. He shook as he took a deep breath, his hooded eyes focusing on his movements. Pushing her knees wide for him, showing every bare inch of her sex.

Lifting just enough to watch him, she felt the first swipe of his tongue against her clit and bucked off the bed.

He placed one hand on her hips to hold her in place. "You taste so good," he murmured as he circled his tongue, sucking every so often.

It was amazing. It was mind-blowing. She wanted it to last forever.

But then he placed a finger inside of her. And another. Pumping slowly as he continued to lick her, and she knew forever was off the table.

With another suck, her climax built. The painfully good moment where she was so close to release, but not there yet. She was hanging on the edge, suspended in time.

As if sensing this, Brooks's fingers and tongue picked up speed. Her body trembled from the rising tension. Everything clenched, bringing her closer and closer.

He sucked her again, helping push her over the edge. Her orgasm came hard, making her see white and stars. She shook almost violently with each pulse. Brooks continued to lick her softly, allowing her to squeeze out every second of it until it was over.

Ava ran a hand through her hair, feeling weak and sated. "Wow."

Before she could even find the strength to do anything, Brooks was sliding her farther up on the bed. He knelt between her thighs and rolled the condom on slowly before settling between her legs. He leaned over her, kissing her neck and collarbone. Her hot skin rose with goosebumps as the rough scruff on his chin scraped against her.

She lifted her hips, silently urging for him to fill her.

He eased himself inside of her and sucked in a deep breath, his eyes fluttering closed as she stretched around him inch by inch. She kissed him hard and moved her hips in response. The slide of him in and out—the friction of it—made her ravenous. More. She wanted more.

Brooks picked up the pace, his hips moving faster, slamming back into her and swiveling his body to rub against her sensitive clit.

"Touch yourself for me," he said against her lips. "I want to know what it feels like when you come around me."

She lowered her hand and pressed her fingers to her swollen flesh. Brooks shifted so he could watch her, his eyes going dark and hooded as his gaze tracked the way she circled herself while his cock disappeared inside of her and reappeared over and over.

"Yes, baby. Like that."

Another orgasm started to build, her body tightening with each stroke of her fingers. Brooks's eyes closed, his hips moving faster, burying himself in her harder and deeper.

"You feel so fucking good. Keep going, Ava."

Her fingers moved in faster, tighter circles as her body tensed more. Finally, she shattered, letting out a loud moan as her body clenched around the thick length of him.

She never knew orgasms could feel so good. She never wanted to have another one without him inside her again.

"Keep touching until you can't take it anymore," he demanded.

It was sweet torture. She was so sensitive, but it felt so good she couldn't stop herself. Brooks pounded harder, his groans growing louder as he finally tensed and let go, his cock twitching as his own release came.

He rode it out, milking every last throb before he let out a breath and lowered himself so he could kiss her.

"Was that okay for you?" he asked as he pushed away the hair stuck to the sweat on her neck and kissed her there.

A delirious laugh escaped her. "Okay isn't even in the realm of what that was. God, Brooks."

A proud smile filled his face. "I've imagined what it could be like between us. I knew it would be good—hoped it would be—but I never imagined it would be *that* good." He rolled to the side and rested his head on the pillow, looking her deep in her eyes. "I could get addicted to you, Ava Espinosa."

"Ditto."

Brooks ran his hand down her arm and hip, trailing lower and grabbing the sheet to pull over her. "Stay the night with me."

"I should get back to the inn. I'm sure Marissa has sent some info over. I'll want to look it over and figure out a game plan—"

"Ava." He ran his tongue along the column of her neck. Her body responded instantly. "If I couldn't show you all the reasons why it would be tempting to stay the night with me, then it sounds like I still have work to do."

She bit her bottom lip and moaned when his hand slipped between her legs again, touching her sensitive flesh. "You may be able to sway me. I need a little more convincing."

"I'll gladly spend the whole night making my case."

CHAPTER NINETEEN

AVA

IT MIGHT HAVE BEEN the first time in years that Ava had slept soundly through the night. She didn't wake up once. Didn't feel the low-level anxious urge to check her emails and voicemails, panicked that something might have blown up overnight and she'd have to do immediate damage control.

After she and Brooks had gotten cleaned up, they crawled back into bed, still naked, and held each other. Brooks's hands ran along her body in lazy exploration as he kissed her slowly, purposefully. The way his fingers traced along her skin, brushing by her sensitive spots but never stopping, was the most erotic thing she'd experienced in a long time. Maybe ever.

After a long while, Ava couldn't handle it anymore. He'd managed to build her up all over again.

Finally—*finally*—when Ava was almost certain he wouldn't put her out of her misery, his hand unexpectedly dipped between her legs and touched her exactly where she ached.

She nearly came on the spot. All that anticipation had her primed and ready. With a simple touch, she'd shattered again.

Of course, she hadn't forgotten to gladly return the favor from her first orgasm of the night. She'd never forget how powerful and sexy she felt with her mouth wrapped around him, looking up to see the pure ecstasy on his face. Or the way his hands gripped her hair as his body tensed when he got closer to his release.

Or the way he roared out her name when he finally let go.

Eventually, they fell asleep in a tired, satisfied heap, all jelly limbs tangled together.

She wanted to stay in bed with him all day, keeping the real world at bay. Their chemistry was more than she could take, but damn if she didn't want to keep pushing the limit.

Unfortunately, they could only ignore their responsibilities for so long. Marissa had come through with the reports they'd been waiting for early the next morning, which helped them pinpoint potential mining spots along the northeastern shore. An hour after getting the message, they'd jumped in the truck to get to the hangar.

They had been flying for hours, trying to spot unusual activity like they'd seen the first day Ava had arrived in Iceland.

Nothing.

The trip could have been tedious with anyone else but Brooks. He'd been a good distraction, especially with the way he was holding her hand, placing soft kisses on the inside of her palm every so often.

His blue eyes gleamed with mischief and lust as he boldly dragged his hand along her thigh until it reached her apex. She was almost tempted to straddle him in the middle of their flight. If he thought he could get addicted to her, what did that mean for how she felt for him? She practically shook with want.

"I can feel how wet you are through your jeans." He looked over, watching his hand touching her between her legs, his eyes hooded with desire.

The helicopter shook, and Brooks grabbed the controls with both his hands to steady them.

"Well, if you can manage to keep us alive long enough, maybe you can find out for sure," Ava quipped with a grin.

"That's quite the incentive. Hungry?"

"Starving, as usual."

"We've been at this for a while. Let's take a break for a bite in Siglufjörður."

Moments later, they'd landed the helicopter and made their way into town. Ava wondered if she'd ever get over the awe she felt every time she visited one of these beautiful places. Siglufjörður, another historic fishing town on the northern shore, not only had the sparkling blue waters of the fjords and a quaint downtown filled with colorful buildings, but the surrounding mountains covered in snow made it look like a winter wonderland.

"I love how festive everything is here." The storefronts were wrapped in forest green garland. Twinkle lights surrounded windows and doors and covered the roofs. Christmas classics sung in Icelandic poured out from the stores as they walked by.

"Yeah, the Icelanders really love Christmas. Örugg Höfn is like that too, but with everything going on, the town hasn't had time to do their normal traditions, aside from the party the other night."

"That's such a shame, but with all that stress, I get it."

Ava bent to look closer at the Christmas ornaments displayed in a shop window. "What's the deal with the black cat? I've seen it a few times now."

"Ah," Brooks said with a smile. "That's the Jólakötturinn, or the Yule Cat. Folklore says he's a massive cat that lurks around and eats people who haven't received any new clothes to wear before Christmas Eve."

Ava raised her eyebrows and straightened. "Is that so?"

"The Icelanders love their folklore. There are also thirteen Santas, which they call Yule Lads."

She laughed. "I heard about their obsession with elves, but never this."

"There are so many stories, I wouldn't know where to start." He nodded at the place next door. "Come on, I hear this place is pretty good."

Ava followed Brooks into a small restaurant made bright and airy by tall ceilings, white-tiled floors, white shiplap, and blond wood tables. They grabbed a small two-seater near the front windows. With how busy the place was, she was glad they found one right away.

"Smells good in here." Ava accepted a menu from their waitress.

"Best fish and chips this side of the island," the waitress said with a wink. "I'm Jóhanna. What can I get you today?"

"You know what? I'll have that," she said, handing the menu back without even looking. "And a coffee—black—and water, please."

"Make it two," Brooks said.

"Absolutely. I'll be back with your drinks shortly." Jóhanna hurried off toward the bar.

"You don't see the restrooms anywhere, do you?" Ava asked.

Brooks pointed to the back hallway to the right of the bar. "There. You see the sign that says *baðherbergi*? That's where they are."

"Perfect. I'll be right back."

Making her way through the dining area, she noticed a small line waiting for the single-stall restroom. She took her place at the back of the queue and people-watched as she waited.

That's when she noticed them. For a second, she'd looked right past them sitting at the bar. They blended in. Forgettable, even.

But it was what was on their laptop that caught her eye first. The interface for ZettaBytes she knew like the back of her hand. When she studied the people using it, she remembered them from Emilia's cafe the other day.

Her stomach dropped.

Could this be our miners?

The men talked animatedly about what was on their screen. She wished she could hear what they were saying.

As a ploy to get closer in the most casual way possible, Ava prayed that her heavy-duty phone case lived up to its purpose and dropped it on the ground. Close enough to her not to be too obvious, but far enough to get a few steps closer to the men at the bar.

She took her time bending down to retrieve it, hearing just enough to make her worry.

"Look at the numbers. This isn't worth our time," the larger, more gruff man said, his accent holding a hint of Eastern European.

The younger man twisted the laptop at his companion and jabbed his finger at the screen. "My calculations say there will be a big payoff here. It's untapped."

"Exactly. There aren't enough data points to take this risk."

"Or maybe it's the risk we need to take. It could be the payload that's been under the radar."

"Miss," the waitress said, her head tilted as she watched Ava bend over and hang there for a moment. "Is everything okay?"

"Just dropped my phone." Heat flushed Ava's cheeks as she straightened and showed her cell. She shrugged. "A little clumsy these days."

Jóhanna gave her a small smile. "Of course. Your drinks will be out in a moment."

"Great. Thank you."

Ava started to take a step back to rejoin the bathroom line when the younger man caught her eye. He paused. A flicker of something she couldn't place flashed through his eyes as he held her stare. She felt caught. Trapped. But she wasn't sure why. She didn't know these men. They didn't know her. Yet something was off.

Did they know I was listening?

Ava gave him a quick, polite smile and busied herself with her phone. She let out a sigh of relief when she felt his stare drift away from her.

She pulled up her Slack app and shot off a message to Marissa.

Ava: SOS

Marissa: What's up?

Ava: I think I have a lead, but I can't be sure. There's a couple of men at the restaurant in the town we're investigating.

Ava: I've seen them before in Örugg Höfn.

Ava: ZettaBytes is on their laptop.

Marissa: You think they're using the database to find their next spots?
Ava: By the conversation I overheard, it's highly possible.
Marissa: What did Brooks say?
Ava: I'm by myself right now. I haven't told him. I don't want to worry him until I have solid evidence.

Ava looked to where the men were sitting, engrossed in their conversation. A jacket with an unfamiliar logo hung on the back of the larger man's chair. Discreetly, she snapped a photo and sent it to Marissa.

Ava: Does this look familiar? The guy has it on his jacket.
Marissa: Nope.
Ava: It could be nothing.
Marissa: Or it could be something. I'll see what I can find.
Ava: Thanks so much.
Marissa: I'll be in touch.

Ava wasn't sure what to think. On the one hand, if she was right about these men, it meant they may have found a solid lead for what was causing all this destruction. On the other hand, if she was right, that meant the company she'd put her blood, sweat, and tears into helped these people with their dirty work.

CHAPTER TWENTY

BROOKS

"YOU GONNA TELL me what's going on?"

Ava glanced at him from the passenger seat of the chopper before quickly looking away. "Everything's fine."

Brooks grunted as he gripped the controls and looked ahead. "You've been quiet. That's not like you."

"People are allowed to not talk, Brooks."

"You've been clutching onto your phone like a lifeline ever since you got back from the restroom."

He'd thought maybe she'd broken herself of that habit as they'd gotten closer these last few weeks, but something had shifted in a matter of minutes and caused her to backslide. The rest of the afternoon, she'd been short, pensive, and distant. The sparkle in her eyes and playful smile had turned lifeless and dull.

He tried again. "Something happen at work?"

She let out a sigh and stared out the window. He almost wondered if she'd even heard him. He placed a hand on hers and squeezed, startling her from whatever she was thinking about.

"Ava, talk to me."

"I'm just tired. We didn't sleep much last night," she said, her voice flat and unconvincing.

Brooks swallowed and pulled back his hand. Maybe it wasn't about work but about what happened between them. They'd said they'd take it slow, but he thought they were on the same page. She seemed happy. Ecstatic. A more than willing participant.

Deciding not to push his luck, he left Ava to her thoughts as he flew them back to town. He'd get to the bottom of it once they were on solid ground.

After maneuvering the chopper onto the landing strip and securing it in the hangar, he opened the passenger door to the truck. Ava slipped by without a word.

He pinched the bridge of his nose. "Come back to my place."

"Um," she started while buckling in, "can you drop me back at the inn instead? I have a few things I need to catch up on after being out all day." She tried to smile at him. Probably wanted to pretend things were normal, but she wasn't so good at faking it.

He didn't expect to spend every waking moment with her now that they'd slept together, yet how she'd reacted almost seemed like a brush-off. They hadn't talked about what last night actually meant. Should he have talked about it with her? They had gotten caught up in the moment. Maybe the endorphins had clouded her judgment and reality was sinking in.

Did she regret it?

He was going to ask her as much, but he saw her attention was buried in her phone again. Shaking his head, he closed her door, got in the truck, and drove her back to Helga's like she'd asked. If she needed a moment to herself, he'd give it to her, but Ava was an overthinker. He'd be damned if he'd let her imagination run wild for too long and get the wrong idea.

He'd give her a little space. After that, he'd make sure they got everything out in the open before things got messed up before they ever really started.

That evening, Brooks made his way to the inn, taking the stairs two at a time, nerves twisting his stomach. He exhaled, then knocked on her door, determined to get to the bottom of things. They'd made too much progress these last few weeks together for him to let her pull away without a fight. Without understanding why. And without convincing her that what had happened between them wasn't a mistake.

Ava cracked open the door. Her brown eyes went big. "Brooks." She opened the door wider but didn't invite him in. "I wasn't expecting you."

He drank in the sight of her. Her hair was in a messy bun on top of her head, her yoga pants hugged every curve, and her wide-necked sweater showed off her silky-smooth shoulder.

For a moment yesterday, this stunning woman had been all his. He hoped it wouldn't be the last time.

"Yeah." He cleared his throat. "I wanted to talk to you."

She checked her phone. "Did something happen in the last few hours?"

"Yes. No. I don't know." He took a step closer. "Look, can I come in?"

"Um," she said, looking back into the room.

Was someone else with her? A flash of red filled his vision before she opened the door further. "Sure," she said.

He followed her in as she scurried to the desk and slammed her laptop shut. She leaned against the desk, crossing her arms in front of her chest casually, but her tense posture made it obvious she was anything but relaxed.

"What's up?" she asked.

Brooks shoved a hand in his hair. "About last night..." The hard edges of her eyes softened. "I thought maybe we should talk about it. About what it meant."

She tucked her hair behind her ears. "It was...amazing. So good, I almost can't believe it was real."

"It was pretty damn incredible, wasn't it?"

Ava nodded, her gaze fixed on him, her chest beginning to rise and fall a little more noticeably.

"I could, uh...prove to you it was *very* real." He took a step closer.

Her eyes went dark, making his pulse spike with want.

Shit, no. This was going sideways, fast. "As great as the physical side of things were," he said, clearing his throat again and shoving his hands in his pockets to stop himself from pulling her in for a kiss, "it wasn't just about that for me."

A small smile lifted her lips. "Brooks, are you trying to inform me that I'm not a booty call?"

His shoulders fell. "Am I doing that bad?"

Her smile grew wider as she came closer to him. "Tell me more," she whispered when she reached him, grabbing his hands.

He squeezed. "Well, at first, you were a pain in my ass. A bossy, self-absorbed, nosy, know-it-all. I couldn't wait to get you out of here."

A loud laugh escaped her lips. "Wow."

"Not a good start, I'm guessing?" he teased as a grin filled his face.

"I'd like to pretend I'm offended, but I'd be lying if I said I didn't feel the same about you. Rude, arrogant, an absolute asshole." She tilted her head, her eyes glimmering as she looked at him.

"A perfect match," he said, his voice low. He ran a hand up her arm and along her bare shoulder to the nape of her neck, resting it there while holding her gaze. "Then something changed. You weren't bossy, you were passionate. You weren't self-absorbed, you were thoughtful. You weren't nosy, you were helpful. And you weren't a know-it-all, you were intelligent. You're really something incredible, Ava. One-in-a-lifetime kind of person."

Her breath caught in her throat. "What are you trying to say, Brooks?"

"I'm saying that—" He sucked in some air and held her beautiful brown gaze. "What I'm trying to say is that despite all the reasons I shouldn't, I'm falling for you."

Her smile could have lit up every major city in the world. His heart filled to the brim at the sight of that smile. "You are?"

He nodded before pulling her in and capturing her mouth in a searing kiss.

She pulled away as she shook her head, breaking their kiss. "But...we live an ocean away. It's impossible. It would be foolish." She looked back up at him, a hint of hope in her eyes. "Wouldn't it be? A bad idea to fall for each other?"

"No. A bad idea would be letting logic steal this from us."

She lifted to her toes, bringing their faces closer together. "Then I guess it's only right for me to admit that I'm falling for you too."

He closed the space between them and crashed his mouth on hers again, grabbing her ass and lifting her so her legs wrapped around his hips.

In a matter of seconds, their clothes had been tossed aside, she was on her back, and he was buried inside her again. Where he belonged.

It wasn't about sex. Not tonight. Tonight, he was making love to her. Showing her how much she mattered. With each slow thrust, he watched her face, studied the way her eyelids grew heavy and how her full lips parted as she said his name over and over.

He wanted to burn these memories in his mind. To remember this deep connection they had as her body clenched tighter around him. How she arched up against him, gripping him as she shook with release.

How her warm breath felt on his neck as she moaned in his ear.

How he realized in that moment that he hadn't just started to fall for Ava Espinosa, he already had.

CHAPTER TWENTY-ONE

AVA

BEING around Brooks and living in this town made her remember what mattered in life, showing her there was a better way. She'd be forever thankful for that. Leave it to her to fall in love with a guy she'd be leaving in a week. A guy who wasn't just a quick trip away. A guy she might never see again.

She snuggled up to him, appreciating his steady, firm body wrapped around her soft curves. Maybe they weren't meant to be forever, but she wasn't about to deny herself the pleasure of loving him now. Being with him now. Embracing all he had to offer her now.

It was going to hurt like hell when she boarded that plane to Boston, but she'd be damned if she let the anxiety of the future ruin the here and now, especially with how good it felt.

So good that she could almost ignore the nagging voice in her head telling her she should share what she learned about the guys in the restaurant.

That it was *her* company that might have made their mission significantly easier, if they were in fact the miners who they suspected were causing these environmental issues.

She held him tighter, pushing the thoughts away. There was no point in worrying him until she knew for sure. If she was right, she'd tell him.

Morning light filtered through the sheer, white curtains of her bedroom, highlighting his body with a stamina that went forever. Normally, she'd be over having sex for that long. After a couple of orgasms, she'd start to get bored and sore. But with Brooks...God, with Brooks, she would make love with him for days if it was physically possible.

It didn't matter that hours had passed from the time he'd first buried himself in her. Time didn't exist. All that mattered was feeling him close and that connection that made her feel invincible. Powerful. Loved.

Flashes of last night filled her mind. The way his watchful gaze drank in her every reaction so he could respond accordingly, giving her selfless pleasure she'd never been lucky enough to know until now. How he knew the right times to whisper dirty or loving things in her ear. The way his body shuddered as he came.

She loved seeing him like that. Bare. Stripped down. Vulnerable. Brooks did his best to keep his emotions in check and put others before himself. But to watch him let his guard down and take as much as he gave, that was a gift that meant the world to her.

Brooks's phone blared from his pants across the room. He groaned and rustled. "It's the SAR mobile," he mumbled and reluctantly pulled away from her, getting out of bed to retrieve it. "Did we really sleep in until eleven?" he asked her before answering the call. He nodded a few times, making a few agreeable noises. "On my way," he said, before punching the end button.

Ava lifted to her elbow and rested her head on her hand, the soft sheets draping across her and hiding her naked, sore but satisfied body. "Good excuse, Jónsson. Did you tell a friend to give you an 'emergency call' so you didn't have to do the awkward morning-after thing with your booty call?"

A smile raised on one side of his lips as he prowled across the room to the bed. The boxer briefs hung low on his hips didn't mask the erection underneath.

"Booty call, huh?" he said, his voice rumbly. He kneeled on the bed and placed a kiss on her neck before whispering in her ear. "If I didn't have to take this call, I'd show you what I'd do to you. But since I can't, let me tell you. First, I'd make you get on all fours facing that mirror." He nodded to the one hanging above the desk across from the bed. "Then, I'd make you watch as I took you from behind, smacking your round, perfect ass as I pushed as deep as I could go."

All the air escaped from her lungs as she shivered. Wetness pooled between her legs. This man never ceased to surprise her. One minute he was worshiping her with slow and intimate sex. The next he was talking filthy to her.

It was things like this that brought fiery passion back to her life. She felt more like herself, confident in her skin and who she was around him. No pretending or worrying about not being good enough. He wanted her for exactly who she was, imperfections and all.

"How important is that search and rescue call? Can they wait a bit?" She chewed on her bottom lip.

A deep groan rumbled in his chest as his gaze raked down her body. "I wish." He kissed her long and deep, and she had half a mind to push him down on the bed for a quickie.

She'd never be able to live with herself if someone was in danger and she held him up though.

"Fine," she said, reluctantly letting him go.

He slipped on his clothes and shoved his phone in his pocket. "I'll call you later, okay?"

"Can't wait."

She flopped onto her back as he closed the door behind him, missing him already.

You've got it bad. So, so bad.

Before she could dissect it anymore, Ava's phone dinged with a message. She rolled over and grabbed it from the nightstand, pulling up the alert from Slack.

> **Marissa:** You're right. There's something fishy going on.
> **Ava:** You found something?
> **Marissa:** The logo is some underground shit. When I dug deeper, it looked like it was for a shell company.

Ava was always impressed by Marissa's skills. As a former hacker for the government, she could get information on anything.

> **Ava:** What company?
> **Marissa:** I'm not sure yet, but there's something there. They're definitely a user of our products, but the information is hidden by some privacy stuff.
> **Ava:** Are you able to get around it?
> **Marissa:** I can try, but it's hard. I can also get in a lot of trouble if I get found out.
> **Ava:** OK. Let's hold off on digging deeper for now. I'm going to try to talk to Benson about this. Maybe he can work with Legal to help us find a workaround. I mean, this has to be an abuse of our product, right?
> **Marissa:** Who knows. Our contracts have a lot of gray areas.
> **Ava:** OK. Hang tight. I'll see if I can get some movement with Benson.
> **Marissa:** Good luck.

Ava would need luck. Benson was a nice guy. Fair. Smart. But this product was everything to him. She wasn't sure how he'd react to an accusation that the product was tied to nefarious things. That the databases made it easier for bad people to do horrible things even easier.

That was a lot to swallow. ZettaBytes had been his brainchild nearly fifteen years ago. Sharing this news would be a hard hit.

Ava jumped in the shower and changed, trying to work out the best way to approach this. She had to be careful not to upset him, but she also needed results.

Her stomach twisted as she grabbed her phone and dialed his number. She held her breath, praying he'd answer. The man had been impossible to connect with for the last few weeks.

Her hope deflated when his voicemail clicked on.

"Hey, Benson. It's Ava. I have something important I need to discuss with you. Can you call me back?"

After hanging up, she messaged his assistant, Ines.

Ines: He's unavailable today.
Ava: The whole day?
Ines: Yes.
Ava: It's important. Is there any wiggle room?
Ines: I'm afraid not.
Ava: Can you please schedule a time with us as soon as he has an open slot?
Ines: I'll see what I can do. I'll message you later.

After how unresponsive he'd been, Ava wasn't hopeful. Ines was a nice woman, but she was the ultimate gatekeeper. No matter how nice Ava was to her, she protected Benson's schedule at all costs. It could be days before she got on his calendar. Even if she did, it didn't mean he'd show up. He had missed one too many of her scheduled calls the last few days because of other meetings running over.

He never bothered to reschedule or contact her back unless he needed a quick answer from her.

Feeling desperate, she sent him a message. She tapped her fingers on the desk as the minutes ticked by. After an hour, her message was still showing as unread.

Where the hell are you, Benson?

Her guilt came rushing back, weighing in her stomach like a lead ball. She needed answers. After everything she and Brooks had admitted to each other last night, the unease of not telling him only grew stronger.

Just like the unease of realizing she might be right. The product she'd spent years marketing worldwide had likely gotten in the hands of some really shady people. Who else had flown under the radar?

If it was true, it didn't sit right with her to continue to do her job until ZettaBytes did something to remedy it and prevent it from happening again in the future.

How could she convince Benson to go for that *and* give her the green light to bypass privacy security to confirm her suspicions before more people suffered? In marketing and PR, there was only one way to deal with negative press: squash it, quickly and completely.

She only hoped that bringing this up didn't put a bullseye on her back.

CHAPTER TWENTY-TWO

BROOKS

BROOKS PLUCKED a French fry from Ava's plate and shoved it into his mouth.

"Hey!" She swatted at his hand. "You have your own."

"Just gotta make sure yours is safe."

Ava rolled her eyes and slid her plate out of his reach, a smile making her eyes sparkle. "I may have been willing to offer fries from other places, but The Chantey's fries are too good to give away. Paws off."

For the last couple of days, they'd fallen into a rhythm. Spending their days working separately or together, meeting for lunch and dinner, making love, and falling asleep together. He may have only known Ava for nearly three weeks, but she'd managed to wedge her way deep into his heart.

She'd come into her own during her time in Iceland, seeming more confident and more willing to show her heart. She was always surprising him. Everything he learned about her had him falling deeper for her. He couldn't stop it, even if he tried. Just like she had cast a spell over the town, gaining their trust and affection, she'd done the same to him.

Except he was the lucky bastard that got to have her in more...*intimate* ways.

Brooks was a man with a healthy libido, but Ava made him insatiable. Crazy with desire. It wasn't just about satisfying a primal need though. It was about the connection with her whenever he got her alone. Being with her felt safe. It grounded him.

As a search and rescue pilot, it was hard to get out of that always-on-alert mode. He was constantly primed to burst into action the moment he needed to. Ava had made that instinctual fight-or-flight mode ease so he could breathe.

He hadn't realized how wearing it was to always feel that way until he finally got a break from it.

"Oh my God." Ava's surprised voice broke through his churning thoughts.

"What's wrong?"

Ava swiveled toward him and leaned closer, showing him her phone. "Look at our campaign site."

Brooks's eyes went wide. "Did someone just donate $200,000?"

"Yup." Ava's smile was full of pride, warming his heart and showing him how much this mattered to her. How much she cared about this town. "That gave us a huge jump. We're almost at $700,000. Just need a little more than $300,000 more and we'll hit our goal."

"Do you think we'll hit it?"

"Ava!" Lotte said as she approached them, her voice full of cheer. She placed her hands on the back of their barstools and rocked on her heels, her eyebrows raised in delight. "Did you see the newest donation?"

"I was just telling Brooks about it."

Lotte patted Ava on the shoulder. "I knew there was something special about you. I can't believe we've made this much traction already. This is more than we got done in months."

"We have a few more campaigns rolling out over the next few days. I'm hoping they'll give us the last push we need to hit our goal."

"I'm confident it will. You're an absolute godsend, Ava. The town will be forever grateful for you. I'm off though. Enjoy your dinner."

"Thanks, Lotte. See you soon," Ava said as Brooks shook Lotte's hand and bid her goodbye.

Brooks's phone chirped with a message. He pulled it out of his pocket and read the text. His stomach lurched in his throat.

This was it. This was the moment he'd been waiting for.

Jumping out of his chair, he pulled cash from his wallet and threw it on the bar. "Put on your jacket. We have to go."

Ava's forehead creased in confusion. "What's going on? Is everything okay?"

"One of my contacts who's been keeping an eye out for us on the northeast shore said there's rumors of suspicious movement about an hour or so flight from here. Thinks it might be our guys."

"Really?" Ava stood and slipped on her jacket. Her eyebrows furrowed with concern. "Where at?"

"About twenty miles outside of Siglufjörður."

"So we weren't far off when we thought that might be the next target?" Ava asked as she followed him out of The Chantey and hopped in his truck.

"Exactly. We were just a few days too early."

Brooks sped down the quiet town roads. Houses and storefronts with warm, glowing windows and twinkling Christmas lights passed by in a blur.

"I sent Marissa a text to let her know," Ava said. "Now that we've confirmed the data she's been pulling might be how these miners are selecting their sites, we could really get in front of them."

"Let's hope we don't have to keep chasing them down. As far as I'm concerned, if the lead is right, this ends tonight."

"I'm coming with you." Ava stomped after Brooks's retreating back, trying to get him to stop long enough to reason with him.

"It's not safe."

She rushed to catch up to him and cut him off, blocking his way.

He sighed. "Ava, please."

"Why did you bother bringing me then?"

"I didn't think it would turn out to be a surveillance mission. I don't feel comfortable with you being this close to it."

She stubbornly crossed her arms, making it clear there was no winning this battle with her. "If it weren't for me and my connections, you wouldn't even have had the insight to look here. I *deserve* to be there."

Chuck, the contact who gave Brooks a heads-up about the activity, shrugged his shoulders. "We should go in pairs."

Brooks narrowed his eyes. *Traitor.* "Fine," he said through gritted teeth before turning to Ava again. "But you're going to listen to me and do what I say. I know that's impossible for you—"

"Ha ha." Ava rolled her eyes.

"I'm being serious, Ava. We don't know what these people are capable of." The tension in his body softened. "I know you well enough now to know I couldn't stop you from doing what you want even if I tried, so at least meet me halfway here so I have some peace of mind that you'll be safe."

She dropped her arms and took his hands. "Okay. Fine."

An hour ago, Brooks and Ava had done a final sweep of the area where Chuck had heard rumors of activity. They searched desolate mile after desolate mile, but they found nothing. As they were about to call it quits, a light flashed in the distance.

It was big enough to illuminate a section of dark, snowy forest, which made Brooks suspect the lead was right. If it were hikers or campers, their sights or flashlights wouldn't make nearly enough light. And being that it was in the middle of nowhere and now well after working hours, it didn't make sense that it would be a legitimate company.

Fearing the helicopter noise would tip off whoever was there, Brooks called Chuck to work out a backup plan to investigate. The decision was to land in Siglufjörður and take snowmobiles into the forest to get a closer look. Chuck had pulled together a small group of volunteers from town to help them divide and conquer.

"I texted you the approximate coordinates of where I saw the activity, but there's no telling how much this spans," Brooks said as he took a first-aid bag from his helicopter and threw it on the back of the snowmobile. "Ava and I are going after that."

Chuck nodded. "The rest of us will break up in groups and circle the surrounding area." He tossed Brooks a radio. "It's likely a dead zone for cell service. We'll be on channel five." He patted Brooks hard on the back. "Don't get too close and blow your cover. We need to get enough intel to share with the authorities. Let's finish this once and for all."

Chuck reconvened with the group to finish packing their snowmobiles. Within minutes, they shot off into the inky-dark evening, traveling nearly silently across the thick coat of snow.

"Ready?"

Ava nodded.

"For the record," Brooks said as he swung his leg over the seat, slipping on thick gloves and goggles, "I'm still not happy about you coming. Hold on tight," he instructed as Ava got on the back. "And cover your face. It's going to be cold as hell."

"Yes, sir."

As soon as her arms wrapped securely around his torso, Brooks kicked the snowmobile into drive and tore through the forest. Ava shrieked as they narrowly maneuvered around trees and rocks.

Adrenaline spiked his pulse. Had they not been on this mission to catch illegal miners in the act, he might have allowed himself to enjoy the excitement and the cold wind against his face as the forest rushed past him.

Maybe when this was all over, he could take Ava on an adventure like this.

If they had enough time before she left.

Brooks slowed as they approached the coordinates. Over the

quiet hum of the snowmobile, he made out the distinct grumbling of a motor. The ground shook as a loud, metallic crash reverberated through the night.

He switched off the snowmobile and brought the radio to his mouth, clicking the talk button. "I think we've got something. Turning the sound down so we can investigate."

"Be safe," Chuck crackled back over the radio.

"You stay put," Brooks said to Ava. "I'm going to get a little closer."

"Brooks—"

"Ava, this isn't up for discussion." He had grown to love her hard-headed nature, but not when it put her in danger. Thankfully, she didn't argue. "I'll be right back."

Brooks lowered the volume on the radio and stuffed it in his pocket as he slowly approached the area where the noise was coming from. Light streamed through the trees, nearly blinding him as he got closer to a cleared area.

That's when he saw them. About ten men in total. A few were operating heavy machinery breaking through the hard, frozen ground. A couple men stood nearby, shouting instructions into a radio. Another group hovered around a laptop, looking at some sort of imaging.

This was it. *These motherfuckers.*

Anger and rage consumed him. He did everything he could to restrain himself from rushing in and confronting them.

"We've got something," Brooks whispered into the radio.

"Looks like I've got something too," a voice from behind him said.

He turned around to find two men flanking Ava.

She twisted against their grip on her arms, trying to shake them off.

"Let her go!" Brooks boomed, taking a step closer. He didn't care that he was outnumbered. He'd fight like hell to get their dirty hands off his girl.

"We've got visitors," the heavier of the men called into his radio.

Seconds later, the motors stopped and several of the other workers appeared.

"What do we have here?" a tall, older man with a thick Eastern European accent said, flicking on his flashlight.

Ava's eyes went wide. Something about her reaction felt off.

The man swung the light around, highlighting Ava's face. "Ah. I should have suspected it would be you."

Brooks took another step forward, but two men grabbed him, dragging him back and slamming him against a large tree. "What's going on?" he asked Ava.

The color drained from her face. She said nothing.

"You may not recognize me," the man continued, directing it to Ava, "but how could I forget you?" He waved a hand in the direction of the drill site. "You made all of this possible."

She shook her head, tears glistening in her eyes.

The man took a step closer. "I'll admit, I was a little surprised to see you here. When you said nothing the first time, I thought it was merely a coincidence. But then I saw you again, and the recognition sparked in your eyes."

"What's he talking about, Ava? What the fuck is going on?" Brooks demanded, straining against the men pinning him to the tree.

The man in charge swung around and flashed the light at Brooks, nearly blinding him. "Didn't she tell you? The whole reason we're here is because I met Ava at a tech convention in Las Vegas three years ago. Head of marketing, I think she said she was." He looked at Ava briefly. "I hope they paid you well, because you had me enraptured during your presentation. And so helpful too. You answered all my questions at the happy hour later that evening. You opened my eyes to all the possibilities.

"You see, with your company's product, I could finally compile the data I needed to locate these precious untapped resources in the heart of Iceland. These idiots have been standing on a cash cow all these years, oblivious to the precious resources they had right under their feet."

"Stop," Ava said, tears streaming down her face.

"If you weren't so good at your job, I wouldn't have ever known the capabilities of ZettaBytes products. I have you to thank for this good fortune."

Brooks's blood ran cold as he stared at Ava in disbelief. "Is this true?" His voice was lethal.

Ava shook her head frantically. The tears streamed faster as her shoulders shook. "That's *not* what it was meant for. I never," she sniffed, taking in a deep breath, "I never pitched it that way."

"But you see..." the man said. "You shared this brilliant idea of how it could be used for anything. It just so happens, this is *my* anything. You already knew that though, didn't you? If your failed attempt at eavesdropping was any indication. You had a hunch."

"Ava," Brooks looked at her again, pleading with her for answers. For truth.

She couldn't have kept this from him, could she? Did she know the product she killed herself day in and day out to promote was the reason these towns were suffering? Is that how she was able to pinpoint the potential locations so easily?

She knew a customer was using it for bad this whole time and didn't tell anyone? Did nothing to stop it?

Said nothing?

"How long?" he ground out between gritted teeth. "How long did you know they were here?"

Time seemed to stop as he waited for her to say something. To say anything.

She hesitated, guilt filling her face. "I...I saw them a few weeks ago in town. And then again at the restaurant in Siglufjörður."

The day she'd acted distant. Like an idiot, he'd believed it was because of what happened between them.

Why? Why hadn't she told him?

"I wasn't sure they were the ones behind this. I wanted to look into it before I said anything."

Her admission sucker-punched him. "If you said something, we could have stopped this sooner. We could have done this together. We were *supposed* to be in this together." His voice went hoarse with emotion.

A loud sob escaped her. "I'm so sorry, Brooks. I'm so sorry."

"We said no holding back. We were a team."

No, they were never a team. She'd only fooled him into thinking they were. He'd opened up to her, gave her his heart. His trust. And she'd betrayed it. She'd betrayed the people of Örugg Höfn.

She'd betrayed him.

CHAPTER TWENTY-THREE

AVA

IT ALL HAPPENED in slow motion, and yet so fast. Before she could find the words to take that look of hurt and betrayal away, the rest of the search party showed up. Outnumbering and surrounding the mining crew, they were able to neutralize them long enough for the authorities to take over.

"This isn't over," the leader of the pack said quietly to Brooks and Ava. He spit at their feet.

Brooks took a step closer, getting right in the man's face. "You're right. It isn't over. Not until I put every one of you fucking scumbags behind bars."

The man snarled and strained against the officer's grasp.

"All right, you two. That's enough," an officer said as he tugged the man away.

Brooks's jaw ticked as the handcuffed men were shoved into police cruisers. The hard edges of his face didn't ease, not even when he glanced at her.

Her chest squeezed. Her throat went tight.

Each angry second that ticked by had him slipping further away. She was desperate to go to him. Cling to him. Pull him back. Tell him she was sorry. But nothing she could say would be good enough to satisfy him.

I should have just told him. Why didn't I trust he'd be okay if I'd just told him?

She'd been so worried about his reaction to knowing it was her company who aided the miners' mission, that she didn't think about what would happen if the truth had come out before she could tell him.

The damage was so much worse than she would have expected.

The flight home was mostly quiet. Anger radiated from his side of the chopper. Even in the dark evening, she could see how white his knuckles were as he gripped the handles. She couldn't stand it.

"Brooks," Ava said, her voice small and wobbly.

His jaw clenched tighter, and his chest heaved up and down as if a spike of adrenaline had hit him again.

"Brooks, please. We need to talk about this."

"What do you want to talk about, Ava?" His tone was ice cold. He'd been rude and distant the first time they'd met, but it wasn't like this. This cut her deep. Searing pain shot through her as if he'd plunged a knife straight into her chest.

"I need to explain myself."

"Why? I found out you kept things from me. I already know everything there is to know. Or do I? What else have you lied about?" He raised his voice, a sharp contrast from the quiet that'd filled the cabin for the last forty minutes.

She needed to make him understand. To lay it all out there and show him the reason she'd kept it from him was because of the shame she'd felt being part of this problem. She'd unknowingly hurt the people she'd come to care about.

She'd hurt him, now in more ways than one.

"When we built the product, we built it for good. When I marketed it, I showed the good it could do in the world. It was supposed to help people. I...I never thought it would be used like this. We were just trying to build a community. To make it more accessible. Not everyone can afford products like this. We were thinking of the nonprofits. Or the kid who wants to make her first app. We wanted to lower the barrier to entry. To give people the ability to see their big dreams come to life."

"And by doing that, you've eliminated your due diligence. By making it accessible, you've empowered people with different motives." He shook his head, disappointment etched on his face. "Where's the responsibility? The accountability to prevent this from happening?"

"We have millions of paid and free users. We can't keep track of them all. Even if we did, there are privacy policies in place. Unless we have a solid case as to why we can override those policies, we can't monitor everything everyone's doing. We don't have the resources to be Big Brother. This isn't just our company, this is every tech company."

"Bullshit."

"Brooks. Please understand."

"I can't. Because of your privacy policy, you're essentially protecting these deviants. Because of your goddamn industry ethics —or lack thereof—you've let all these towns down. People suffered because of this. Don't you see that? He said you knew. He said you were onto him. Was that not enough to build a case?"

"I had a hunch. I wasn't sure. I had Marissa look into some clues I'd seen to try and build that case."

He snapped his head to look at her again. "You knew enough to be concerned, and you still didn't tell me?" His anger held a hint of sadness. "Why?" His voice had gone quiet and gravelly.

If she'd thought the look of betrayal had killed her, the sound of its pain his voice made it that much worse.

"I didn't want you to worry until I was sure." The excuse sounded lame to her own ears. "If I was right, I wanted to gather enough information so we could be strategic and have a solid plan. Not approach it like we did today." She shook her head. "Things could have turned out way worse than they did."

Brooks barked out an acidic, dry laugh. "So now this is my fault? Who gives a fuck if I was worried about it? When things got tough, we had each other. We would have figured it out together, or so I thought." He flashed a disappointed look at her before focusing on the empty space ahead. "You keeping this from me shows me how much of an idiot I was to believe in you. To believe in *us*."

"Brooks, please—"

"I'm done, Ava. I don't want to discuss this anymore."

Painful silence surrounded them once again. All she could hear was the steady thumping of the chopper's blades, the pounding of her erratic heart, and the swirl of damning thoughts floating through her head.

Was it over between them?

She wanted to ask. Wanted to beg for him to understand the position she was in. Wanted to go back to the good place they were in, when it felt like anything was possible.

When he'd stolen her heart and she was happy.

The truck ride home to the inn was just as quiet. Even worse now, because he wouldn't look at her. At least he'd glanced at her a few times on the flight. Now, he was rigid and did everything he could to pretend she wasn't there.

"I think it's best that you leave in the morning," Brooks said as he pulled to a stop outside the inn.

"What?" she burst out the response, unbuckling herself and reaching for him. "Hold on. We need to talk about this."

He shook her hand off his forearm. "There's nothing more to talk about, Ava. This was going to end eventually anyway. Now is just as good a time as any."

"Brooks—" She couldn't find the words to express how sorry she was. Her world was shrinking into tunnel vision.

This can't be it. This can't be over. Not like this.

"I'll call a car to take you to the Akureyri airport. You can take a flight to the city from there."

The knife twisted deeper. It was agony. It was the worst feeling in the world.

"But the campaign. We still—" She was grasping for anything to get purchase before she spiraled away into the darkness.

"There's no we, Ava."

Her breathing stopped as the words sunk in.

Her tears came slow and hot, as if her tear ducts had been so shocked into disbelief, they forgot how to work for a moment.

Brooks slipped out of the driver's seat. The headlights illuminated his stiff posture as he walked across the front of the car. He yanked open the passenger door, making it clear she was no longer welcome near him.

She grabbed her purse and got out of the truck with slow, shaky movements. She wanted to collapse on the ground and cry. The pain was searing.

When she heard him slam the door and drive away, the tears she'd held back came out in a strangled sob.

Brooks wanted nothing to do with her anymore. There was nothing she could do to get him back.

And it was all her fault.

CHAPTER TWENTY-FOUR

BROOKS

THERE WAS value to compartmentalizing things. If one thing went to shit, at least it all wouldn't come crumbling down around him.

He should've never opened up to Ava. Letting her in every nook and cranny in his heart and mind. Invading him. Overwhelming him. Filling his every thought.

He knew better than that, and yet he let it happen anyway. This was how mistakes were made. He blindly trusted an outsider, and she'd let them down. He'd been so wrapped up in his feelings for her, he'd never seen it coming.

Now look at him.

Brooks had driven away from her last night, his aching heart feeling like a pincushion. Sharp pricks poked away at him every second that passed, only getting worse throughout the night.

He'd driven long and far, needing to put space between them. He'd thought maybe he'd gotten his heart in check by the time he made it home hours later. But then Stella came running up to him, a hopeful look in her eyes as she peeked around him, likely looking for Ava. She'd become a fixture around his place these last few weeks, even so much as helping watch Stella when he had an overnight SAR mission. Stella had fallen in love with her.

Just like he had.

Stella walked away with her head hung low and snuggled on the couch with a sad sigh.

Her disappointment only reopened the wound he'd tried desperately to tourniquet. Truth was, as angry and hurt as he was by Ava, he couldn't stop himself from loving her.

The next morning, a pounding at his front door caused him to stir. For one fleeting moment, he'd prayed it was Ava. For one weak moment, he wanted to forgive her. If it meant he could keep her, he wanted to forgive her.

And it's that kind of stupidity that got you into this mess in the first place. You didn't let her earn your trust. You just handed it to her, and she took it for granted.

Brooks did his best to swallow down the conflicting emotions racing through him, making his mind and heart waffle between letting her go and letting her in. But, apparently, he wouldn't have to make that decision.

"What the hell did you do?" Jón said as the door opened, before pushing inside and limping to the island barstool.

"What are you talking about? And what's going on with your leg?"

"Tweaked it rushing up here. I'll be fine." Jón waved him off. "You want to know why I felt compelled to rush here?"

"No. Though I'm sure you're going to tell me." Brooks ambled to the coffee maker, as if caffeine would change the fact that he didn't sleep a single minute last night. He put in the grounds and set it to brew.

"Why did you send Ava away?" There was a hint of outrage in his dad's voice.

There it is. Brooks turned to face his father and leaned a hip against the counter, rubbing at his eyes.

"I saw her loading a cab to go to the airport," Jón continued, without giving Brooks a chance to respond. "She told me what happened. She was so devastated, she could barely get the words out."

His chest squeezed. He closed his eyes, trying not to picture Ava looking sad. "Then why the hell are you asking me about it?" he asked through gritted teeth. He didn't need to rehash what happened last night. He didn't want to have this fucking conversation.

It hurt enough the first time around. And the countless times he'd thought about it last night. He didn't need to stab himself in the heart again by talking about it. It was better to forget.

"So she should have told you what she suspected sooner. So what?" his father said. "It was an error of judgment. That one small thing couldn't have overshadowed all she's done for us these last few weeks."

No, but it showed him it was best to keep people at a distance so he could keep better control over his life. To not be blindsided. His father had convinced him to let people in, and look at what good that got him.

"And I didn't realize you were so perfect that you had the right to damn others for having flaws," Jón continued when Brooks said nothing.

He blinked at his dad. Out of all the years he'd tortured him, all the years Brooks had been a menace, his father had never spoken like this before.

So this is what it feels like to have your parent be disappointed in you. No wonder it's so effective.

He shook away the guilt eating at him. It was *her* who should feel guilty, not him.

"What she kept from us put us all at risk. Our town is struggling enough. We don't need an outsider to make it worse."

"She worked at the company that made the product those miners were using. She wasn't the one feeding them the information."

"She knew they were potentially using the product and did nothing to stop it. Her silence let it continue on for weeks when we could have been taking action."

"How would you know what she was trying to do? Did you even ask her?" Jón let out a dry laugh when Brooks came up short. "Let me guess. You went cowboy on her. Got all hotheaded like usual and made up your mind before you even gave her a chance to explain herself."

"Ava had plenty of time to tell us what was going on, and she didn't. Her excuses weren't good enough."

"Maybe she had her reasons, son."

"We were in this together. Her reasons should have been my reasons too."

He swallowed, recognizing the statement for what it was. Truly letting it sink in. When he was with her, he didn't feel like they were simply teaming up to stop the town from suffering. In a way, he felt like they'd become a team all around. It was fast, he couldn't deny that, but having her around made his burdens feel less, and he felt like a better man.

Which is why the betrayal hurt him so much. It wasn't *just* about the town. It was about her taking away a piece of him he hadn't had in a long time: his hope.

The coffee machine buzzed, giving Brooks the perfect excuse to turn away so his father couldn't see the pain on his face.

Jón wouldn't let up though. Maybe that was where Brooks got his stubborn determination. "You can't shut down again after one setback," he said as he approached Brooks, putting a hand on his shoulder to force Brooks to look at him.

"It's better this way." He couldn't handle another loss. Losing his mom had devastated him. Changed him.

Losing Ava had the potential to do the same. He needed to forget her before the loss consumed him again.

"Love isn't perfect. You're bound to let each other down over and over, but it's your ability to forgive and not lose faith that makes it worth it."

"Love? We've barely known each other for a month." Brooks

turned away, busying himself with making their coffees. "Leave it alone, Dad."

"Don't be a fucking fool, Brooks."

Brooks stopped mid-pour, unsettled by his father's outburst and furious he wouldn't stop pushing. He slammed the coffee pot down and spun to face his dad.

"I'm not a fucking kid. This is my decision, and I have my reasons for it. I don't owe you or anyone an explanation."

"I've lived enough life to have the right to tell you when you're being an idiot. This is a mistake you'll regret. After everything Ava has done for the town. After all she's given us. You think she deserves exiling? Pull your head out of your ass and stop being an idiot. You're making the wrong call."

"That's your opinion, and I think I've had all I can take of it. You can see yourself out."

Jón shook his head, his jaw set in a tight line. He turned toward the front door and opened it, turning back for one last comment. "Time is precious. You don't know how short it is until the things that matter are gone. I'm only giving you this advice because I don't want you to feel the pain and regret I have in my life not realizing that sooner."

"She was going to leave anyway."

"All it takes is one decision to change everything." Jón closed the door, leaving Brooks alone with his aching heart.

CHAPTER TWENTY-FIVE

AVA

SHE'D MANAGED to sound confident when letting Freyja and Lotte know she'd had an "unexpected work emergency" come up, cutting her trip short. After handing off the rest of the campaign strategy and access to the fundraising site, Ava had given them both a tight hug goodbye with a promise to be in touch as soon as she got settled in Boston.

She didn't tell them Brooks all but forbade her from helping them anymore.

Ava had managed not to fall apart in Jón's arms when he practically pulled her luggage from the cab's trunk, urging her to stay so they could talk some sense into Brooks.

Her brilliant smile didn't waver when her building's concierge welcomed her home, asking Ava all about the exciting details of her trip to Iceland.

On the elevator ride up to her condo, she'd kept her lip from quivering.

But once she'd made it into her apartment, the brave face she'd kept firmly in place during her long journey home had crumbled as soon as the front door clicked shut behind her. Her bags slipped from her grip and hit the wood floors with a thud. Ava pressed her back to the door, sliding to the ground, her sobs reverberating throughout the foyer.

She rested on the cold floor, sucking in what little air she could manage. It was agonizing, the way she felt. Everything inside of her ached and twisted and stole her breath.

Hollow. Cold. Alone.

Brooks's dismissal didn't just rip her heart from her chest. He ripped the sense of community she'd found while in Iceland, something she hadn't realized she'd needed for so long.

He took away her sense of purpose. Her sense of meaning.

He'd taken her heart and clutched it in his hand, disintegrating it into useless ash.

Ava had known it would hurt once she had to say goodbye, but this...

How could she survive this?

I still love him.

That was the worst part. She was an expert at moving on, closing the door on broken plans, pivoting easily when needed.

When it came to this, it wouldn't be so easy.

The afternoon light had disappeared and given way to dusk. Her tears had finally slowed to a trickle, her body tense and sore from bone-deep sadness that had torn through her for hours. Weak and miserable, she dug her phone out of her purse and crawled to the living room, pulling herself onto the couch and folding herself into a tiny ball.

Her hands shook as she turned on her phone, finding a few messages from the townspeople wishing her a safe trip.

Nothing from Brooks, not that she'd expected it. She'd hoped though. If he'd called her and told her he'd made a mistake, she'd be on a plane back to him right away.

He wouldn't call to say that to her. He'd never speak to her again.

Her cold blood went hot when she clicked through her emails and realized Benson had never gotten back to her either. She'd tried calling him, emailing him, and texting him. Tried finding a way to get his executive assistant to get him on the phone.

Of course, when she had something serious to talk to him about, he was ghosting her. Yet he had no problem bothering her when she was on vacation, taking away the little precious free time she'd taken for herself for the first time in years.

Ava sat up straight, wiping the last remaining tears from her cheeks. She'd make it so he couldn't ignore her any longer. He didn't know she was back yet. She could easily stop by his home and force him to hear her out. The element of surprise would work in her favor.

He was going to listen, damn it.

She was done being pushed around.

Certain she looked every bit of the mess she felt, Ava didn't even bother cleaning up her raccoon eyes or washing away the scent of hours-long travel. No more wasting time.

In a matter of minutes, she was out the door and in her car, taking I-95 to Weston. Even with the evening hours, rush hour traffic dragged on, only making her pulse race even more. Finally, she got off the interstate and drove through the quiet streets lined with multimillion-dollar mansions, their expansive lawns beautifully landscaped with lights illuminating the massive homes, putting them on display. Tasteful Christmas decorations only added to their charm.

It had been a while since she'd been to Benson's. He'd had a holiday party at his house a few years back. Thankfully, she remembered his was one of the few homes that didn't have gate access to get into his driveway. She drove to the cul-de-sac where his house stood, lit up just like the rest of the perfect properties surrounding it.

Once she'd parked in his driveway, Ava slammed the driver door closed, then took the wide stone steps two at a time. She rang the doorbell three times in rapid succession before she pounded on the door.

"Ava? What the hell is going on?" Benson asked when he pulled the door open, a look of surprise across his face.

"Why are you avoiding me?"

He shook his head. "What are you talking about?"

"I've been trying to contact you for days. You haven't returned any of my calls." She pushed past him and stepped into a foyer fit for a five-star hotel.

"Sure. Come right in," he said drily before closing the door again. "I've been busy. If you remember, we're trying to launch our product before our competitors." He couldn't keep the annoyance out of his voice.

She crossed her arms, doing her best not to tap her foot. "We have bigger things to worry about than beating out the competition."

He sighed. "Come on. Follow me."

Benson led them to a sitting room off the foyer, walking to the built-in wet bar near the tall windows. He poured them both a glass of Scotch. She took the glass from him and placed it on the end table, uninterested in taking a sip.

Benson lowered himself in a chair across from her, crossed his legs, and took a sip of his drink. "Well?"

"We have a problem with our product." For the next few minutes, Ava shared what she'd discovered in Iceland and how it showed her a major issue they'd failed to address. "Instead of trying to beat out the competition with new features and products, we need to be taking care of the one we already have. Our teams should focus on making it safer and more socially responsible."

Benson didn't bother to hide his bored expression. "That's not how business works, Ava. You know this. If we slow down, we run the risk of being outpaced by other companies. It only takes one good idea to make our tech obsolete. We need all the resources we have to focus on R&D. I'm afraid we don't have the bandwidth to do what you're proposing."

"So that's it then? You're not even going to consider this?" Her fingernails dug into her palm.

"It's not up to us to monitor how people use our products. We have terms and conditions, sure, but we're not in a position to decide what's morally good or bad. There are so many unique use cases and gray areas that can land us into a whole heap of legal trouble and bad PR. It's not in our interest to police this."

It felt like she'd been sucker-punched. All the time she'd spent here, being part of the history of ZettaBytes, helping them build and grow it. All that dedication. The loyalty. All the blood, sweat, and tears. She'd given so much to this company. To its founders, employees, and customers. All this time, she'd never asked for anything.

Now she was, and this is what she got in return: a slap in the face.

This choice wasn't just letting her down, it was letting so many others down too. By not taking action, there was no telling how many people would be impacted by those out there using their products for horrible things.

"This seems pretty fucking black and white to me. This is bad business."

Benson swirled his Scotch and shrugged a shoulder. "That's a matter of opinion. However, my decision is what's going to ensure the company has a solid future ahead of it. That's all that matters." He leaned forward and held her stare. "You've been part of this company since the beginning. You know what our goals are. You knew what you signed up for. You made a promise to stand by our side and help drive ZettaBytes to success."

The statement said it all. He was asking her to be complicit. Using her loyalty to the company against her.

But she'd seen firsthand what turning a blind eye could do. Flashes of the events of these last few weeks filled her mind. The struggle of the townspeople. Their worries. The tears shed over their lost economy and their dying ecosystem. It could have been so much worse, and it still could end up that way if no one did anything to stop it.

"I quit." She blinked a few times, stunned by the sudden declaration. It was as if she'd been possessed for a moment. As she let the resignation settle in, it felt right. Ava stood. "We're not seeing eye to eye. I'm afraid I can't in good conscience be part of something like this."

Benson stood, his eyebrows furrowed as he took a step closer. "Don't forget, as part of your employment contract, you have an ironclad NDA. I don't think I need to remind you of the legal implications if you tried to go public with this."

She'd made the right decision. She knew it then and there.

"I won't go public with this, but I sure as hell am not going to be part of selling your flawed dream anymore." She grabbed her crystal tumbler and downed the expensive liquor. "It's been a pleasure doing business with you this last decade, Benson. I learned a lot from you, and I have ZettaBytes to thank for my career. I'm sorry it's ending this way. I just hope someday you'll see my perspective and do the right thing."

Benson gave her a tight-lipped nod. "Best of luck."

With that, Ava made her way through the foyer and out the front of the house, closing the door on one of the most important things of her life. Something that had shaped her into who she was.

Now, something that helped her see that she could be doing so much more for the world.

All she had to do was figure out how.

First, however, she was going to finish what she started. Maybe Brooks didn't trust her anymore, but she'd made a promise to help, and she wouldn't go back on her word.

Whether he liked it or not.

CHAPTER TWENTY-SIX

AVA

AVA WAS CURLED up in the corner of her couch, aimlessly staring out the floor-to-ceiling windows. "I can't believe I did that." She stuffed a heaping scoop of dessert into her mouth.

"And I've never seen someone eat that many cookie à la modes in one sitting without getting diabetes on the spot," Jess said as she reached for the bowl.

Ava slapped her hand away. "Off! This is all I have left in life."

"Hello?" Jess narrowed her eyes. "I'm literally right here."

"You're okay, I guess. But you're not à la mode good."

Jess shook her head and rolled her eyes, walking away to fuss around the apartment. Ava had called Jess as soon as she left Benson's, driving back to Cambridge half in shock. By the time she'd made it home, Jess was already waiting for her inside.

Waiting wasn't all she did though.

Ava tracked Jess's movements. "It looks like Christmas threw up in here."

"Just because you're all depressed and having a midlife crisis doesn't mean you can ignore the fact that Christmas is less than a week away." She placed ornaments around a faux tree sitting in Ava's living room and nodded with approval. "Perfect. Well...perfect for a fake tree."

"Sorry to disappoint you. Been a little too busy to get to a tree lot," she said with sarcasm. "And kinda hard to get into the Christmas spirit when I basically blew up my whole life." She put her empty bowl on the coffee table. "How am I supposed to pay my bills? My contract offers three month's salary as severance, but it's going to take a lot longer to find a job. And unemployment isn't going to come close to covering my expenses."

"You were a chief marketing officer, how hard can it be? People are going to be clamoring to get your expertise," Jess said as she plugged in the white twinkle lights, illuminating the space.

"Technically, I never started as the chief marketing officer. I was supposed to go official after the holidays, but I quit before then."

"Whatever. You still have the skills to even have been offered the job. You'll be fine."

Not that she'd want a job like that anymore. After the whole ordeal, she was turned off at the thought of working for another for-profit company. Experiencing all the good she did in Iceland—before everything went to shit—she realized there were more fulfilling options in life.

Jess eyed her and frowned. "It's not just about your job, is it?"

"No," Ava tilted her head back and groaned. "I'm worried about what's going on in Iceland."

"And Brooks."

Ava shot her a look. "We're *not* talking about him right now." She didn't think her heart could take it.

On her ride home, she'd called him to tell him what happened. To see if she could make things right. Not only did he send her straight to voicemail, he'd never called her back.

A knock pounded at the door.

"Are you expecting someone?" Jess asked as she made her way to the foyer.

"No, but I wouldn't mind if someone's pizza accidentally got delivered here. I'm starving."

"I'm getting sick even thinking about the crap swirling in your stomach right now." Jess swung the door open. "Hi, how can I help you?"

"Um, maybe I have the wrong apartment. I'm looking for Ava Espinosa." Ava recognized that voice.

"You've got the right place. I'm her sister, Jess."

"Nice to meet you. I'm Marissa. I work with Ava, er, or I guess I used to."

Ava shuffled to the door, feeling worse for the wear and a million pounds heavier from the ice cream. Maybe she shouldn't have had that third bowl. "Marissa, you didn't have to come."

When Ava had returned home and pulled into her parking spot, Marissa had called her, demanding to know why her account was no longer in the company directory when she'd gone to message her. She gave Marissa the rundown, which only sparked Marissa's outrage.

That's why she liked Marissa. She was a passionate woman with a strong backbone and even stronger values. It was nice to have her validate Ava's decision, even if there was nothing they could do about it.

"I have something to share with you."

Ava's eyebrow quirked up with interest. "Come on in."

She led Marissa into the apartment, offering her a glass of water and wine as the three of them took a seat at the small kitchen table.

"Nice decorations," Marissa said.

"Thank you." Jess smiled sweetly. "I thought so too," she added as she stuck her tongue out at Ava.

"What's going on, Marissa?" Ava asked.

"Well, when you told me what happened with Benson, it got me thinking about everything we went through these past few weeks. How he handled it was some bullshit."

Ava lifted her shoulders in a defeated shrug. "It's just business," she said, her words coming out empty.

"No. That's bullshit. It's never *just* business. There are companies out there that care about being socially responsible. I can't believe Benson would turn a blind eye to this."

"There's nothing I can do about it."

A smile lifted on Marissa's lips. "Right. The NDA. Thing is, I'm still an employee."

"Even so, your NDA will prevent you from going public with it even if you're still employed there."

"But it doesn't say anything about talking about it internally."

Ava furrowed her brows and cocked her head. "What?"

"After I got off the phone with you, I started a petition about the unethical handling of our product. Benson has the engineering and product teams killing themselves to beat the competition so the company can turn an even bigger profit, but he's not willing to listen to us? It didn't sit right with me. I knew there was more I could do, so I sent the petition around to engineering, product, IT, research, and security."

"Wait. *What?*" Ava sat straighter.

Marissa's smile got even bigger as she withdrew her laptop from her bag and pulled up a screen showing a live form. "See all these names?"

Ava nodded as more names appeared on the form in real time. She took the laptop from Marissa and scrolled through. There were hundreds already, many names she knew from over the years. Some with incredibly important jobs at the company. Tears stung her eyes.

"These people are willing to walk if Benson and the rest of leadership don't do something about the issue."

"That's a huge part of the company." Ava's gaze caught Marissa's. "They'd really all leave?"

"Yup. In my petition, Benson has until the end of next week to give us an action plan of what he's going to do to ensure our products aren't getting into the wrong hands, or we'll all walk out."

"But he could fire you all for this."

Marissa shrugged. "Either way, he's left with a huge talent

shortage. Some of the people on this list are the only subject matter experts in their jobs at ZettaBytes. With that many people leaving and all the knowledge they'd take with them, Benson would be fucked. If he thinks he has any hope of saving his company, he needs to follow through on what we're demanding." She bit her lip. "I'd hate it if we made the company go under, but sometimes we have to do something radical to set a precedent. Maybe if word gets out, more employees will take a stand when they see something unethical. Maybe we can make technology for good rather than just for profit."

Something about Marissa's idealistic speech clicked for Ava, giving her hope.

"You're kind of amazing, you know that?"

"You inspired me," Marissa said with a grin. Her eyes lit up. "Oh! That's not all I came here for."

"There's more?"

"After you confirmed the location of the last mining site, I was able to use the data to pinpoint the other locations." Marissa took the computer and pulled up a map with marked spots, swiveling it back for Ava to study.

"How accurate do you think this is?"

"Ninety percent?"

Ava nodded and tapped her chin in thought.

"Uh oh," Jess said. "I know this face. This is the face you make when you're about to do something big."

Marissa leaned forward in her chair. "What are you thinking?"

Ava held Marissa's stare and grinned. "I'm thinking we're about to go back to Iceland and finish this once and for all."

CHAPTER TWENTY-SEVEN

AVA

"Brooks, do you copy? Over." Jón released the radio button and waited. Minutes ticked by, but only crackling static came through.

Lotte shot Ava a look, one filled with concern and desperation. "It would be stupid to go after them by ourselves." She scanned the tourism office filled with a hodgepodge of townspeople. "Wouldn't it?"

"Even catching the one group, things are getting worse," Kristofer said. "Viktor, Lars, and the rest are out to sea, trying to find a spot for a fresh catch but coming up empty-handed. Who knows how long they'll be searching." He shook his head and turned to Ava. "In the couple days you were gone, more of the marine life washed to shore. Dead. Dying. It's not good."

"Brooks, son. Do you copy? Over." Jón let out a curse when nothing came through again. "He'd gone to the south shore to help with a search and rescue mission. Contact has been spotty."

Marissa clicked a few buttons on her laptop resting on the lobby coffee table, her knee bouncing. "If my calculations are right, we only have tonight to nab these guys before they move on again. After that, the trail runs cold. They probably protected their data once they knew someone had found them out. It has to be tonight, or we might lose them for good."

Ava pinched the bridge of her nose and took a seat next to Marissa on the couch. The last two days had been a whirlwind. Marissa and Ava had managed to catch a last-minute flight from Boston to Iceland. It had two stopovers, only extending the grueling trip. Her jet lag had whiplash from the rapid change of going back and forth.

Thankfully, Kristofer had brought his special coffee, which had enough caffeine to jump-start a corpse.

She'd tried to contact Brooks several times since she and Marissa had come up with the plan. At one point, the three little dots appeared, and she'd hoped beyond hope he'd finally respond to her. But after a few minutes, the dots disappeared with no reply.

She prayed it had everything to do with him being in a bad service area and not because he couldn't stand the thought of talking to her.

At least the rest of the town was happy by her unexpected arrival. After a few hugs and chatter, Ava got down to business, getting them up to speed on the real reason why she left, what happened when she got back to Boston, and how Marissa thinks they found the next big dig.

"I'd feel better if we had more manpower behind this," Jón said. "You said these people are dangerous. I don't want to have another run-in and put any of you at risk. I couldn't live with myself."

"Officials will meet us there for backup if we find anything, Jón." Lotte touched his arm with affection. "We may not have enough people, but we'll divide and conquer with protection. I promise we won't get too close. If we find something, we'll let the police handle it."

"After our last run-in, the miners might be on high alert. They'll expect we're coming," Ava said. "We need to be stealthy."

"No planes. No helicopters. No getting too close," Lotte agreed. "We'll take the vans, get close enough. Go on foot. They may be hidden in remote areas, but there's no way they can hide that activity. We can spot them a mile away without ever getting caught."

"You think so?"

Lotte nodded.

Marissa pulled up a map on her phone. "The three locations are all on the northeast side of the country, but several miles apart from one another. Either way, it's going to be a few hours' drive to any of them."

"Let's break into groups and scout out those three spots." Lotte grabbed radios and flashlights. "All of you run home and get some warm clothes, snacks, and water. Meet back here in thirty minutes. It's going to be a long night."

CHAPTER TWENTY-EIGHT

BROOKS

"I'm here. Over," Brooks said into the radio.

"Thank God." His dad's voice was overwhelmed with static. "Where are you?"

"On the way back."

"We've been trying to reach you, cowboy."

"We?"

"Me. Ava."

How does he know Ava's been calling and texting?

He'd seen a few messages come through once he got into the service area, but he didn't have the heart to talk, no matter how persistent she was about it.

He had to admit, his ego didn't mind her determination, but his heart reminded him that it wasn't worth opening that wound again. Eventually, she'd get the picture and would stop calling him.

There was no point. Even if she hadn't let him down and broken his trust, she was on a different continent. It wasn't meant to be.

"Yes. She came back." The statement rang in Brooks's ears.

"Wait. What?" *She was back in Iceland?* "Why?"

And why was he suddenly speeding through the night sky to get back home to see her? He knew better than that. They were a lost cause. If anything, he should turn his chopper around and wait it out until she was gone.

"She and her colleague are sure they know where the next dig site will be. She came to rally the town and find them." There was a long pause while Brooks sat speechless. "She quit her job, son." Jón's voice sounded softer.

She quit her job. He couldn't stop his traitor heart from hoping it was for him. For them.

"Where is she?"

Jón rattled off the coordinates. "Officials are on call. She'll be safe. In any case, don't fly too close and tip them off."

"Copy that."

"Be safe."

"Dad?"

"Yeah, Brooks."

"Thank you for everything. I couldn't have asked for a better father."

"I love you too, son."

Brooks took a hard right and pushed the chopper's speed to its limits toward the coordinates, praying Ava and the rest of his people were safe.

After what he'd seen last time, he hoped things wouldn't go sideways before he got there.

Snow crunched under his feet as he weaved his way through the thick forest, crouching down every so often when he heard a noise. He had no doubt the miners would be on high alert, likely keeping people in the shadows to protect them from intruders.

Why would she walk into danger like this?

He knew why. Ava was a woman who wouldn't let anything or anyone slow her down when her mind was set. She said she wouldn't let the town down, and Brooks guessed this was her way of keeping her word, regardless of how reckless.

She wanted justice and to take care of those who mattered to her. No matter the consequence, it would be worth it in her eyes.

He'd been wrong about her.

Even more insane was that his father and Lotte went along with it. He hoped their desperation to end this mess wouldn't land them all in hot water.

Or a grave.

He walked farther, the cold night air numbing his bare cheeks as he got deeper into the dense woods.

He ducked behind a tree when he heard movement, peeking out just enough to recognize a familiar shape that would be burned in his mind forever. Even through the thick layers of clothes, he knew what was hidden underneath.

A body he craved and worshiped and loved.

A woman who had changed his life in a matter of weeks.

He took a step closer, following Ava and who he believed to be Freyja and an officer.

At least they were protected. Would one officer be enough if this all went sideways?

"Ava," he whispered loudly. He called out again when she stopped in her tracks and swiveled her head in his direction.

That's when he heard it. The distinct sound of a pistol being cocked, ripping through the quiet night.

"Get down!" Brooks yelled as he ran toward them.

The snow was like wet cement, slowing down his progress. He needed to get to her. The officer called for backup on his radio as he grabbed his taser.

Cops in Iceland rarely use firearms, and if they do, they have to call for permission.

Why, why, why didn't they sign off on this beforehand?

Maybe the police didn't use guns, but bad people do. They weren't prepared at all.

Brooks leapt and tackled Ava to the ground as a bullet ripped through the air, zinging past them. A burning sensation tore through his shoulder.

"Shots fired! Shots fired!" the officer screamed into his radio, requesting armed backup in Icelandic. He shot off a taser, knocking the assailant to the ground and cuffing him.

"Brooks! You're bleeding," Ava yelled frantically from underneath him.

"Oh Jesus." Freyja ran up and pulled off her scarf, wrapping it around his arm. "We need a medic!"

The sound of sirens approached, but it was all so hard to hear over the slow thumping of his heart. The echoing of his breath.

He rolled off Ava and onto his back. The oppressive trees and night sky swirled around him, closing in until there was nothing but black.

CHAPTER TWENTY-NINE

AVA

"I KNEW you were trouble the moment I met you."

Ava jumped at the sound of Brooks's voice, rough and weak. She lifted her head from where she'd fallen asleep on his hospital bed, her gaze latching on to the inky-blue eyes she'd lost herself in countless times.

"Oh God. You're okay." She couldn't stop the happy tears from streaming down her face. The last twenty-four hours had been the hardest she'd experienced in her life.

"What happened?"

"You saved my life for starters." She grabbed his hand and squeezed. "You got shot. It clipped the artery in your shoulder. Somehow it was just shallow enough that you didn't bleed out before the medics came, but they had to do a rush surgery." She sucked in a breath. "I was so scared I'd lose you before I could make things right."

She'd tried to stay awake as long as she could, fearing the beeping heart monitor would flatline as soon as she let her guard down. Eventually, restless sleep took over, but she never left his side.

He winced as he shifted to get the cup of water near his bedside and took a massive gulp. "You can't get rid of me that easily."

A small smile lifted her lips. "We stopped them though. All of them. Lotte called me a few hours after we got to the hospital. Their operation is over."

Brooks let out a sigh of relief. "And now our town can heal."

"I'm so sorry. About everything. You were right. I should have said something. I should have done more."

"Dad said you quit?"

Ava nodded. "I confronted my CEO. He wasn't willing to make a change, so I quit on the spot."

Brooks's face softened. "I'm sorry I pressured you to do that."

"You were right. If anything, you pushed me in the direction I'd known I needed to go but was too scared to do it." She looked away, trying to find the right words. "ZettaBytes had been my home for ten years. I helped build it. I was sucked into the company, and it was hard to see the truth. In working to create the best branding campaigns, I completely missed that the brand wasn't living by the values it touted.

"Maybe that's why I've felt hollow, especially these last few years. Deep down, my intuition knew better, but I wanted to be successful. But I realized success doesn't mean becoming a C-level executive by thirty. Success is leaving the world a little better than how you find it."

A small grin lifted Brooks's lips. "All of that in one breath. I'm not surprised, yet still amazed."

She glared at him playfully. "I hate you. I just poured my heart out, and that's all you have to say?"

He grabbed her hand. "You love me. And I love you, Ava Espinosa."

Her eyes misted. "But you said you couldn't trust me anymore."

"I was wrong. Besides, even though I pushed you away, I didn't stop loving you."

"I didn't stop loving you either." Her heart swelled as she pressed a soft kiss to his lips and rested her forehead against his. "You've been an adventure...an unexpected but absolutely necessary one."

"Told you'd I'd show you all the best parts of Iceland." He waggled his eyebrows.

She grinned and pulled away. "By the way, I have some news. While you were busy being off the grid, the campaign reached just slightly under our goal. Still, our plea was enough to get the attention of a nonprofit in Norway. We have enough money to get them here and work to restore the marine ecosystem, especially now that we have a sense of what was causing the issues. With that insight, they can get started a lot sooner."

Brooks's eyes lit up. "Really?"

"Really."

"Ava, that's amazing. We only have you to thank."

"It was a team effort."

"I couldn't imagine doing this without you by my side." He studied her a moment, a look of concern on his face. "What about you though? You quit your job. Now what?"

Jón popped his head in. "You're awake. We were so worried. How are you?"

"Sore. Groggy, but it doesn't hurt so bad with Ava here." Brooks shot her a smile that warmed her insides and restored her hope that things truly could work between them.

"I'll let you two have some time alone. I'll be back later. Glad to see you're okay, son."

"Thanks, Dad."

Jón disappeared, leaving them alone again.

Pride and hope swelled inside of her. "Marissa and I had a *lot* of time to talk about things between the endless stopovers here. We're going to start our own company."

Brooks cocked his head and lifted an eyebrow. "I love seeing that passion in your eyes. What's the company?"

"We'll help tech businesses do their due diligence. We'll advise them on how to ensure their products are ethical and do social good in the world."

"That's amazing. I'm so proud of you," he said, raising her hand to his mouth and placing a kiss on her knuckles.

She leaned closer and gave him a coy smile. "What's even more amazing is that I can pull a few strings with the boss."

"That boss being you?"

"Mmhmm. And since I have it in good with her, I'm pretty sure I can swing some long working vacations in Iceland. Maybe even have an office here."

If Ava could have photographed the look of joy and hope on Brooks's face, she would have. She'd cherish that unguarded reaction for the rest of her life.

"Sounds like I need to thoroughly thank your boss for her generous flexibility," he whispered before kissing deeply.

EPILOGUE
AVA

DECEMBER, THE FOLLOWING YEAR

AVA'S PHONE buzzed on her wooden desktop, disrupting her daydreaming while she stared out at the bustling harbor.

Brooks: You better not be working.
Ava: Absolutely not.

Apparently, a lot could change in a matter of weeks. Ava had found her new calling, Iceland had stopped the menace wreaking havoc on their coastal towns, and she'd found the love of her life.

Brooks: Liar. Don't forget, you promised me dinner at The Chantey in ten minutes.

She checked the time and cursed. The day had somehow gotten away from her.

Ava: Fifteen minutes.

Brooks: Fine. I'll be waiting here. You're lucky you're worth it.

A lot could happen in a year too.

After the Norwegian team came to town, Örugg Höfn saw a major rehabilitation of its ecosystem. Although not quite at the level as before, the town had made massive strides and things were getting better every day.

Her business with Marissa had taken off. As the younger generations came into the workforce, more companies were facing this demand to make a positive social impact and be held accountable. Somehow their little company had been in desperate need. In a matter of months, they'd had more work than they knew what to do with. So much so, they'd already expanded their team from two to nearly thirty people and growing.

Unfortunately, ZettaBytes hadn't taken up her offer to help fix their product. As promised, countless employees quit on the spot, tanking the company. It hurt to see, but it was Benson's own selfish ego that caused his company to fail.

Despite that, Ava loved her new purpose in life. It was the first time in a long time that she felt good about what she was doing. No money or job title in the world could compete with that sense of fulfillment.

With Ava visiting Iceland for long stretches of time, Brooks had bought a house by the water, giving her a special room that was dedicated to office space for the weeks she was in Iceland. Although she wasn't there full-time, because of all the crazy laws of getting established overseas, she milked as much time as she could, savoring every moment with the man she loved more than anything.

Shutting down her laptop for the day, she cleaned herself up and spritzed herself with perfume, petting Stella on the way out of the house and into the cold December evening to meet Brooks.

She swung open the door and paused. The Chantey was always busy at this time on a Friday night, but no one was there. The place was dim, aside from the flickering candles lit on every table and along the bar. Soft music played from the kitchen.

"Hello?" She walked cautiously into the dining room, confused.

Brooks strolled out of the kitchen, donned in a form-fitting suit that practically made her drool.

A laugh escaped her. "What's going on?"

He strolled up to her, taking her hands. "You look beautiful, as always."

"Where is everyone?"

Brooks shrugged a shoulder. "Around."

"What's *really* going on, Brooks?"

"What's *really* going on, Ava..." he started as he began to kneel. Her breath caught in her throat. "...is that I brought you here tonight to tell you how this was where I began to fall in love with you. Things between us didn't start off great—"

She raised an eyebrow. "You mean when you almost ran me over?"

"The reality of those events is a matter of opinion." She snorted at that. "When I walked in and saw you talking to my dad, I felt it in my gut. I just knew. Even though my head was too stupid to catch up to my heart, deep down I knew you were the woman meant for me. You're everything. Smart. Passionate. Caring."

"And I don't let you get away with anything."

He grinned. "Yes. I love when you boss me around," he wagged his eyebrows. Ava flushed thinking about their more adventurous sexcapades over the last few months. "More importantly, you showed me I can trust. That I can share my whole self with someone. I didn't realize how much I needed that until you came along. I also realized that having you part-time isn't enough. I'm lost when I'm not with you. Stella is too. I don't care where we are. Here. In Boston. Somewhere else. I want you all the time, for always."

Tears pricked her eyes. "Brooks," she breathed out.

He reached into his breast pocket and pulled out a jewelry box.

"So I want to ask you a question." Flicking it open, he revealed the most beautiful emerald ring she'd ever seen. "Ava Espinosa, my fiery, pain-in-the-ass woman who I love more than life itself, will you do me the greatest honor and be my wife?"

"Oh. How could I ever deny you with that stellar proposal?" she said dryly. A smile lifted her lips as tears began to flow. "Yes! Yes. Of course, I will."

He stood and pulled her into his arms, swinging her around and kissing her with fevered passion. He placed her down and slipped the ring on her finger. It sparkled in the candlelight.

"It's gorgeous," she said in awe.

"It was my mother's. A family heirloom passed down from generation to generation. During her last few months, she gave it to me and told me to hold out for a woman who challenged me and loved me fiercely. To only give it to a woman who I couldn't imagine my life without."

"I can't tell you how much this means to me." Ava's voice choked up as Brooks swiped away her tears with the tips of his thumbs.

"It's okay, honey. You've said the most important thing in the world to me. You said yes."

"It's about time," Jess said as she pushed through the swinging doors from the kitchen.

Ava stepped away from Brooks and met Jess near the bar. "What? What are you doing here?" she asked, choking out a confused laugh.

Jess shrugged a shoulder. "I know a guy." She winked at Brooks.

"Safe to come out now?" Ava's head snapped in the direction of the kitchen and her mom's voice.

"Mom's here too?"

"And Dad." Jess smiled. "Come on out, guys! She said yes."

Ava's parents appeared, both with gleaming pride in their eyes. "We're so happy for you, mija," her father said as he wrapped her in a hug.

"My goodness. Would you look at that?" Her mother lifted Ava's hand to inspect the ring. "Don't go swimming with that on. You'll drown."

Brooks pulled Ava to his side and squeezed. "I wanted your family to come here so they could see where this all started. I also wanted them to be here when I asked you to be my wife."

Ava raised an eyebrow and smirked. "Pretty sure of yourself that I'd say yes, huh?"

He kissed her head. "Let's just say I was taking a big swing and hoping I was right."

"We're staying at the cutest inn in town, but I'm looking forward to when the in-law suite is done. We'll be here all the time, especially for wedding planning!" her mother said.

Ava's eyebrows furrowed. "In-law suite? I thought those plans you had on your desk were for some sort of man cave."

He grinned. "Another big swing?"

She wrapped her arms around his neck and smiled. "Seems like all these bold moves are going to pay off for you."

"Oh?"

"I love it here. I love the community. I love how it showed me what mattered in life. Although I appreciate how open you are to going anywhere with me, I want to stay here. With you. So, Brooks Jónsson, it's safe to start making those blueprints a reality. The rest of our lives together starts now."

Brooks's eyes misted. "I love you, Ava, forever."

Ava kissed him deeply, her mind swirling with all the hopeful possibilities. Never in her life would she have thought a last-minute trip to Iceland would give her so much, but it was exactly what she needed.

She wouldn't have had it any other way.

Thank you for reading! Did you enjoy? Please add your review

because nothing helps an author more and encourages readers to take a chance on a book than a review.

And don't miss more of the *Her Journey* series coming soon.

Until then, discover <u>WAVERLY LAKE</u>, by City Owl Author, Mary Shotwell. Turn the page for a sneak peek!

You can also sign up for the City Owl Press newsletter to receive notice of all book releases!

SNEAK PEEK OF WAVERLY LAKE
BY MARY SHOTWELL

Somewhere among the bustle of the morning pedestrians lining the sidewalks of Manhattan, Kara Carter strolled with a bounce in her step. Her energy could be blamed on the high-octane caffeinated coffee she guarded with her bony elbows, or the three packets of sugar she had poured in it. Perhaps it was the fact that the horns honking, sirens blaring, and neighbors shouting through the pane of her one-bedroom apartment window had become soothing for her, lulling her to sleep in an ironic security blanket. But anyone who knew Kara, or at least knew Kara as she was in New York City, knew that today was an important day.

She had awakened nowhere near refreshed, the anticipation too much to allow rest through the night. The meeting had been marked on her calendar for a week, after her return from photographing elephants in Namibia for an ivory trade piece. There was no hint to the meeting's topic, but she knew what it was about. She could feel it in her gut. Her photographs helped win *International Ecologic* the reputed Carroll Award for Excellence in Environmental Reporting. It was time for her to call the shots—literally. The stories she wanted to cover. The art she wanted to capture and create.

Her phone buzzed in her purse pocket, the one kept closest to her chest for such an occasion.

"Hey, babe." Marcus Goodwin's soothing deep voice greeted her. "I just wanted to talk to you before you arrived and say happy anniversary."

"Happy anniversary to you. To us," she said. Two years. They had met at the magazine—she the junior-level photographer, he the new assistant executive editor. They had kept their dating low-key. Society said it was tricky dating a colleague, but they were the exception.

"I didn't want to make a scene at work."

"I know." She stopped at a crosswalk, the crowd growing in all directions. "You hate PDA, especially at work."

It was effortless with Marcus. Work together yet separately, dinner together, weekend together. Repeat. Sure, it was routine, but it was reliable. Two years of reliability.

They had technically celebrated their anniversary last night. Marcus had insisted on taking her to Maître D', the newest eatery in the Village, but he couldn't get a reservation for Friday night, so they settled for Thursday.

"You're radiant," he had said, lifting his glass of champagne. The candlelight and instrumental music added to the surreal movie feel of it all. "No matter what tomorrow brings, know I love you and believe in you."

He had done it. Two years in the making, and he had gotten on one knee and opened the box, adding, "Enough to want you as my wife."

Just thinking about last night, rolling the diamond around her finger, nearly brought back tears of joy. She couldn't have planned it better. College, internship, job, dating, marriage. And now—crossing fingers—promotion. It was all working out.

"I'll see you in a few, fiancée?"

The word tickled her ears. "Yes, Mr. Goodwin. Crossing over to the building now." She slid the phone into her purse.

"Good morning, Miss Kara," said Barkley, the doorman to the First American Bank building in Midtown. His beyond six-foot stature dwarfed her five-and-a-half-foot frame. He glanced at his watch and smirked. "Is it possible you're here early this morning?"

"You'd better believe it. Today is my day."

"Well, you go and grab it then, Miss Kara."

His morning pep always put a smile on her face. She headed to the elevator, a gaggle of men in suits already waiting for the doors to open.

She rode the elevator up to the eleventh floor. The elevator opened as Suzie walked by the front doors of *International Ecologic*, the green leaf logo etched on the glass.

"Morning, Kara." Suzie, one of the office assistants and, quite frankly, one of her best friends in town outside of Marcus, held the office door open, eyeing the elevator.

"Morning."

"That was quite the crowd in the elevator with you."

Kara shook her head. "They say New York has a shortage of men, but I have yet to see it in the corporate world."

"Amen to that. Maybe I should move to corporate." Suzie chuckled, a high-pitched genuine laugh. "Care to join me?"

"No, thank you. You know I'm taken." Kara briefly flashed the ring on her hand. They had agreed not to make it a big deal in the office today. But what was the harm in telling Suzie?

"Are you kidding me?" She hugged Kara. "Here I thought I'd try to introduce a little fun in your life, and you've gone and nailed that coffin."

Kara gave her *the* look—the one she gave whenever Suzie took a backhanded stab at Marcus. *That* was the harm in telling Suzie. Ever since his arrival, she had put up her guard and wanted Kara to do the same. To Suzie, Marcus was either a liar or, in fact, as boring as he seemed.

Kara embraced his sense of order. What was wrong with structure, with knowing what to expect? Heck, her first love, Danny Bennett, had given her a taste of unpredictability and unreliability and all the other negative "uns." He had toyed with her heart, and she learned her lesson. No more Danny Bennetts.

Marcus walked into her office as Kara organized the top layer of her desk. He always made sure his shirts were crisp and ties perfectly knotted. Kara especially liked his choice for her special day—a perfectly fitted charcoal suit with a splash of blush on his tie. It brought a flash of color to his fair complexion. And made her feel underdressed in her navy pants and white high-collared shirt. "Why would I need to cross over to corporate to find a man when I have the perfect one right here?"

Kara rested her head on his shoulder and kept her eyes locked on Suzie.

"Ugh. You guys are depressing."

"Kara, come on now." Marcus slipped away, straightening his jacket.

"It's just Suzie. Lighten up. We're all friends." She rolled her eyes. "See you in the meeting, Suzie?" Surely, Suzie would be there at least to record the meeting's minutes.

"I wouldn't miss it. Considering it's my job and all." She walked off down the hall.

Kara patted Marcus's arm, thin yet solid under his firm-fitting suit jacket. "Come on. We have to get going."

He scratched his neck beneath the shirt collar. "Well, just remember. Whatever happens in there, I'm here for you."

Kara raised her right eyebrow. The rogue eyebrow had a mind of its own when she was confused. No *Good luck*? No *I'm proud of you*? What did *I'm here for you* mean?

"You coming, Kara?" Jamie, the newest addition to the administrative team, stopped in her doorway.

"Yep. Be right there," Kara said.

"See you later then?" Marcus said.

"Later? Are you not coming?"

"Afraid not." He adjusted his perfect tie.

"But I thought—"

"Hey." He placed his hands over hers. "You'll be fine. You're a great photographer. Have some confidence in yourself. Okay?"

Kara nodded. "Okay."

"Good," he said. "Now get."

She grabbed a notebook and pen. Marcus held his arm out for Kara to leave the room first. She turned out of the office and walked down the hallway, smoothing down the flyaways back into her sleek ponytail. The only privacy the conference room afforded was one of sound, with a glass wall separating the room from the general office space. The long table was occupied by five coworkers.

Kara checked her watch. Even though she had arrived at the building early, she made it to the meeting room at nine o'clock on the dot.

"You're all here." Editor-in-chief Rick Simon clapped his hands upon entering. "Let's get this going. I don't want to waste your time."

Rick's bluntness was also reliable—and very much appreciated.

"Many of you already know of the success stories *International Ecologic* has had in the past few weeks," he said. "Mainly, the Carroll Award for Excellence, for which we would be remiss to not acknowledge Kara Carter, who is with us here today." He gestured to the distant end of the table at Kara. She nodded in recognition. Suzie clapped and the others joined, reluctantly, based on their lack of enthusiasm behind it.

"That achievement is the good news," he said. Kara's heart sank. What was happening?

"Unfortunately, the bad news is, well, bad."

Her mouth turned dry, and she swallowed hard. Her hands grew sweaty.

"Subscriptions have declined the last six quarters, this last quarter being the worst. It's been my opinion, as well as that of our sister company, that it's time to go completely digital."

Kara sighed, releasing the tension built up in her body. Going digital wasn't bad news at all. In fact, she had been awaiting the transition for over a year. It was long overdue to keep up with the times, let alone the competition. She didn't need to see the numbers to know the sales of physical copies weren't worth the print costs.

"It may take some time, but we believe the magazine will endure the transition and eventually rebuild its fan base. We have already procured a new generation of readers in the online environment with the little we've done with it so far. All around, we will become more efficient and cost-effective."

"Sounds good to me," Meredith, a junior writer, said.

"Yeah..." Rick stared at the table. "It is good. Unfortunately, in our efforts to streamline, we will have to make some cuts. That means employees."

"How many are we talking here?" Calvin, an art designer, squirmed in his seat.

Rick held up his hand. "We've looked it over, many times. Crunched the numbers. We tried to find alternatives. But we're going to have to let six of you go."

"Six!" Meredith shook her head. "When will this happen? Does everyone else know?"

Kara looked at her coworkers. All five of them. Suzie met her gaze, a look of dread on her face. Kara cleared her throat and found the strength to speak. "You've already decided, haven't you? It's the six of us."

Her colleagues looked each other over, back and forth, like tourists crossing Seventh Avenue for the first time.

"I'm terribly sorry," Rick said. "I wish there was a better way. Of course, once we get our footing back, you may be able to reapply for your positions when announced."

"Reapply?" Calvin said. "I've worked here for six years."

And Kara the last four. But not as long as at least two other photographers.

Marcus stood outside the room, leaning on Vince's desk and chatting. Kara locked eyes with him briefly before he turned away.

"I'm sorry we couldn't do more," Rick said. "We've organized a severance package for each of you. I know it's not much, but I'd be happy to serve as a reference for your next endeavor."

His assistant, Giles handed out sealed manila envelopes. Poor Suzie had to sit there with her competition, who was keeping his job.

No one bothered to open their packets. The newly unemployed huffed out of the room, the air sucked out of their lungs and joy sapped from their faces. Kara took a breath, stood tall, and approached Marcus at Vince's desk.

"You knew about this, didn't you?" She slapped his arm with the envelope. It was painful to believe it, but it was obviously true. "You knew and you didn't tell me."

"Kara—"

"How could you not tell me?"

He couldn't manage to look her in the eyes, opting for the floor.

She sighed and put her fist on her waist. "Everything I've built here. It's over." She turned away and stormed off to her desk. Or her former desk.

"Kara! Come on." Marcus trailed behind her. "What do you want me to say?"

Giles interrupted, delivering an empty box on her desk. It sat there, awaiting the contents of her life, her goals, her dreams in its four cardboard walls.

"Nothing." Kara stacked her papers and camera equipment into the box. "Say nothing, Marcus."

"What are you going to do? Where are you going to go?"

She paused to look him in the eyes. "I don't know."

"You can find something else. I'll help you. We can look together."

She picked up the weighted box, struggling to keep her fingers underneath to support it. "Together? You should've thought about together when you decided not to tell me I was going to lose my job."

"Come on, Kara. It's our two-year anniversary. Let's talk about this tonight and we can celebrate our engagement. You know how you overreact. Don't make a decision in the heat of emotions."

"I don't—I can't even look at you right now. You made a very bad decision by not telling me. But as much as I hate to say it, you're right. I don't want to make a bad decision in reaction to it." This certainly was a curveball. Her gut told her to leave him in the dust, but her head forced her to weigh two years of history. Not to mention they were planning to marry sometime in the near future.

"I think I'm going to need time to process this and plan what's next. Time to think. Which is what I have an absurd abundance of now."

She brushed past Marcus and refused to look back. "Please open," she mumbled, pushing the elevator button. "Please, please, please." If Marcus was coming after her, she didn't want to argue. Not now, after her livelihood had been pulled out from under her.

The elevator doors separated, welcoming her into their cold, steel arms. As the elevator descended, her emotions rose. She fought back the tears. It wasn't worth it. "Just a job," she whispered.

She arrived on the ground floor and rushed out.

"Got the good news already?" Barkley said from behind the reception desk.

She walked by, unable to say a word. She exited the First American Bank building onto Seventh Avenue, the brake screeches and vehicle rumblings hitting her at the same time as the smell of dirt and meat vendors and sweat. Half an hour ago, she was an award-winning photographer with a promising career and a fiancé, and everything had flipped upside down. She made the journey to her apartment building but didn't quite make it up the stairs before she let the tears roll freely.

Don't stop now. Keep reading with your copy of <u>WAVERLY LAKE</u>, by City Owl Author, Mary Shotwell.

And find more from Sofia Sawyer at www.sofiasawyer.com

Don't miss the next book of the *Her Journey* series coming soon, and find more from Sofia Sawyer at www.sofiasawyer.com

Until then, discover WAVERLY LAKE, by City Owl Author, Mary Shotwell

Kara Carter has her future set— the right photography job, the perfect reliable boyfriend, and her own apartment in New York, until one morning changes it all. She has no choice but to move back home to Waverly Lake, North Carolina, a town she had sworn off for ten years.

It's one thing to return as a failure, it's another to find her neighbor is the one and only Danny Bennett, the boy who broke her heart senior year of high school.

As Kara helps with the family's furniture business—and steers clear of Danny—she is pressured into teaming up with her dad for the Annual Waverly Lake Regatta. But when her dad's accident results in forfeiting his sailing team slot, no one in Waverly Lake can forgive her past—except Danny.

Danny Bennett, now a single father of seven-year-old daughter Hannah, can't help but be drawn to Kara. When he offers to help Kara race in the regatta, little does he know how the woman who stole his heart long ago will change the way he sees family, love, and parenting a child with autism.

Can these high school sweethearts sail through the pain of the past?

Please sign up for the City Owl Press newsletter for chances to win special subscriber-only contests and giveaways as well as receiving information on upcoming releases and special excerpts.

All reviews are **welcome** and **appreciated**. Please consider leaving one on your favorite social media and book buying sites.

Escape Your World. Get Lost in Ours! Romance and speculative fiction from City Owl Press at www.cityowlpress.com.

ACKNOWLEDGMENTS

All my life, I've used writing as a way to overcome hard times, work through challenges, ease anxiety and heartache, rediscover joy, and to remember not to take life too seriously. Whether for pleasure or an escape, I always knew I could grab a pen and paper (or a keyboard) and get lost in a world of my own creation. This always made the not-so-glamorous parts of writing (cough: the editing process) feel less daunting. But even on a good day, writing is no easy feat.

Unfortunately, I faced health issues this year that made my writing "happy place" feel out of reach. The toll chronic pain took on me—from full body pain, numbness, and stiffness, especially in my back and hands— made writing even for a few minutes feel like an impossible task.

But I did it. It took *a lot* longer than I would have liked, and there were plenty of days full of tears. However, despite it all, I finished. I couldn't have done it without the compassion and understanding from my editor, Mary Cain at City Owl Press, and my agent, Jana Hanson at Metamorphosis Literary Agency. There were days I'd beat myself up over the fact that I couldn't work the way I used to, and I worried I was letting everyone down. Instead of putting on the pressure to meet deadlines, Mary and Jana showed me empathy and offered flexibility so I could work whatever way my body would allow. This made a difficult situation a lot easier and helped me push through to the end.

Publishing partners aside, I want to thank my husband Jim Sweeney for finally convincing me it's okay to put myself first for once and supporting me through it all, even when I'm being an absolute monster. I'd also like to thank my new team of doctors who, after years of being dismissed by other doctors, finally listened to me and are working to support me and this new reality of life.

It's been a tough year, but there's a glimmer of hope on the other side. Thanks to all these wonderful people, I'm looking forward to enjoying writing again soon (hopefully, pain free!).

ABOUT THE AUTHOR

When Sofia Sawyer's fifth-grade teacher handed her a journal, encouraging her to keep writing, she vowed she always would. A lifelong storyteller, Sofia writes contemporary romances featuring tenacious women who won't stop until they get their happily ever after.

Based in Charleston, S.C., she follows her wanderlust whenever she can to new and exciting places, often finding story ideas throughout her travels.

When she isn't reading, writing, or jet-setting across the globe, you can find Sofia playing with her dog, taking advantage of the amazing Charleston restaurant scene, hiking, or hanging at the beach.

Sofia is represented by Jana Hanson from Metamorphosis Literary Agency.

Sign up for her newsletter at www.sofiasawyer.com/newsletter

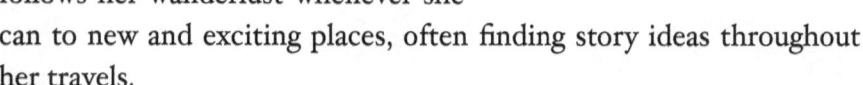 facebook.com/sofiasawyerwriter
twitter.com/sofia_sawyer
instagram.com/sofiasawyerwriter
pinterest.com/sofiasawyerwriter

ABOUT THE PUBLISHER

City Owl Press is a cutting edge indie publishing company, bringing the world of romance and speculative fiction to discerning readers.

Escape Your World. Get Lost in Ours!

www.cityowlpress.com

facebook.com/CityOwlPress

twitter.com/cityowlpress

instagram.com/cityowlbooks

pinterest.com/cityowlpress

tiktok.com/@cityowlpress